TATTERED & TORN

Sacred Hearts MC Book IV

AJ Downey

Second Circle Press

Published 2015 by Second Circle Press
Book design by Lia Rees at Free Your Words (www.freeyourwords.com)
Cover art by Clarissa Yeo at Yocla Designs (www.yocladesigns.com)

ISBN: 978-0692396773

DEDICATION

To the women of A.J.'s Sacred Circle. My very own, much needed, street team. You all have made my life so much easier, most notably, Jennifer Mitsada and Michelle Bigioni Slagan. If I have missed calling you by name it is not any kind of intended slight, you all have been exceedingly awesome at spreading the love, shouting the word and cheering me up when it feels like everything is burning down around me. Much love. Keep on keepin' on!

THE SACRED HEARTS MC BOOKS IN ORDER

CONTENTS

PROLOGUE

"Tell me about Ghost, you mentioned him earlier."

"What about him?"

"Well, you said that he was different from the rest. Different how?"

"Is that what you write in that fancy notebook of yours all the time?"

"You sound angry. Does my note taking bother you?"

"No."

"So why are you angry?"

" ... "

"Shelly?"

" ... "

"Shelly..?"

"I don't want to talk about him."

"What do you want to talk about?"

"I don't know! What do I *need* to talk about to get you, my cousin, Ashton... Hell all of them, off my back?"

"Is that how you see it?"

"Yes! ... No... I don't know."

"Shelly, the goal of coming to therapy is to help you, but first you have to decide what you want help with. No one can make you work your issues. You have to be willing to do that on your own. I'm sensing you don't want to be here."

"You're right I don't."

"Then why are you here?"

"Short answer? It was the condition my cousin gave me to let me move in with him and his wife. I kind of lost my shit a little and forgot to pay my rent and got evicted."

"I see. Well. This is your third visit, do you feel like you have made any progress?"

"Hell no."

"Why is that?"

"I still dream about it. You know? At night, I wake up in a cold sweat with this crushing weight on my chest and it's like... I don't know! This is stupid!"

"No, no it's not... Please... Keep talking."

"Why? Talking isn't going to fix it. It's not going to undo anything that's happened."

"No, that's true. That's very true, but it's my hope that what it will do is allow you to come to grips with it, to deal with it and move past it."

"Maybe I don't want to."

"I don't think that's true Shelly."

"Well what the fuck *do* you know?"

"I know that you're hurting. I know that when you talked about Ghost during your first session here that you seemed to hurt a little bit less. Why is that? What is it about him?"

"I like him. Okay? Is that what you want to hear?"

"It's a start."

"He's just different."

"What makes him different?"

"I don't know, it's like he sees me, you know? It's weird. I don't know how to explain it."

"Can you try?"

"Look, I don't want to talk about him! Can we please just talk about something else? Please?"

"We can talk about whatever it is you would like to talk about for the remainder of our session."

"Thank you... I guess."

CHAPTER 1

Shelly

I left Dr. Hubbard's office feeling like I'd been run over by a truck. I got into my battered old Volvo and started it, shivering. It was the end of fall and the days were shorter, the nights longer and it was getting a hell of a lot colder. It had been warmer earlier in the day, if rainy and windy, and stupid me, I thought I would be fine in what I had on. I was wearing a pair of black leggings with an oversized white 'V' neck tee-shirt and had a light gray cardigan with an asymmetrical hemline over the top of it all. I probably would have looked a hell of a lot better if I'd bothered to do anything with my hair or had put on any make up, but lately, I didn't care so much about what I looked like.

I huddled miserably behind the wheel of my car and hugged myself. *Fuck, I was cold!* I wrapped the cardigan around me tighter and sighed out miserably, my breath pluming the air. Great. That was just great. I yanked the seatbelt savagely across my body and buckled it with fingers going numb and put the old car in reverse. It protested moving so quickly without being fully warmed up but it would warm up quicker if I got it moving.

I put my headphones in my ears and set some music to playing on my phone before pulling out onto the street. I was Dr. Hubbard's last appointment for the day so the parking lot for the little squat two story office building was empty, except for what I assumed was Dr. Hubbard's silvery gray, old school Mercedes.

The streetlights were coming on, glimmering against the wet pavement as I turned out of the drive, my headlights sweeping across the row of parked cars along the side of the road. I was grateful to be motoring up the street. God! It was good to get away from all of the probing questions and uncomfortable silences of my latest cross to bear. I still couldn't believe Reaver was making me go to therapy! I loved my cousin, I really did, but sometimes he could be really fucking irritating. Like with this whole going to therapy thing. Seriously? What good was it going to do?

I sniffed, my nose running from the cold, and tried the heat in my car. The air blew from the vents and defrosters slightly warmer than the ambient air and I was grateful. Wouldn't be long now before she was really heated up and I could be *warm* again.

It was eerily quiet and deserted as I drove through town, heading out for the country road that would take me to the 'burbs and ultimately to Reave and Hayden's townhouse. It had been storming all day, rain and wind and sometimes even hail with thunder and lightning added to the mix, so it was no wonder that the world felt deserted at barely eight o'clock on a Thursday. I imagined most people were bundled into their nice warm houses with a bowl of soup and a grilled cheese sandwich. Yeah, it had been *that* kind of a day.

I drove down the country back road past tree lined farmland and even had to skirt around a fallen tree limb or two. I was just beginning to think that maybe I should have taken the highway, squinting into the rising mist and cursing my dim headlights when I realized that something was wrong. My headlights were steadily growing dimmer, my car was losing power. I cursed.

"No!" I cried when it stalled. I cranked the wheel hard to the right and coasted to the shoulder of the narrow two lane road and let out a harsh breath. Well this was just fucking perfect on top of everything else! I slumped back into my seat and stopped the music on my phone and realized that it was dying too.

"Damn it!" I yelled and did what I always did in situations like this... I dialed my big cousin to bail me out of trouble and like always, he answered pretty much on the first ring which made my shoulders drop in relief.

"Yellow?"

"Reave! Listen, my phone is about to die. I'm on Abbey Country Road on my way home and my car just quit, can you come get me?" I rushed out.

"Whoa, hey, what was that Baby Cuz? Your car died?" he asked.

4

"Yeah, it just lost power and died," my phone chirped the two percent battery warning in my ear and I swore.

"Shelly? Shelly?" Fuck he couldn't hear me!

"Yeah Reaver, I'm here! I'm on Abbey Country Road!" I called into the phone.

"Abbey Country Road, got it! Hang tight, we'll get you taken care of Runt," he said and I heard things being moved around, like tools and stuff.

"Thanks Reaver, I'm really sorry," I said softly.

"Don't be Baby Cuz, just stay –"

My phone died and with it my only means of communication, entertainment and way to tell time. Shit. I tried to restart my car but as I suspected, nada. I pulled the hood of my thin sweater over my hair and undid my seatbelt, forcing the angry tears that were threatening down. *Fuck that.* I would not cry. I was not a fucking crier. I violently jerked the sweater around my body and huddled miserably on my driver's seat and waited for Reaver. I heard a distant motorcycle and locked my door and tried to make myself small.

The Suicide Kings travelled this road almost as much as the Sacred Hearts did lately and besides that, Reaver wouldn't come on the bike. Not to say any of our guys were fair weather riders, they rode whenever they fucking felt like it, but I was closer to the county line and The Suicide Kings clubhouse than I was to town and The Sacred Hearts and it'd barely been two weeks since the Suicide Kings had blown up Open Road Ink. They'd tagged the hell out of Open Road Garage with threatening messages just two nights ago. Dray had been fucking pissed and had pretty much been on the warpath ever since... and here I was, not just a sitting duck but the cause of it all.

I bowed my head and sighed, the guilt weighing heavily on my soul, the damp chill from outside creeping into the car as the minutes ticked by. I sniffed and started to shiver. I had no way of telling how much time had actually gone by, but it certainly felt like forever.

"*Come on Reaver!*" I said impatiently, my voice harsh in the quiet interior of the car as if my impatience would somehow make him appear. I shifted for what must have been the thousandth time and tried to get comfortable which was easier said than done in a car that was almost twice my age. Well, okay... it was really more like fifteen years older than me but that was still the 80's which by car standards made this bitch a classic. I mean wasn't it something like 30 years and older it was a classic?

I exhaled sharply and ground my teeth together to keep them from chattering. Where the fuck was my cousin? Not a single damned soul had passed me on the road since I'd pulled off to the side so when the sweep of headlights caught in my side view I felt relief spiked with a hard measure of anxiety. I couldn't tell what kind of truck was pulling up behind me but what I could tell was it wasn't Reaver's Ford and it wasn't Hayden's Escalade so the relief was quickly swamped by the anxiety.

I huddled in on myself harder as I watched the driver's door on the big black monstrosity open and a pair of legs appear beneath it. The door on the truck swung shut and the person, who was so *not* my cousin, walked up along the driver's side of my car. I swallowed hard and hugged myself tighter and turned my face away from the penetrating ray of light from his big black flashlight. My door was locked but if he wanted to get at me he could, and if he wanted anything else... well I already knew it didn't matter how hard I fought.

"Shelly! Open the door Princess. It's me Ghost," he called through the window, rapping his knuckles lightly against the glass.

Ghost? Reaver had sent Ghost? I swallowed hard and with trembling hands pulled up on the lock. The door opened up.

"You okay?" he asked. I put up my hand to block the flashlight he was shining at me and squinted.

"I'm fine," I said and sniffed, my damned nose still running from the chill.

"No you're not. Come on, let's get you into the truck where it's warm," he tried to take my hand but I recoiled from the touch.

"Fine! Just please don't touch me," I snapped.

"Sure. Sure thing. Sorry Princess," he said and he sounded it, I still couldn't help but to put up a hard front.

"Don't be sorry, just don't touch me," I said unfolding myself from the driver's seat. Bits of twig and leaves grated under my simple flats as I stood up and slung my small purse across my chest.

"Come on," he walked with me to the passenger side of a tow truck and opened the door for me. The heat was blasting inside and the warm air puffed out to greet me, I turned my face into it and sighed inwardly with relief. I was *freezing*!

"Can I help you up?" he asked me and I shook my head.

"I can do it," I said and braced a foot on the metal step and gripped the handle set above the door on the inside of the cab. I pulled myself up and startled when his hands went to my hips and helped me anyways when my foot started to slip. He quickly took them away once I was stable and I was at once grateful for his assistance and thoroughly put out with the fact that I'd needed it.

"Thanks," I grated sourly and Ghost nodded. I could see him now, the light from the interior of the cab of his truck shining down into his upturned face. He was your all-American boy kind of beautiful. Compact and lithe, the high school star quarterback all grown up but without losing any of those damned good looks. He had high cheekbones and these hazel eyes that sparkled when he smiled, more brown than green. His milk chocolate brown hair flopped over his forehead and looked soft to the touch but it's not like I would ever know. No, no and nope. Ghost didn't want me, and once upon a time, before The Suicide Kings, it had turned me upside down and inside out.

No matter how hard I'd tried to get into Ghost's bed or him into mine before, well, before... anyways, it never happened. He wouldn't so much as kiss me. For a minute I had thought he was gay like Disney but only for a minute because sometimes I would catch him looking at me, sort of like he was looking at me right now and I knew he wanted me but I couldn't wrap my brain around why he *didn't*. It hurt. A lot of things hurt right now, in fact I was pretty sure the whole damned world was nothing but one big ball of hurt anymore and it made me so tired that I just didn't want to poke at it. So I turned my face away from him. I saw him nod out of the corner

7

of my eye and he shut me into the warm brightly lit bubble of the truck's cab.

I watched him come round the front of the truck, and wistfully admired the way he moved in the beams of the headlights. Ghost moved with purpose, no matter what he did. Like he was set to take on the world even when the task at hand was simply getting a glass of water, or in this case to get up into the truck to pull up in front of my dead Volvo. He climbed up into the cab and put the truck in gear, I turned my face and stared out the window. If Ghost hadn't wanted me before, he damn sure didn't want me now and I didn't want to see the cold look of pity or the sadness in his eyes. It was hard enough seeing it on everyone else's faces.

"I'm sorry it took me so long to get here. I had a tow across town when I got the call and had to drop it off before I could come get you."

He expertly piloted the monstrous black truck in front of my car. I let my gaze wander the reflection of his hand resting on the seat between us. The girl I was before would have given anything for that hand to touch me, to trail across my skin in that way that left a shiver down my spine and a sweep of tingling sensation in its wake. Now I just felt so dirty, so reviled and unclean I didn't want anybody to touch me and unfortunately the stain left behind on me from the fourth of July weekend wasn't something I could scrub off in the shower. God knows I'd tried often enough since then.

"Shelly?" my name snapped me out of my downward thinking spiral and I turned unbidden to that look of concern I was so sick of seeing on everyone's faces painted all over Ghost's. The last person I *ever* wanted to pity me.

"What?" I demanded and it came out a little more sharply than I intended. Ghost lifted the hand I'd been studying so hard the moment before, and reached out. I flattened myself against the door and he dropped it.

"I'll be just a minute Princess," he said and I snorted.

"Stop calling me that!" I snapped and he smiled to himself and was out into the night, the door swinging shut behind him leaving me in the dimly lit but blessedly warm interior of the truck. I closed my eyes for a moment and simply soaked in the warmth. The truck jerked and rocked a few times as Ghost expertly flipped switches and dragged chains and bound my poor old car to the metal framework behind it.

I felt so tired. I always did after my sessions with Dr. Hubbard. I wondered faintly if that meant they were working, but then quickly dismissed the notion. Dr. Hubbard wasn't a bad guy. Short and portly he reminded me of my junior high science teacher with his pressed shirts, bow ties and sweater vests. Dr. Hubbard always wore slacks and decent shoes. Every time I looked at him I thought how much he *looked* like a shrink, or an old-school family doctor or, a lawyer... With the way he interrogated me sometimes he really could be any of the three.

The driver's side door opened and I jumped. Ghost froze midway into climbing into the cab and raked me with his gaze, a quick, hard once over.

"It is A-Okay Darlin'. It's just me," he uttered and hoisted himself up into his seat. I turned my face to the glass and didn't speak. I didn't know what to say and truthfully I had so many burning questions to ask... *Why don't you want me Ghost? Why do you pretend to care when you've already made it so clear you don't?* But I looked at it this way, I may have been born at night, but I wasn't born *last* night. You didn't ask questions unless you were prepared for the answer and I just didn't think I was ready, or could take even just one more blow right now. Life was just hard enough without Ghost in it. Trouble was, at least for me, is that it was hard without him around too.

"You warming up?" he asked. I nodded mutely and kept my eyes fixed on the glass and his reflection, or what I could see of it.

"Okay, we'll get your car dropped off and I'll take you home," he said and pulled onto the old country road.

"I don't have a home. At least not really," I didn't think I had said it aloud but obviously I did because he responded.

"Well, we'll get you to your cousin's in any case."

I watched the reflection of his shoulder give an indelicate shrug. I let out a pent up breath, *why the hell couldn't Reaver have just come and gotten me and sent Ghost for the damn car later?* I frowned, brow wrinkling, a small voice in the back of my mind reminding me, *because he was working you idiot!* And it was true, and very unfair of me to wish for my cousin. He'd taken enough time off recently warring with his ex over their son and getting settled into his new life with Hayden who was great for Reaver, she really was, but I couldn't help but be jealous.

I missed my cousin and I felt like I needed him now more than ever and it wasn't fair to him or Hayden me moving in like I'd had to, but there was Reaver, ever my Captain Save-A-Ho. When it had been the choice of homeless, moving in with my mother or moving my shit into storage and me into their guest room my cousin hadn't hesitated. I closed my eyes and rested my temple against the cool dark glass of Ghost's passenger window.

His phone went off in his breast pocket and I turned my head to look, he extracted an iPhone in a thick, ugly, neon yellow case that was grease stained. I made a face at it and he smiled at me a genuine smile.

"May be ugly but it's easy to spot in the dark," he gave another one of those one shouldered shrugs of his and answered the phone with, "Pauley's towing; this is Derek how can I help?" I rested my head back against the rest and closed my eyes, listening to the timbre of his voice as he spoke to whoever on the other end of the line.

"I'm on a tow out on Abbey Country Road right now, I still have to drop the car over at Open Road Garage sooooo," he paused, "ETA an hour and a half? Maybe. Uh huh. Yeah. Good deal. Yeah, you too," he hung up and we rode in silence for a while. He didn't have the radio on and the monotonous sound of the rushing pavement and diesel engine in combination with the warmth of the cab lulled me, I went from tired to sleepy in the blink of an eye but I didn't sleep well these days. Still, moving along in the closed space of Ghost's truck, wrapped in warmth and the smell of his cologne, I think I fell asleep.

CHAPTER 2

Ghost

I pulled up at Open Road Garage and looked Shelly over. She looked like hell, her platinum blonde locks shaggy and lank against her forehead which was furrowed with deep lines as she slept. Dark circles stained her too pale skin beneath her eyes and she'd always been a narrow woman but now she was positively *gaunt*. Her sharp cheekbone standing out further than I'd ever remembered; her cheeks had become so drawn they were shadowed beneath them. I looked down at the hand that had slipped from her lap to the seat between us, her once carefully filed, painted and manicured nails, barely held onto the chipped polish now. To top it off, they had been bitten damn near to the quick. Even in her sleep she was tense, tucked tight against the door as far as she could get from me.

It was a damned shame. One of the things that had first attracted me to Shelly was her surety and confidence. She had been a vibrant spitfire of a woman, a real fireball, and now... well now she was barely a shadow of that girl. A ghost of who she once was and the guilt of that weighed on me.

My personal cell went off and I scrambled to answer it before it woke her up. I was so used to answering the work cell I did it without thinking,

"Pauley's towing this is Derek, how can I help?"

"What the fuck. Ghost?" Reaver laughed on the other end of the line. I frowned.

"You didn't tell me she wasn't sleeping," I said, and I knew my voice was thick with displeasure, tumbling into the too warm cab of my truck and lost to the dark. Sort of like Shelly seemed to be.

"Yeah man. It's pretty bad. Nightmares all of the time," Reaver sighed out on the other end of the phone and sounded about as tired as Shelly looked.

"She's sleeping now. I'm at the shop about to drop her car. I'm hesitant about waking her up so I'm just gonna let her sleep. I'll bring her home when she wakes up," I said.

"Yeah man, might not be a bad idea. I know Hayden could use a good night's too so yeah, okay. Just…" he hesitated like he was afraid he was going to offend me by saying it but I knew what was coming just like he knew it went without saying. "Just take care of my Baby Cuz."

"You know it, man," I said and we said our goodbyes and hung up. I sat there a little longer than I should have and just let myself drink her in. Even as worn and tattered as she was she still had this air about her, this pride or just, I don't know… The girl was tough as nails and would get past this but she was stubborn as hell too. I got out of the truck and got her car dropped. I was pretty sure it was her alternator which was a pretty quick and easy fix if Dray could get the part. I got back into the truck and damned if she hadn't stirred a bit. She was out like a traffic light.

With a rough exhale I put my truck in gear and went for my next tow. Shelly slept on through the next three which were all no passenger deals and the fourth was supposed to be too so you can imagine my surprise when I pulled up to find a dude sitting there. He waved me down and I took a nervous last look at Shells. She'd been out a solid three or four hours by now which was good and it was nice having her along, in my truck with me. Even with her asleep it was less lonely somehow. I shifted it into park and I got out to see what was doin' with the dude.

"Thought this was a no ride tow," I said simply, but held out my hand to shake his anyways.

"Was supposed to be but my damned brother wouldn't answer his phone," the guy grunted. He looked to be in his twenties, maybe thirties, "Is it a problem?" he asked.

"Naw. I'll figure something out," I said and he looked back to the truck and squinted.

"She's pretty, what's the matter with her?" he asked. I felt my lips thin down as I pressed them together. Guess it was pretty obvious to everyone.

"Nothing," I lied, "Just a friend along for the ride. Gimee just a sec to get your car hooked up."

I pulled on my gloves and started rigging up the guy's Mustang. I was so busy making sure I didn't crush myself somewhere that I had stopped paying attention to the dude. Big mistake because the next thing I know I hear Shelly shriek like all holy hell. I stood up and cracked my head on the underside of the 'stang. My eyes watering I didn't take the time to process the pain. I jerked my head up. Dude had my passenger side door open and Shelly was plastered back against my driver's door. Dude had his hands up, eyes wide and I leapt over the tow arm and went around to my door.

I didn't think about it. I just opened it and Shelly spilled out backwards with a short bleat of unexpected terror right as I caught her. I wrapped my arms around her lithe form and crushed her back to my chest. Her legs out in front of her but not supporting her, if they had been she'd have been taller than me, as it was, her head was tucked neatly under my chin, her arms crushed to her sides so she wouldn't flail.

"Easy Princess! I gotcha," I said and her chest heaving she went limp with, I think, relief.

"Jesus Ghost!" she barked and began to struggle in my grasp, but I was having none of it, holding her fast. "Let me go!" she shouted.

"Nuh-uh, not until I'm sure you're not going to hit me," I told her and she gasped, indignant and started to struggle with more fury but I had her fast. I grinned, I couldn't help it. An echo of the fireball was in there somewhere and I loved it when she put up a fight.

"Please let me go!" she cried and her voice was tinged with such a desperate fear it wiped the grin right off my face. I did what she asked and immediately relinquished my hold on her. She got her feet under her and took several steps away, chest heaving.

"Easy Baby. You're okay. Deep breaths," I took a slow deep exaggerated breath for her benefit and she unconsciously mimicked me. I locked eyes with her, nodded slowly and took several more breaths until she seemed steadier. Her sapphire eyes lost some of their panic, the fear quickly turning to the old standby spark of anger.

13

"What the fuck Ghost?" she shouted.

"Yeah!" the guy echoed from behind me. I held up an index finger in his direction where he'd come around the front of my truck.

"You fell asleep Princess, Reaver and I thought it best to let you stay that way. He wasn't supposed to be here, I was gonna wake you as soon as I got the car hooked up. Didn't mean to scare you Shells but you're exhausted…" I tried to reason, but she cut me off, that stubborn set to her chin coming out to play.

"Seriously? You were supposed to take me *home* you asshole!" she cried. I gave her a baleful look and she swallowed hard, glancing at dude. While I enjoyed the banter and the healthy debates we'd had in the past, I wouldn't be disrespected. Especially not in front of a customer.

"Sorry," she said and smoothed down her sweater in the front. She'd caught my look full meaning and apologized to the guy.

"Hey, no worries. I really didn't mean to scare you," he gave her a smile and she nodded. She still looked spooked and when I took a step forward she immediately fell back a step of her own. I sighed inwardly but kept my outward appearance steady for her benefit.

"You're okay Baby," I murmured consolingly and she pursed her lips.

"Except I'm not!" she blurted and her eyes filled up with the hurt I knew was in there, but just the hurt, no tears.

"I'm really not," she said. I found myself nodding. I knew this was big but I had no idea why she'd picked me, or right now to open up, but as quickly as she had she shut right back down when dude spoke.

"I'm Ron," he said and took a halting step forward, holding out his hand to shake.

"Shelly," she stepped forward and shook his hand quickly then immediately bounded back out of reach.

"I really am sorry I scared you," he said and she nodded, her eyes fixed on me.

"It's okay. I didn't realize I'd fallen asleep. I uh, I don't sleep too well these days," she swallowed. Ron laughed.

"I'm not a morning person either," he ventured. Shelly's brows knit and she came at me abruptly. I held my ground; held still as she grabbed me by the shoulders and turned me into the light spilling from the cab of my truck. She hissed, that sound you make when something looks like it hurts and I was a bit mollified by the fast change in her demeanor.

"You're bleeding Ghost," she informed me and dug around in her purse. She pulled out one of those travel packs of those Kleenexes, stripped the plastic off them and pressed the whole wad to the back of my head which instantaneously gave a giant throb and started stinging like a son of a bitch. I grimaced.

"Cracked my head a good one under the car," I said and replaced her hand with mine. The Kleenex's were soaking through pretty quick. "First aid kit is behind the seat, let me finish hooking this up," I said and went to work. Shelly got the kit out and thrust a flashlight at Ron.

"Here, I need an extra set of hands," she said and he smiled and nodded. I wrapped up quickly and got the Mustang up and ready to roll. Ron was in the truck holding the flashlight beam where Shelly directed it and I stood obediently under it.

"Scalp cuts always bleed like a son of a bitch," she complained and pressed some gauze to it. She moved my hair aside combing it with her fingers and I guess inspected the cut. My eyes were fixed on the dark asphalt of the roadway. Couldn't stop the pleasant tingling of her fingers in my hair if I wanted to so I tried to focus on that sensation rather than the angry throbbing my head was starting up with.

"How bad is it?" I asked because it was sure starting to just plain *hurt*.

"I don't think it's going to need stitches. It's really not that big, I think you hit it just right. You're shirt's toast unless I can get it into some hydrogen peroxide sooner rather than later." She held the gauze bandage tight to the back of my skull for a minute or two, checking under it once or twice.

"We good?" I asked when she left it off for a moment or two longer than she had any of the previous times.

15

"Yeah, it's stopped," she said.

I turned around. Ron scooted back across the seat and settled on the passenger side. I looked at Shelly with a faint smile and said, "Up you go Princess," murmuring loud enough for just her ears, "You're safe as long as I'm here."

She pulled herself up, stopping midway to say, "That's the problem Ghost, you're hardly ever here."

She settled into the center of my bench seat and I pulled myself up after her and got behind the wheel, contemplating what she'd said and I realized, she was right. I aimed to fix that in a real big damned hurry. I just didn't know how I was going to do it yet.

Ron chatted amicably with Shelly on the ride to his house. She sat stiffly between us and politely answered his questions, though the answers she gave were the bare minimum. The more he talked and the more he showed an interest in her, the more her thigh pressed against mine which secretly gave me a thrill, which then made me feel guilty as hell for feeling that way. I dropped the Mustang and Ron in his driveway and took care of all of the paperwork. Once I was back in the truck, no sooner had my driver's door clicked shut Shelly's head turned sharply in my direction.

"You *never*, and I mean *ever* do that to me again! You arrogant *jackass!*" she seethed. She crossed her arms over her chest and the only thing that kept me from believing it was in righteous anger was the way her shoulders rounded forward, hunching in the dark. I pursed my lips to keep myself from saying anything regrettable and counted to ten in my head.

"First off, why aren't you sleeping? Secondly, I didn't do shit to you Shelly. You fell asleep and I *let you*, so you can get your wadded up panties out of your ass and see it for what it was!"

"Oh and what's that?" she snorted.

"Doing you a fucking favor Princess."

Shelly's head snapped around and she stared resolutely out the passenger side window, my proclamation met with a stony silence. Shit. So much for not saying anything regrettable. I let out a pent up breath I hadn't realized I'd been holding.

"Shelly look at me," I said, her jaw tightened and she continued to give me the cold shoulder.

"Shelly…" I tried more gently but she cut me off.

"Just take me home Ghost," her voice held sorrow and the bitter tone of regret.

"Not until you look at me," I said and switched off the truck to prove my point. She threw up her hands and looked at me incredulously, sapphire eyes wide with annoyance.

"I'm sorry," I said and her expression went from annoyed, to confused, to skeptical each one chasing the other across her fair face.

"Okay," she nodded, her brow furrowed as she searched my face, trying to decide if I was sincere or if I was lying to her no doubt.

"No lie," I said softly, "You're right, I should have taken you home Babe, but you look exhausted and…" I could see I was losing her, her scowl deepening "That's no excuse so I'm sorry." She searched my face and after a moment or two her skepticism dissipated, she nodded slowly.

"Instant karma," she said judiciously and it was my turn to frown.

"What?" I asked, genuinely perplexed.

"Your head. Chalk it up to instant karma. Now can you please take me home?" I winced, my head throbbed like a mother now that it'd been brought up, but I nodded anyways and started up the truck. We drove in silence for a while, me paying attention to the road inside the reach of my headlights, her staring blankly, somberly out the window at the blur of passing dark.

"Will you get in trouble?" she asked softly.

"Trouble for what?" I asked frowning.

"For having me with you, if that guy complains or something… Will you get in trouble?" I smiled.

"Well according to you my boss *is* a dick," I said grinning. She frowned at me.

"How do you mean?" she asked and her expression was tempestuous. I laughed.

"I'm my own boss Princess," I clarified, "Pauley's towing is mine."

"Oh, I knew your name was Derek, I never knew your last

name," she shrugged a shoulder.

"Didn't?" I asked surprised. She turned back out the window.

"No, didn't seem important," she said.

Ouch.

"I didn't mean it like that," she said exasperated and I caught her rolling her eyes in her reflection in the darkened window glass. "Don't look so butt hurt," which made me smile. I liked that she was watching me.

"If you grew up with Reaver you would understand," she muttered.

"Was his name really Rhett Butler?" I knew it was but I just wanted her to keep talking so I tried to put a convincing amount of skepticism into my voice when I asked. I missed the mark I think.

"You know damned well it was," she said, her tone colored with exasperation. We lapsed back into silence but I can't say it was an uncomfortable one. We'd just run out of things to say. I kept stealing glances at Shelly who stared vacantly out the window, thoughtfully chewing her lip.

"What're you thinking about so hard over there, Princess?" I asked. She let out a pent up breath in a whoosh of air and pinched the bridge of her nose, closing her eyes.

"I'm not a fucking Princess," she snapped, "Princesses need saving, I'm a motherfucking Queen. I got this shit handled." I snorted and tried to cover it with a laugh which I think was just as bad. That mask of anger snapped right back into place. Those sapphire eyes burning a hole through me where they were reflected through the glass. If looks could kill I would have been incinerated but Shelly didn't know I had her game. It was too late for all of her fronting and bucking up. She'd slipped up back when Ron had scared the shit out of her. She wasn't half as angry as she pretended to be. She was scared and unsure of herself and lashing out because of it.

"Okay Princess, whatever you say," I said and turned down the perfectly paved road of Hayden and Reaver's subdivision. I pulled up to the sloped curb in front of their driveway and killed the engine. Shelly immediately went for the door handle.

"Night beautiful," I said without thinking and she froze, her back to me, shoulders hunched like I'd hit her. I blinked wondering what I'd said wrong and opened my mouth but she was out the door, the sharp report of it shutting in my face echoing through the cab and the girl practically ran for the front door of the townhouse.

What the Hell?

CHAPTER 3

Shelly

"Night beautiful," he said to me and it sounded almost wistful. I froze, so many confusing emotions clashing against one another. Maybe once upon a time, but I felt like I was made of pure ugly on the inside now. I bolted out of the truck as fast as I could and slammed the door behind me on a surprised curse. I raced up the walk and let myself into the townhouse closing and latching the door behind me, resting my forehead on the cool, painted metal of the front door for a minute.

I heard a sigh behind me but I knew it was Reave. I could always depend on my big cousin... or at least I used to... I didn't know anymore! I felt my shoulders tremble as I suppressed a sob. I would not cry! I wasn't a crier!

"Aww no. C'mere Runt," Reaver's hands kneaded my shoulders and I turned around and buried my face in his chest and took several deep breaths of clean laundry soap and freshly showered big cousin, forcing the tears down hard. Reaver hugged me, rubbing up and down my back with his broad hand. I shoved away from him after barely a moment and sniffed.

"Enough of this touchy feely shit," I said and rolled my neck which was stiff from sleeping in the truck.

"Yeah you learn to appreciate the touchy feely shit more when you're with the right person," he said and I knew he was talking about Hayden but I made a face anyways.

"I'm your *cousin* and *you're married* you sick bastard," I pronounced and made to go up the stairs.

"Shelly," he said, not rising to the bait, I paused in my step but wouldn't look at him. "You need to let someone in, if not me or one of the girls..." he sighed when the set of my shoulders tensed.

"I'm fine," I lied, he snorted.

"Yeah, well..." he palmed the back of his neck and I took the stairs two at a time to the guest room closing the door quietly behind me. I wrinkled my nose. I smelled like metal and grease and automotive leavings, but over that was the woodsy outdoorsy smell that was Ghost. I tentatively raised my sweater to my nose and breathed in, my eyes closing, savoring for just one second...

I dropped the material and ripped it off, pulling my shirt over my head and stripping deftly in the cool dark of my borrowed room. I pulled on my bathrobe and listened at my door for Reaver. When I heard the door down the hall to the master bedroom shut in the quiet hush of the house I slipped out and into the guest bathroom, taking my most comfortable pair of pajamas with me.

I shut myself into the small space, locking the door and started up a hot shower. I mean *really* hot. There wasn't any sense in pretending when I was alone like this. Ghost wasn't my knight in shining armor, more like just some asshole in aluminum foil. It *was* as I'd said though, I wasn't some weak ass princess in need of saving... but unlike what I'd said, I wasn't no queen either. That'd been pure bravado on my part but there wasn't any way I could admit it to anyone else. That I could tell anyone that late at night, when I was by myself like this? Well, I so did *not* have any of this shit handled.

It was like I couldn't shut out the memories, no matter how hard I tried and it was only worse when I was sleeping because then I *really* didn't have any control over it. I would dream about it, in full, high definition, living color. The awfulness of that night playing over and over in my mind like some macabre movie I couldn't shut off until I woke screaming just as long and loud and clear as I had tried to in the woods. Only then his hand had been over my mouth as he took whatever he wanted from me while now, I woke everyone in a god damned three block radius.

I hung my robe on the back of the door and stared at myself in the mirror, hard, for several minutes. I'd always had a rough time keeping weight on myself and now that I was running harder and more than ever I was painfully thin. I looked like shit, I just didn't have the energy to do anything about it. Plus, who was I trying to impress anyways? I moved the curtain aside and stepped under the scalding spray with a hiss. Hot! Too hot! But I needed it to be and I would adjust in a second.

I thrust my face into the spray and scrubbed at it with my hands before bowing my head and letting the water pound the back of my neck and skull. I wanted *him* off me, out of me, out from under my skin and the inside of my head! I wanted him gone, banished forever more... and I wanted so badly for Ghost to live there instead and I didn't know why. I didn't know what it was about Ghost that was different from any other man I had ever met, but wouldn't you know? It was just my luck. If I really were a Princess then Ghost is what I had always pictured my Prince Charming to be and for whatever reason, he just plain wasn't interested.

Oh he'd flirt all right, he flirted with the best of them, but when it came to actually *doing* anything? He would never follow through. No matter how hard I had tried I couldn't get him to so much as kiss me and it had been infuriating for the longest time. Now I didn't want him to touch me, but that was because I wasn't *fit* to be touched. I hadn't really been before, I guess, but at least I could hide it then, now though... Now everyone *knew* I was damaged goods.

I poured some shampoo into my hand and started scrubbing the hell out of my hair. It was too long but I barely had it in me to get my ass out of bed on a daily basis, let alone deal with making a hair appointment. Now that I wasn't working I didn't have the money for it anyways and I was loathe to bum it off my cousin or his Ol' Lady. Maybe it was time to grow it out. I huffed out a huge sigh and let the water sluice through my hair and down the drain, the soap swirling around the silver plug before disappearing.

I hated myself so God damned much for not listening to Dragon. If I had just been less of a petulant damned baby, if I'd just taken the rag he'd offered, pretended for *one* damned weekend to be his! I fell into a crouch on the shower floor and sucked in breath after breath trying to get the storm inside my head and my heart to go away but the harder I tried to hold it back the harder it raged until finally, like always, it broke through and the hot tears rose up and fell, my throat closing up so tight I almost couldn't breathe.

I hated that I couldn't fight the tempest raging inside me. That even though they'd killed the son of a bitch, he still had so much control over me. Him *and* Jimmy. I grabbed the soap and started scrubbing until I was pink and raw and still the dirt wouldn't come off. I felt slimy and filthy and I didn't have clue one on how to make any of the stain left in my soul to come out. This was all my fault. If only I had been a better person if only... *If only.*

Ugh! This wasn't getting me anywhere. I stood up and pulled myself together as hard as I could and shut off the water. I wrapped my hair in a towel and dried off with another and pulled on my PJ's. Black satin shorts and a black satin camisole edged in cream lace. I swallowed back the bitterness and beat back the demon in my head, the near constant voice of self-doubt I lived with these days, and pulled my warm fluffy winter robe on over it all.

I slipped back into my cousin's guest room and shut the door quietly behind me. I hugged myself and stood for several moments and tried to decide if I wanted to sleep or do something else for the time being. I moved about doing a few little things, plugging in my cellphone to charge, setting my purse on the dressing table where I usually kept it...

My eyes landed on my discarded pile of clothes and in a moment of incredible weakness I plucked the sweater off the top and brought it to my nose again, breathing in deeply. Fuck. No one was here to see me so to hell with it! I shrugged out of my robe and back into my cardigan before I got into bed. I tugged the sweater up against my nose and burrowed under the covers. The smell of Ghost comforting me the way no words or hands from anyone ever had. I closed my eyes.

I wanted to be mad at him, wanted to blame him for what'd happened to me, for what he said to me, and for a time I did... I'd lashed out and blamed everyone for what had happened. I'd blamed Reaver for being distracted by Hayden. I'd blamed Hayden to her face for being a distraction to Reaver. I'd blamed Ghost for not wanting me and hated everyone for not trying harder to talk me into taking Dragon's property rag when really, deep down inside, I was absolutely humiliated and angry with myself for letting it happen. For not fighting harder, for being so weak, for freezing up solid... for so many things.

I mourned the girl I had been before. Stubborn and headstrong sure, but I used to be *confident*, I used to be *fearless*, and now... now there was nothing *but* fear. Sparks had stripped me of all of those things and more. I didn't feel *safe* anymore. Whereas before I had felt pretty and desirable, now I felt like a piece of meat. I didn't want to be pretty anymore. What once was a confidence booster now hung around my neck like an Albatross, a great big visible mark of my shame and a heavy burden around my neck, dragging me down. I felt like an object, just here for the using and that *killed* me. Where once I had felt powerful, now I felt powerless. I'd been stripped of all my illusions, I guess.

I sighed and closed my eyes and prayed that for just one night the nightmares would stay away. I breathed deep Ghost's smell and secretly wished I were still in his truck. I liked that he didn't feel the need to fill the silence when I wouldn't talk to him. I liked that he didn't pry, that he didn't ask how I was doing when I so obviously wasn't doing well. I didn't feel pressured when I was around him. I never had. He was different somehow, it was what had attracted me to him in the first place, well, after his damned good looks. The fact that he didn't want me had driven me crazy before but now, now it was a comforting thing but it still hurt... Wasn't that fucked up?

I drifted off to sleep slowly, my thoughts whirling around images of Ghost, replaying the sound of him on his ugly yellow cell phone, of his murmured words in my ear... *You're safe when you're with me.* I wanted to believe him, but what I'd said was true, he wasn't really ever around that much. Especially after what'd happened. To top it off, I wasn't sure I would ever *really* feel *safe* again. Safe was the paramount illusion that I'd been stripped of.

Still, with my nose pushed into my sweater, breathing him deep, I slept more fitfully than I had in months and woke the next morning to my big cousin waving a steaming mug of coffee under my nose like smelling salts.

"Morning Sleeping Beauty," he said with a smile, his blue eyes, an almost perfect match for my own, sparkling with entirely too much good humor given the early hour.

I snorted, "Sleeping Beauty my ass. I look like shit first thing in the morning, always have." I pushed myself into a sitting position and took the coffee.

"True enough," he agreed and ruffled my hair, I jerked my head back out of his reach and scowled.

"To what do I owe this displeasure?" I asked sardonically.

"Ghost called. He's coming by to pick you up," he said. I blinked.

"What? What for?" I took a larger swallow of the hot coffee, bigger than I intended. I blew out and sucked air into my scalded mouth. Lots of flavored creamer. Just the way I liked it, which meant Reaver was trying to butter me up for something. I narrowed my eyes in suspicion when he shrugged laconically.

"Reaver," I started, warning in my voice, using the tone that foretold terrible fury and a myriad of ways of attaining my vengeance in the form of practical jokes that could end up very, very messy if not downright embarrassing for him. His eyes widened and his smile got bigger.

"Sleep did you some good Runt! He's coming by to take you to breakfast then to your car. You must have made an impression on him." I blinked stupidly and stared down into my coffee. I could feel Reaver's smile disappear.

"Shelly," uh oh, he used my name, that was never a good sign.

"Mm?" I took another careful sip of coffee and wouldn't meet my cousin's eyes.

"What happened last night?" he asked in that deathly quiet way of his, the way that told me my loving big cousin had gone on vacay and left the monstrous cold one to house sit inside of his head. I flinched.

"I may have had an embarrassing epic freak out," I said dryly staring into my coffee. I didn't want Ghost to be in trouble, he hadn't done anything wrong.

"Spill it," Reaver ordered and I could tell just by his tone of voice he was back from wherever he'd gone. I told him about his customer opening the door and waking me up. Reaver listened in silence and when I finished gave a great big sigh.

"Just saved your boy an ass beating. He told me as much this morning when he called," I looked up at him sharply and backhanded his shoulder. He laughed and put up his arms in mock defense. Sadly I couldn't hurt him if I wanted to. Reaver was solid.

"How's things going with Dr. Hubbard?" he asked me then and I sobered. I think my silence on that matter said everything it needed to. Reaver let out a breath and scratched the back of his neck.

"Baby Cuz, you need to talk to *somebody*, if not the Doc, or me, or one of the girls..." he gave me such a pleading look.

"Reave, I don't... this wasn't... I don't know how! It's like I want to, I really want to but I'm scared you know?" I swallowed hard.

"Don't you trust me?" he asked and he sounded like his heart was about to break.

"I trust you with everything. I just, I don't know! It's like I want to talk about it and then the words, they just get stuck. I don't trust Doc Hubbard, how do I know he isn't gonna tell me I'm crazy?" truthfully I was afraid everyone was going to confirm my worst fears and my deepest shame, that what had happened to me was all my own damned fault.

Reaver hooked a hand behind my neck and pulled me forward and down so his lips connected with my forehead. He murmured against my head, "You're scaring the shit out of me Cuz. This ain't you. I don't know what else I can do to fix it. I killed him, you know I killed him and I did it bad Baby, I made him hurt so much for what he did to you." I shuddered and squeezed my eyes shut and huffed a deep breath of my own. I know my cousin meant well telling me these things but that wasn't it.

Sometimes, in some ways, I was *jealous* that Sparks had gotten to die. Sometimes it hurt so badly, in my heart and inside my head that I wish I could be afforded the same luxury. I didn't dare say any of these things out loud though. Reaver was scared enough and I hadn't gotten around to do anything about it mostly because I didn't know how well he'd do if I was gone. All though with Hayden around, I figured he had a much better shot at happy than I ever would now.

"Remember when we were kids?" I asked softly. Reaver's expression darkened.

"Wish I could forget, but which part?"

"When you found out Jimmy was coming around, that he was messing with me."

"Yeah."

"Remember how you started coming over?" I prompted.

"I started climbing in through your window and would sleep on the floor every night between your bed and the door," he said nodding.

"I never thanked you for that," I said and set my coffee aside, taking one of his bigger hands between the two of mine.

"You don't have to thank me for that or for anything I've *ever* done for you Runt. We're family. It was you and me against the world from the moment you were born. I love you. Now get your ass out of bed. He's gonna be here in like ten minutes." He got up and extracted his hand from between my own and I lost my nerve, I was trying to build up, to talk to him but the moment was gone, done and over with. I nodded mutely and he frowned at me.

"You okay?" he asked.

"Yeah you big dumb ox. Get out so I can get dressed." I swallowed past the lump in my throat and Reaver nodded. He went out, shutting the door softly behind him. I flopped onto my back and pressed the heels of my hands into my eye sockets. *What was wrong with me?* I stared at the ceiling for a heartbeat or two before throwing back the blankets. I untangled myself from my cardigan and rooted through the chest of drawers and the closet for something to wear.

Everything that I owned clothes wise was from the girl I was before. Revealing or form fitting, which is part of what got me into trouble in the first place. Don't get me wrong, I loved sex. I loved to feel good and I loved to make my partner feel good, and I used to love to engage in it as often as possible. I mean who wouldn't? It was fun times and even when it was empty of all emotion behind it, it had been a damned sight better than being alone.

Which was pathetic, I know, but I had always been the girl that had been good enough to fuck but not enough to love and eventually I'd grown to accept that sad fact. After a while a 'if I couldn't beat 'em, might as well join 'em' attitude had taken hold and I figured I was young and might as well have some damn fun... So I'd embraced my sexuality and had run with it and I had been moderately happy with the compromise. Still, I had always held out for a Mr. Right to come along someday versus a Mr. Right *Now*.

I pulled out a pair of skinny jeans and a thick, cream, cable knit sweater off a hanger. I pulled on a matching bra and panty set, again, a throwback from the girl I had been before and felt a little tired and sick to death that this was what it had devolved into for me... The girl I was before versus the girl I am after. I just wanted to be *me* again but I didn't know how after something just so... *life altering*.

I pulled on the jeans and a fitted white crewneck baby doll tee to keep the sweater from being scratchy. I was sitting on the edge of the bed pulling on my knee high red Doc Marten boots, lacing up the front of the last one meticulously when Reaver shouted from the bottom of the stairs.

"Runt! Your ride's here!"

"Just a sec!" I yelled back harshly through the closed bedroom door. I threaded a belt through the jeans and pulled the sweater on over my tee. I ran a comb through my hair and made a face in the mirror. There wasn't shit else I could do for it without it either getting longer or me going to get it cut. Maybe I *could* ask Hayden if she would make me an appointment with her stylist...

"Shelly!" Reaver yelled up the stairs impatiently.

I blinked stupidly at myself in the mirror of the antique dressing table and looked down at the tube of lip gloss in my hands. What was I doing? I threw the tube back down on the lacquered surface. It clacked and skittered across the polished wood and bounced against my cup of makeup brushes I hadn't used since forever. I heard Reaver's running shoes bounding on the tread and yelled at him.

"I'm fine! Jesus Christ! Let a girl run a brush through her hair! Fuck me Cuz!" I jerked open the door to my room and looked up at

28

my cousin with a frown.

"What was that?" He asked suspiciously. I rolled my eyes.

"Found a random tube of lip gloss in my jeans pocket, tossed it on the dressing table. Stop being such a freak." I went back to the nightstand, grabbed my phone and snatched my purse off said dressing table before I finally pushed past him. His eyebrows went up.

"Never claimed to be anything else, and speaking of which, who's the fucking pervert now?" He smiled and bounced his eyebrows. I frowned harder.

"What are you talking about?"

"Last night you get on my case about being married and your cousin and this morning you... hey!" I slapped him in the chest with both hands and shoved him, scoffing.

"So violent Missy!" he said and I could tell he was pleased that I was at least trying to banter back like we used to. I rolled my eyes and let the smile happen and tried not to let it slip when I realized it had been so long that the gesture actually felt foreign on my lips. Ghost cleared his throat from down below. Reaver and I both looked over the railing.

His hands were thrust deep into his jeans pockets which rode over sturdy scuffed brown farm boy work boots. I let my eyes sweep from his feet to his head. He wore one of his mechanic type button down work shirts over a white crewneck under tee. It was a two toned shirt. Black on top, gray on the bottom with a two inch wide red stripe separating the two colors midway down his chest. It looked good on him. A man in uniform always did funny things to me, even if that uniform was just a mechanic's or tow truck driver's. Just something about a hard working blue collar man did it to me every time.

Over the shirt was a sturdy blue jacket with a name patch sewn on the breast that proclaimed his name to be Derek. I felt myself blush and struggled with the fact that even after Sparks, I still had it bad for Ghost. I mean I shouldn't should I? It'd been four and a half months since it happened. I didn't really know how long it was supposed to be before I should start to feel or deal with attraction

29

again. I mean what happened had a profound impact on me, obviously. That meant it should take longer than four months for me to start feeling these things again shouldn't it? I didn't know and the whole mess of logistics and emotions confused the hell out of me. I secretly worried that enough time hadn't gone by and the last thing I wanted anyone to think was that I was a whore, or that I'd deserved it.

I felt Ghost's gaze on me keenly all of a sudden, his hazel eyes sweeping over me speculatively as I took him in while the war waged on between my heart and my head as I tried to just *deal with this*. His brown hair was hidden by a blue trucker's hat with 'Pauley's Towing' on a white patch on the front and I hated it. The hat. It didn't look right on him.

"Hi," he said.

"Hi," I echoed back at him. Reaver twisted his body and bumped his shoulder into my back propelling me forward a halting step towards the stairs.

"Get the fuck out, Cousin Dear. I want to fuck my wife," he said. I sighed heavily.

"You're disgusting," I muttered and went forward and down the stairs. I pulled my gray rain jacket down out of the hall closet and Ghost took it from me holding it out for me to shrug into. I turned to let him help me into it; that place between my shoulder blades tingling with apprehension as I gave him my back.

Reaver is here and this is Ghost. Reaver is here and this is Ghost. I repeated in my mind like a mantra. My thoughts were spinning at a dangerously fast pace. The hamster working overtime. *Why was I letting this happen? How could I agree to this? Wait.* When *did I agree to this?*

"See yah kids." Reaver gave a nonchalant wave and disappeared towards the master bedroom, a moment later Hayden let out a surprised shriek and Ghost and I went for the door.

"How do you live with those two?" he asked with a smile but I had none to spare. The girl I was before would have laughed her head off and said something about him being a prude. The girl I was now just felt confused over *everything*. Okay, well, not confused.

I was lonely… isolated. I loved my cousin, I loved Hayden but I felt so out of place living here it wasn't even funny. Which totally wasn't their fault! Not at all. No, it was just mine. I sighed as he shut the front door tightly behind us. It was crisp and overcast outside. Just a few more days and it would be Thanksgiving.

"Hey," I turned and there was that look of concern I was growing so accustomed to seeing on anyone and everyone who looked at me lately. I changed the subject abruptly before he could ask me anything. I wasn't sure I could lie to Ghost.

"How's your head?" I blurted.

"It's doing okay. Thanks, Princess. That tip you gave me about the shirt was solid. Replacing these is kind of a pain in the ass." He started walking down the drive to his tow truck which was parked at the curb. I walked along with him lest I be left behind.

"Reaver said you were going to take me to breakfast?" I asked skeptically.

"Yeah," he looked me over considering, "Consider it a peace offering for not taking you straight home like you wanted."

I nodded slowly, "Okay."

He opened the passenger side door for me and stood back. I pulled myself up into the cab of his truck and he shut the door behind me and I was suddenly struck by it. No guy had ever opened doors for me before. Huh… It was kind of nice. He came around the back of the truck and opened up the driver's door and got behind the wheel. He stuck the key in the ignition and I pulled the seatbelt across my body.

"Got anyplace in particular you'd like to eat?" he asked putting the truck into gear.

"I'm not really a breakfast person." He glanced at me.

"Gonna have to change that," he commented dryly and I felt my eyebrows go up.

"Oh really?" I asked, suddenly ready to fight him on it if he was getting ready to go all high and mighty on me.

"Easy Princess, didn't mean it like that. I'm just sayin' breakfast is the most important meal of the day."

I turned my face to watch the last of the brown and curling

leaves pass by the window as we drove.

"Stop calling me that," I said darkly and I watched his lips curve into a smile in the faint reflection in the window glass. *Why did I go along with this?* I wondered again, and just as quickly answered my own question... *Because it's Ghost, and girl before or girl after, you're still crushing on him like some stupid preteen.* Wasn't that the ever-loving truth?

CHAPTER 4

Ghost

She stared bleakly out the window, lost inside her own thoughts and I felt both frustrated and helpless to do anything for her. I didn't feel one bit guilty about lying to her about the real reason I was taking her to breakfast. Peace offering my ass, I just wanted to be in her company, to talk to her, to see if she'd let me have a peek inside that pretty head of hers. I looked her over and decided on Ghorm's, this greasy spoon over on Douglas. It wasn't pretty, it wasn't fancy; it was a working man's joint, plain and simple. I think she was the kind of girl who could appreciate something simple right now.

I let her think. Didn't disturb her at all on the ride over. I'd never really needed meaningless conversation to fill the empty spots and this right here was no exception. Sniping had taught me to be comfortable with silence and so I just drove and relished the simple pleasure of her sitting beside me. I was surprised when she spoke up as I made the turn onto Douglas.

"That's what I like about you Ghost," she said, voice strong but sounding faraway at the same time. I rolled up to a stop sign and turned to look at her.

"What's that?" I asked.

"You don't ask me how I'm doing every five minutes. You just let me be, let me be still and think." I smiled.

"That what you need? To just think?" I asked softly. She turned and looked at me and had such a sad and stricken expression on her lovely face I felt my heart twist in my chest. She looked like she had so much to say and so I stayed still, stopped at the sign even though someone was coming up on us in the side view mirror.

"I don't know," she said at last and I opened my mouth but the bastard behind us honked. Shelly jumped, startled and turned to look back out the window. I closed my mouth and rolled us through the intersection, making the turn into the diner's parking lot.

I backed us into a parking stall and threw the truck in park and switched her off. Shelly stared out the window for several more seconds before her hand reluctantly went for the latch on her seatbelt. Damn. Moment gone.

I was really hoping she'd talk to me. Patience. It was just like staring down a scope all day, just had to be patient. The shot would present its self. Just had to wait and not hesitate to take it when it did. I undid my belt and opened my door.

"Here, wait, let me get your door," I said to her when she reached for the handle and she looked over to me colored surprised. I got out and went around the front of the truck and got her door for her.

"I can do it," she said gently when I held a hand out to her to help her down.

"I know Princess. Ever stop to consider it was more for me than for you?" I asked and it was true. I couldn't fix her tattered heart but I could do this. Little small things that showed her I gave a damn. I couldn't fix what was wrong but I could try to fix a million little other things to make life easier for her and maybe if I mended enough of the little things the whole would start to come back together too. She pursed her lips and with a grim set to her expression got down on her own. That was okay, this was just day one and it didn't mean I would stop offering.

"Classy joint," she said but she had a charmed little half smile when she said it, even if it was weighted down by her sadness.

"Not much to look at but they have real good food. Come on," I held the door for her and she bowed her head and slipped through, her hands gripping the strap of her purse, which lay across her chest, like it was some kind of life line.

"Hi Derek! Go on and sit anywhere hon, who's your friend?" Margie was my usual waitress, plump with frizzy dyed red hair pulled into a severe bun, she wore the diner uniform of black slacks and dark green polo in such a way that she always looked harried and like she'd pulled it on as she was going out her front door. Which she probably had. She had four boys ranging from four to twelve, two of them identical twins.

Shelly swallowed and looked at Margie a little wide eyed as she breezed around the little diner at top speed filling coffee mugs and setting down plates chattering a mile a minute about this and that like none of the other customer's existed.

"Well, what's your name dear? I've never seen Derek bring a girl around these parts. Go on! Have a sit!" she waved a hand in the direction of some empty booths.

"I'm Shelly," she slipped wraith like to one of the open booths and slid in, I slid in across from her.

"Usual Derek?" I nodded, "And what would you like to drink Shelly?" Shelly looked up at Margie.

"Orange Juice?" she asked.

"Oh look at you! Aren't you just a pretty thing? One coffee and one OJ, coming right up," Margie bustled off and Shelly blinked at me.

"Ever bring any of the guys here?" she asked.

"No. This is the only little slice of life I really keep separate from the club. Don't know why I've never brought anyone here; you're the first." I gave her a small shrug. She looked anywhere and everywhere but directly at me. Her bright, clear, sapphire eyes roaming the place. Over the yellowed and peeling wallpaper, the cracked burgundy vinyl booths, the oak bar that customers sat at to eat, over the customers themselves which were almost all retirees or working men like me.

"Why did you really bring me here?" she asked.

"I've been thinking a lot about what you said last night." I'd decided truth was best if this particular question came up, and what I said got her attention because those eyes of hers snapped to mine, her lips thinning. She looked about to say something, opening her mouth to speak but that's when Margie showed up with our drinks and a menu for Shelly. She set the items down.

"You take your time Baby. Derek I'll put your order in as soon as she's decided." I nodded.

"Thanks Margie." I silently cursed her bad timing but couldn't be mad at her. Shelly had disappeared behind her menu and I decided to press on even though she hadn't asked.

"Specifically about me not being there. You're right, I'm sorry." Her eyes flicked to mine over the screen of the menu and the laminated paper dipped low, forgotten in her hands.

"Ghost, I shouldn't have said that I…"

"No, you were right. I never should have said what I did at the lake, I drove you right…" Anger sparked to life and high spots of color appeared in her cheeks. Uh oh.

"You drove me right to him? Is that what you're going to say?" she demanded. Actually no, it wasn't so I said as much.

"No. I was going to say I drove you right into a no win situation and I feel like it's my fault. What happened to you, I mean." I shifted, uncomfortably while her mouth dropped open in a little 'o' of surprise.

"I'm the slut," she said simply and I felt my features darken, "Don't look at me that way," she said tiredly.

"You're not a whore," I said curtly.

"I didn't say that, I said I was a slut. Whores get paid Ghost," her voice grew thick with a mixture of derision and sarcasm, "Those bitches have way more class than –" I smacked the flat of my hand against the diner's table hard enough that the flatware jumped and some of my coffee sloshed out of the mug and onto the table.

"Stop! Just stop Shelly, you don't need to do that; I won't have you do that," I grimaced. Damn the disrespect out of this girl sometimes, especially when she turned it on herself. I fucking hated that shit.

"It hurt," she said softly, "What you said – "

"I know and I was a total fucking douche pickle for saying it." She laughed a little under her breath and it made me smile to see it.

"Was that a laugh?" I asked, smile growing wider when one graced her lips, bursting across them like one of those time lapse photos of a rose blooming to life.

"Douche pickle?" she asked and the words, though crude, did nothing to lessen the effect those smiling lips had on my heart… or my dick. I shrugged laconically.

"Got a better one?"

She turned her head and looked at me sideways like she was trying to decide. "Not at the moment no," she said and we lapsed into a more comfortable silence, a little less strained than it had been before. She went back to deciding what she wanted to eat.

"I mean it Shelly," I said quietly.

"Mean what?" she asked, distracted by the menu. I sighed.

"I'm sorry. I was being an immature idiot wrapped in moron dipped in dumb shit at the lake." Her eyes flicked to mine and something passed through them, a deep and desolate darkness that shrouded her in sorrow.

"Can we please talk about something else?" she asked quietly.

"As long as you promise we'll talk about it someday," I ventured. She pressed her lips together and finally nodded reluctantly. I felt a tiny surge of triumph and Margie came back to take Shelly's order but my mind was back on that night.

Shelly had come up behind me and wrapped her arms around my shoulders and smiled at me.

"*So how about you and me go celebrate that shiny new cut?*" she'd asked with a sweet smile.

"*Celebrate how?*" I'd asked and not for the first time she'd laughed and scoffed at me. By now I was more than a few beers into my evening.

"*Don't be such a prude Ghost!*" she'd cried. I'd been sitting with a bunch of the men from the Kraken and Suicide Kings MC and they'd laughed which had hurt my manly pride or some shit and I opened my mouth when I shouldn't have.

"*No thanks, Princess. I'd rather find me a woman who hasn't whored for half the MC,*" she'd pushed off me with an expression that was a mixture of anger and pain. I'd never out and out said anything about it before. I'd kept it to myself, the disapproval over her status within the club.

"*Actually it's more like three quarters of the MC, and at least they know how to have a good time!*" she'd lashed back.

"*Good go whore yourself out to one of them then!*" I'd told her and she'd flipped me off as she'd stalked over to a different fire up the beach, closer to the tree line. It was Zander's words that haunted me most now. He'd watched her go and looked at me and shook his head in disbelief.

"You know she hasn't touched another guy in months? Ever since the first time you made a comment about it? She heard you man." He'd stared into the fire, resolutely *not* looking at my dumb ass.

"What do you mean?" I'd asked.

"I mean, you dumb fucker, that she likes you. Like, really likes you and she hasn't touched another dude. She's talked about it and implied, sure but she hasn't been with anybody since she overheard you tellin' Trig that you thought she was pretty but couldn't deal with sharing. She went cold turkey and hasn't touched another dude since, even though by all rights it could get her bounced from coming around the clubhouse. So why don't you stop being a jackass, put on your big boy pants and go say you're sorry?" he'd gotten up and wandered off leaving me at the fire with the other guys who had moved off onto conversations about how to best control mouthy club whores. The general consensus being with a dick in their mouth or with the back of a hand *to* their mouth. Neither of which I was on board with. At least not the way they suggested it.

"What are you thinking about so hard?" she asked me gently and I sniffed and adjusted the way I was sitting in the booth.

"Nothin'," I lied. She nodded slowly and stirred an insane amount of cream and sugar into a coffee Margie had poured for her. I took a swallow of mine which I'd left black while the silence became thick and awkward between us.

"How are classes?" I blurted in a desperate attempt to keep us from bogging down in the uncomfortable past. She fidgeted in her seat.

"I stopped going. I'm, um, on hiatus." She wouldn't look at me and I felt like I'd stepped in it hip deep.

"I didn't know," I said at last.

"There's a lot you don't know apparently," she said under her breath in a barely audible mumble.

"So why don't you fill me in Princess?" I raised an eyebrow and rose to the challenge. She froze, looking at me.

"Why do you care?" she blurted and I could see she was gearing up. I used to love pissing her off. She was so fucking pretty when she was pissed. Except this time I could see it for what it was. She was using her anger as a shield. I deserved her being pissed at me though, so I let it roll like water off a duck's back.

"I fucked up. I can admit that Shelly. So in all seriousness, why don't you fill me in Sweetheart?" she stared at me coldly but the anger in her eyes lost its edge pretty damned quick.

"I don't... I can't..." she turned her face away and stared out the windowpane through the dusty slats of the old venetian blinds. She was unconsciously hugging herself but it wasn't cold in here. Far from it. I'd touched a nerve and thrown her off base. Good.

"Why'd you quit school?" I asked gently.

"I quit everything. I quit life," she said and her mouth closed and set into resolute lines of silence. I nodded. It was a start.

"Thank you," I sat up straighter and so did she as Margie approached and set down our plates.

"For what? What'd I do?" she asked confused. I smiled and cut into my omelet and took a bite. She closed her eyes and her shoulders dropped in defeat.

"My heart is not your dick, so stop playing with it," she said and it was my turn to freeze up. Truthfully I was surprised as hell I didn't choke on my food. *Where the hell had that come from?*

"I would never... Why would you say that to me?" I asked, totally taken aback and I really hoped she would fill me in because I was at a total loss.

"I've always been *that* girl. You know?" she said and her hands trembled as she took a sip of her orange juice, her waffle sitting forgotten in front of her. Whatever this was, it was important so I set down my knife and fork and gave her my full attention.

"What girl, Baby?" I asked her.

"The one who was always good enough to fuck, to fool around with and have a good time with but not... not for anything else. I got tired of having my heart busted so I just kind of gave in. Figured I might as well enjoy myself until someone came along who saw me. Then you showed up and wow, I *really* liked you but you didn't want to have anything to do with me," she shrugged and I blinked, at a total loss. I'd never heard her say *anything* like this to *anyone*. Silence stretched between us and she picked up her fork, cutting into the whipped cream and berry covered breakfast confection in front of her. I looked at her, I mean *really looked at her.*

"I don't know what to say," my voice was hollowed out. I sat in stunned disbelief. I never in a million years realized that Shelly felt that way. She'd always seemed so, confident and sure and… she'd always just been so on top of things and was such a fireball. I sat back.

"You don't need to say anything. I don't even know why I said any of that, just please… eat your food it's getting cold." She wouldn't look at me. She was entirely too tense and the only thing that gave her total state of anxiety away was this flinching around her eyes as I scrutinized her. A lot of shit suddenly made some sense. I picked up my fork but it hung useless in my hand as I considered her.

"You were right," I said finally, switching gears.

"Right about what?" she asked, picking at her food.

"About what you said last night. I haven't been around and I'd like to change that. I'd like to try and be friends," I said and she snorted indelicately and dropped her fork with a sharp clack against the plate.

"Sure, okay," she said and let out a pent up breath.

"Not okay," I said and she looked at me.

"I'd like to try and be friends to start but ultimately I'd really like to get to know you… Maybe take you on a date." I ventured and she stared at me, poleaxed and started to look around.

"What are you doing?" I asked.

"Looking for the guys, or the camera," she said. Well that was a shit thing to say but I couldn't say I hadn't earned her mistrust.

"What?" I asked frowning.

"This is some kind of cruel practical joke right?" she asked and her words were like a blow to my chest. I wanted to rise to the bait, to get pissed off and tell her to fuck right off because what she was saying hurt for a multitude of reasons but I stopped myself and considered her.

"You don't trust me?" I asked. She gave a rude snort.

"Only person I trust is Reaver and I don't even know if I can really even do that anymore, he's been a little… distracted." She shrugged and had the grace to look uncomfortable with her admission and I let out a breath I hadn't realized I'd been holding.

"You've really been dicked over haven't you?" I asked and wanted to kick myself when she frowned.

"What was your first clue?" she asked. I shook my head incredulous and replayed a whole lot of things, a whole lot of interactions over the last couple of years over in my head using these new sets of filters I'd just been given and felt almost like an even bigger jackass than before.

"Okay Princess," I said and started eating. She stared at me.

"Okay what?" she demanded.

"You don't trust me then I'm gonna have to earn it." I shrugged. She looked at me like I had grown horns or something. I took a bite of omelet.

"So I'm going to earn it," I finished and chewed carefully. She cocked her head to the side and considered me.

"Yeah, we'll see about that," she sounded skeptical and fucked if she didn't have every right to be.

"I guess we will," I smiled at her and she looked at me with some serious misgivings. This wasn't going to be easy, but then again, for as *easy* as Shelly had been when I'd met her, she was one of the most difficult people I had ever met.

We lapsed back into silence, and I watched her as she stared at her plate like the answers would come to her in the patterns the melting whipped cream left in the strawberries.

"Shelly," I said quietly, she flinched at her name and looked up, clear blue eyes troubled.

"What?"

"Eat your breakfast," I said gently and she picked up the fork and took a tentative bite, but it was plain for anyone to see, she either had no appetite at all or the one she may have had, had fled. This was going to be one long and winding road.

CHAPTER 5

Shelly

Ghost was throwing curve balls faster than I could bat at them. I picked at my food. It was good, I just wasn't all that hungry all of a sudden. I took a deep breath and forced my way through half the waffle even though my stomach was churning. I didn't know why I had told him any of those things and I found myself really wishing I could take it all back. I guess I was just tired of him judging me.

I huddled miserably in my seat and tried to look anywhere and everywhere but at him. The view of the parking lot through the disgusting venetian blinds suddenly became really, really fascinating.

The diner was clean for the most part, just shabby. The table top wood had been heavily lacquered at one point but now that lacquer was hazy; pitted and scarred with age. Still, it was undeniably clean when we'd sat down. The dishes and flatware were clean too, if chipped here and there. Really it just seemed as if whoever did the regular cleaning for the place had simply overlooked or forgotten the blinds. I closed my eyes and took in a slow deep breath and let it out slowly.

The damned blinds didn't matter. Nor did the rest of my surroundings. I was just fixating on them so I didn't have to think about anything else, because everything that Ghost was putting into my head had the potential to destroy the last little bits of me if it all went wrong. And honestly, when was the last time anything had really gone *right* for me? I really didn't think I was up for what he was proposing, the last part anyways, I mean *dating?* Really? I mean come on! *Really?*

"I can't," I said and my voice surprised even me after our long silence, while he'd eaten and I had picked at my food. His hazel eyes flicked to mine, puzzlement shining in them. I felt like my soul was folding in on its self. What he was proposing, the shiny carrot he was dangling in front of my nose… Why *now*?

"This isn't fair," I said and it sounded childish even to me.

"You can't just all of a sudden decide that I'm worth trying for, that I'm worth *dating* after… after what happened! I mean come on! It's not fair or even very realistic Ghost." I wanted it. I wanted it so very badly but at the same time I was terrified, if I did and he decided I was too broken or too fucked up and he disappeared on me… I swallowed hard. I would not cry. I was so not going to cry.

I wrapped both hands around my anger which was trying to leave, to retreat in the face of my fear and yes, even hope. No, I wrapped both hands around my anger and with every bit of strength I possessed I tried to pull it back to me, trying to hide behind something familiar so I didn't have to feel anything else. I tried so hard to hold onto it so nothing else had room to get in and so nothing else could get through. I needed to protect myself. I couldn't allow myself to believe in any of this.

"Shhhh, it's okay Princess," he soothed and I blinked at the unexpected reaction. I expected him to buck up, to be harsh, to say something incredibly mean or to shrug me off. I expected derision, condescension even, but the warmth and compassion that was coming from him made my brain melt. I broke open and spilled my awful truth out across the table at him.

"It's not okay Ghost! I'm not okay and I don't know if I'm ever going to *be* okay again. I'm never going to be the same. That was stolen from me and I don't know if it's possible to ever get that back! So save your pity for the poor slut who got what was coming to her, I don't want it or need it!"

I slid out of the booth, his hand shot out, an angry look on his face and I felt a surge of success as I dodged his grasping hand, but just barely. I turned and swept out of the diner, making strides into the crisp fall air and across the parking lot. Eating up the asphalt in long strides until I was all the way across it. I stopped at the corner by the edge of the road and put my hands on my knees taking deep cleansing breaths. Letting my heart rate cool. I pretty much instantaneously felt bad for ripping on Ghost but at the same time

43

felt just a bit lighter for having gotten some things off my chest.

"I want to kill him all over again," I heard him mutter dispassionately behind me. I turned and he stood a few feet behind me, hands buried deep in his jacket pockets head bowed, eyes hidden by the bill of his hat but the downward twist to his lips screamed his displeasure.

"Well you can't, and neither can I," I said bitterly, maintaining my front.

"I want to hug you," he said, but made no move towards me. I felt something in my chest loosen but I wasn't ready to let go my walls just yet.

"I don't like being touched anymore," I said and gritted my teeth because I really, *really* wanted to be held. My pride denied me though. He sighed and looked at me.

"Let me take you to your car?" he asked. I wasn't too familiar with this part of town but I was pretty sure that ORG, Open Road Garage, was only a mile or two away. I *could* find my way there on my own and walking never hurt anyone.

"Come on Princess," his voice was gentle and a little sad, "Just let me be your friend, let me take you to your car and we'll go from there. One step, one day at a time." His words were like a siren's call and I found myself relenting. I nodded slowly and he took a few steps back towards his truck. I reluctantly followed when what I really wanted to do was scream at him to stop confusing me, but I couldn't... because I was pretty sure I was only confusing myself. I was so bitter and so fucking angry and I was taking it out on everyone and it wasn't fair to them. I just didn't know how to stop. I didn't know how to process this big horrible no good very bad thing that had taken over my life and my dreams and dogged every step I took. I knew what my heart wanted. Had always known what it wanted but my god damned head always had to get in the way.

"Oh shit! Hey, no Shells, no don't cry, Baby." He took several steps at me and I back pedaled as fast as I could, dashing at the cresting moisture in my eyes.

"I'm not crying, my eyes are watering. Wind caught me just right," I lied and I sucked it up and shut it down. Pulled myself up by the proverbial boot straps and strode past him. I stood at his passenger side door for the moment it took him to catch up to me. He unlocked it and opened the door for me despite me being such a total manic cunt and I felt my shoulders drop along with my mood, even further into the abyss of self-loathing.

"Thanks," I muttered and heaved myself up into the passenger seat. I startled and looked down into his upturned face when he rested a hand on my knee.

"I was a complete and total selfish asshole, Shelly. I'm going to try really damned hard to make that up to you," he said. I felt my mouth open. I had just found my voice and was going to speak when he patted my knee twice and withdrew his hand, shutting the door tightly behind him. I stared at where he had been, mutely until the sound of him opening his door broke me from my silent reverie.

"I'm sorry, I shouldn't be taking it out on you," I tried.

"You go right ahead Sweetheart, I've earned a few licks for what I said to you that night... More than a few." His jaw clenched and a muscle ticked and I chewed my lower lip thoughtfully.

"You didn't rape me," I said at last, my voice hollow. I hated that word. It held a new and terrible, extra special loathing and I had studiously avoided it up until right that second. I turned my head to look at Ghost and his hand slipped from the key in the ignition, before he managed to turn the truck over.

"No, I didn't, but I did hurt you just the same, and by the sound of things, pretty deeply," he said and he was right, his words had hurt. I had never, not once, felt ashamed of my extracurricular activities until he had berated them. He'd called me a whore, except no one had ever made me *feel* like one until that moment.

I really didn't want to think about this anymore. I didn't want to think about any of it, but it was there just the same, breathing down my neck, crushing me into the forest floor just the same as that night. I swallowed hard.

"I'm sorry Shelly," he said and he reached forward and turned the truck on.

"Yeah, me too," I said softly. He put the truck in reverse and pulled out of the lot and into the street.

"Friends?" he asked several moments later.

"I'll try," I said and he gave me a crooked smile and nodded, turning on the radio. Country music filled the truck and I made a horrified face.

"Make it stop or I take it back," I said disgustedly, attempting at some levity. He laughed and switched the station.

"What do you listen to?" he asked. I slapped his hand and pushed buttons until I found my regular station. The Fray's, Over My Head filled the truck and I turned my face back to the window. The cab growing thick with emotions evoked by the song I reached over and powered off the stereo. God. I couldn't even have a minute without all this heavy shit weighing me down!

"Sometimes silence is better huh?" he asked and I nodded. I wanted so badly to be able to say that it was rarely ever silent in my head anymore. That the me on the inside was screaming, over and over and slamming myself into the inside of my skull. I wanted so badly to be able to trust someone, *anyone* with my deep dark secrets. To be the real me and to not have to be afraid of their judgments and recriminations, but I couldn't. Ghost gave a gusty sigh and I turned.

"What?" I asked.

"You," he said finally and I felt myself cringe. *Here it comes.* I thought. "The longer you sit there, the longer you're silent, the more you look tore down. You're tearing yourself apart in there aren't you?" he asked.

"Maybe," I hedged.

"Well stop. Just stop, Honey," his voice had dipped in that way that was purely comforting.

"I don't know how," I said and it was the most honest thing I think to come out of my mouth today, even with all the truths I'd been spilling.

He gave a slight chuckle, "Well then it's just something I have to add to my list then isn't it?" he asked.

I didn't rise to the bait, remaining resolutely silent instead. He turned us into the lot at Open Road where Dray had put a couple of the new guys with mechanical know how to work. A couple more were out with ladders and buckets of paint going over some fresh graffiti curtesy of The Suicide Kings. Disney was one of the guys on the ladders and I sighed softly to myself.

"What's wrong?" Ghost asked as we rolled to a stop.

"Nothing," I lied.

Truth was I pretty much felt like it was my fault that Dis had so much free time on his hands. I felt responsible for Open Road Ink's destruction, because let's face it. It all circled back to me in the end. I got out of the truck before Ghost could get my door and Dray came out of one of the bays. He looked me over, his dark eyes holding something that he'd never turned in my direction before. Compassion. It felt awkward and uncomfortable. The new, softer Dray still took some getting used to. It wasn't *bad*, I mean I kind of wished I knew what this Dray was like. The Dray I knew and had fucked around with had always been rough and intense. We'd shared some brutal fucks he and I, brutally *awesome* but really rough just the same.

He came up to me and before I could move or make a protest, hooked an arm around my shoulders and pulled me into his side. He planted a gentle kiss on my temple and asked those dreaded three words.

"How are you?" I stared resolutely at my red Docs on their asphalt backdrop.

"I'm fine," I mumbled. Dray was too much like his damned daddy because he barked a short laugh.

"Bullshit! Don't lie to me Shells, don't you ever lie to me," I shuddered in his grasp and his arm tightened.

"Easy," he said and his tone had gentled.

"Really Dray, I'm fine," I glanced up to see Ghost leaning against his truck's front fender, his posture stiff as he watched mine and Dray's interaction.

"Shelly," Dray's tone held warning and I felt my muscles tighten.

"Please don't Dray," I pleaded softly, "I'm okay, but I'm not gonna be if you keep pushing it and I really don't need it today, okay?" I said and he let me get away with it. He kissed my temple again through my hair and shook me a bit by my shoulders before letting me go.

"I'll accept that, but you're not fine," he said. I turned my face away from the lot of them watching me and stared for long moments out towards the street.

"I keep hoping that if I say it long enough and wish for it hard enough that it'll come true, okay?" I asked, and I looked at my one time fuck buddy because lovers we were not, lovers we had never been... to be someone's lover there had to be love and I was pretty sure Dray had never loved me. I know I had never loved him. Our physical relationship had been based on respect and on the understanding that there were no strings attached. My eyes drifted to Ghost who was looking me over with a slight frown on his face.

"I get you Shells," Dray said and I was pretty sure he did. He'd flown the same banner for years after his mom died. *I'm fine. I'm all right, I'm okay...* Say it long enough and often enough maybe it would come true. Yeah. Wish in one hand shit in the other and see which one filled up faster?

"What's wrong with my car?" I asked gently and looked to where she sat, backed into one of the work bays. Dray sighed.

"Alternator's shot. Waiting on the part. Might have to rebuild the one you got. Parts are getting scarce for a car that old." I bobbed my head softly in a nod at what he was saying.

"I can't pay you," I said and Ghost spoke up.

"It's taken care of," I looked over to him sharply. He was fishing his ugly ringing phone out of his breast pocket beneath his jacket. He gave me one of those one shouldered shrugs of his.

"What are friends for?" he asked before answering his phone, "Pauley's Towing this is Derek how can I help?" I blinked at him a bit incredulously and looked at Dray.

"Don't look at me Sweetheart," he said with a shrug and let me go. He took some backwards steps towards the open bays. With one last lingering look of concern, he turned around and waved over his shoulder before getting back to work.

"Shelly!" I looked up and had to smile. Disney was waving at me from the top of his ladder. I raised my arm and waved back. Ghost was talking on his phone and was totally absorbed so I figured I had a minute. I stepped across the lot, closer to the men who were painting over whatever The Suicide Cunts had scrawled on the cinderblock building.

"What are you covering?" I asked curiously.

"You don't want to know, but since I'm out of work for now while Trig tries to find us a new shop I figured I'd keep up on my skills. I talked Dray into letting me do a mural on this wall. Just gotta lay down primer and paint the building. Blessing in disguise if you ask me. This place needed a new coat of paint." I stood back and craned my neck back to look up at him. Disney's positive and sunny disposition was usually pretty infectious. I already felt a little lighter just from being near him.

"You going to be at the club later?" one of the guys on the ground asked me. I snapped my attention down to him. He was a new guy, from a chapter in Arizona. I couldn't remember his name but he had long light brown hair with streaks of blonde in it and a dimple in his chin. His eyes were hazel, but not like Ghost's. Ghost's eyes were clear with a differentiation between the brown and the green. This guys' eyes just looked muddy to me.

"I don't know, why?" I asked. He looked me over from my head to my feet and back again and where once I would have appreciated the look he was giving me, like I was something good to eat, where once I would have felt empowered and sexy and beautiful... Now all it did was nurture that seed of fear planted in my heart and mind by a man, who I had to remind myself daily, was dead. I swallowed hard.

"Just like to get to know you better is all," he said and he sounded genuine, but still, I had to swallow hard again to get it past the sudden lump in my throat. I painted on a smile. I didn't need anyone to think I was as crazy as I felt like I was these days.

"I don't know yet," I said and shrugged. I gripped the strap of my purse with both hands to keep them from visibly shaking.

"Aaron and I will be there," Disney said and I shaded my eyes and looked back up to him. His smile was thin as if he could read my mind and knew exactly how uncomfortable I was and I loved him for it.

49

"We'll see, I'm kind of out of a car right this minute," I said.

"Be happy to pick you up, Baby." The man said with a smile. He wiped the paint off his hands and strode towards me. It took everything I had to stand my ground but I did.

"I'm Grinder," he said and I held out my hand with trepidation and shook quickly before taking it back.

"Shelly," I murmured. I knew he was a Sacred Heart and I knew what the club stood for and how they operated here but at the same time, these new guys who had freshly patched over? They were an unknown quantity and that put me off my game.

"Oh I know," he said and winked. If ever there was a time I *didn't* want my reputation to precede me, this was it.

"Shelly," Ghost was right behind me, I jumped sky high and yelped. The guys painting laughed. Disney didn't. His eyes dimmed in sympathy.

"Sorry Princess, didn't mean to scare you," he said and I bit the inside of my cheek to keep from snapping at him or barking at him. He'd scared the crap out of me all right but it wasn't his fault. I nodded a bit too rapidly.

"I got a tow," he said and I nodded again.

"I'll come with you," I said quickly. Grinder's eyes shifted back and forth between me and Ghost.

"She yours?" he asked as if I wasn't standing right in front of him. The bubble of irritation I'd been holding back peaked and burst with this new outlet.

"I'm no one's!" I snapped and turned on my heel. I immediately wanted to cry, but I would be damned if I would do it! Wasn't that part of what had gotten me in trouble? I'd refused to wear Dragon's or anyone else's property cut that weekend. My pride and my obstinacy, a direct result of trying to prove to Ghost; to *will him to understand* that I'd really wanted something legit with him, had been my downfall. I'd told myself a million times since then, that what had happened to me was my own damned fault and that's what really sucked about it. It was. It was all my own damned fault, for not taking the cut and for not staying closer to the guys from our club. Ghost walked with me and let me get my own door. When we were safe inside the truck he started it up and put it in gear immediately.

"Easy Princess," he said in that smooth and soothing tone of his. I nodded.

"I feel like such a freak," I uttered and huddled in my seat, wrapped in my misery and guilt.

"Naw I've seen it before, I'm a soldier, remember?" he looked me over.

"Seen what before?" I asked, a mixture of suspicious and curious.

"You went through a traumatic experience," he said as if that should explain everything.

"And?" I prompted.

"PTSD Baby, Post-Traumatic Stress Disorder." I felt hot and cold at the same time for a second.

"I know what PTSD means!" I snapped and looked out the window, so I didn't have to look at him. I had always thought of myself as stronger than that. I pursed my lips before finally settling for raking the lower one between my teeth.

"You okay?" he asked somberly a little while later.

"No," I said curtly. No I wasn't okay. I didn't want to be crazy, I didn't want to be sick!

"You just want to ride with me for a while or you want me to drop you off somewhere?" he asked. I didn't want to be alone, but I didn't want to be around a whole bunch of strangers either. I swallowed hard.

"Yes please," I eked out.

"Yes, you want to ride with me or yes, you want to be dropped off?" he asked.

"I'll um, I'll ride with you for a bit if that's okay," I said and he nodded.

"Yeah Princess, it's fine, I like your company," he told me. I snorted incredulous that anyone could and would want to be around me anymore.

"Please stop calling me that," I said softly. He nodded and I turned my attention back to the passing scenery.

The first tow we went to was a woman who'd rear ended a man

on the highway. The woman was on the side of the road in tears, her small daughter clutching her waist, terrified of the lights and police and the man, who was standing by his SUV screaming at the woman, despite the police officer telling him to calm down and to stop shouting.

"Shit, this is gonna be fun." Ghost pulled up behind the whole mess and threw it in park.

"Stay here Baby," he said and I nodded numbly, my eyes fixed on the little girl's tear soaked face where she looked at the monstrous tow truck from beneath her mother's arm. Ghost went up to the State Patrolman and they shook hands like they knew each other.

The man shouted something at the mother and the little girl jumped in her mother's arms, clinging to the woman's coat as she started to cry harder. Suddenly the girl I'd been before decided to come out of nowhere because before I knew it I was out of the truck, my Doc Marten's thudding against the gritty highway blacktop and I was striding forward.

"Hey jackass! You aren't the only one having a bad fucking day here! So why don't you just calm your shit before I come over there and really give you something to bitch about? I'm sure his dash cam would provide the next greatest YouTube sensation of you having your ass handed to you by a girl! So sit the fuck down and shut the fuck up before I give it to you!" I wound my fist around and pointed at him and the small population on the side of the road blinked at me incredulously. I went up to the woman and her girl.

"C'mon Mamma, let's get you and your little one in the truck where it's pleasantly warm, not heated from all the hot air he's spewing." I led them over to the truck. The guy yelled at the cop who was with Ghost.

"You going to let her talk to me that way?"

The cop looked back and forth between us and called back to the guy, "Yep!"

"She threatened me!" he cried incredulous.

"Threatened you? That skinny little thing?" Ghost asked, "I think you're making that up!" he grinned and winked at me, the cop nodding along with what he was saying.

"I didn't hear any threat sir, now for the last time, get back in your vehicle and wait for your tow to arrive!" I swung the door shut on the mom and daughter closing them in Ghost's truck. I crossed my arms, leaning a shoulder against the truck's door, daring the guy to smart off to me with my sour expression. Ghost and the cop finished their exchange and he came back to the truck and we both got in sandwiching the mother and daughter between us.

"Nice going Princess," he said, his voice holding a shine of pride to it. He held out his fist across the mom and daughter's laps and I bumped it with my own.

"No sweat," I said and swallowed convulsively. He pulled in front of the woman's totaled Toyota.

"I'm Lindy and this is Kaylee," the woman said, voice shaky.

"Shelly. Nice to meet you," I said and smiled at the little girl, "Kaylee is a pretty name..." By the time we dropped the woman and girl off at the body shop, they were smiling. I waited in the truck for Ghost to come back and when he did he stopped and looked at me for several heartbeats before putting us in motion again.

"I've missed that girl. I'm glad she could make an appearance," he said, turning us in the direction of his next call.

"Me too. I just wish I had the ability to back her mouth up," I said and went back to staring out the window. Ghost made a noncommittal noise and we rode in silence through two more non-passenger tows. Around lunch time he pulled into the lot at Soul Fuel, Everett and Mandy's coffee and chocolate shop.

"What are we doing here?" I asked.

"I need coffee and you need to do something other than hang with me while I work all day. Let me get your door," he said and had efficiently switched off the truck and was at my door before I could protest that I could do it myself. He opened the door and stood aside. I got down and he smiled at me.

"Thanks," I said nervously.

"Any time..." I put up a finger.

"You call me 'Princess'; I'm kicking you in the balls," I said and he laughed.

"Any time Beautiful," he said and I bit my lips together and blushed. I still wasn't sure that was an accurate description anymore... Pretty to look at, maybe, but I wasn't beautiful by any means. My soul was still stained with too much ugly for that.

"Heya Lass!" Everett called from behind the chrome and mahogany monstrosity of an espresso machine. She twisted levers and knobs and banged this and that like a pro. "Usual Ghost?" she called.

"Yeah!" he called back from behind me. One of the club's new guys looked up from his phone in the corner. Protection detail. Dragon had one on every Ol' Lady at their place of work since Open Road Ink went kablewy.

"Dray said you both were at the shop. I kind of expected y' t' come 'round a lot sooner than this," she said. She poured coffee and steamed milk while she talked. I looked past her to see Mandy back in the kitchen, carefully shaking a chocolate mold back and forth. Air bubbles, or something, I think she once told me.

"Yeah, Shelly rode along on a couple of tows," Ghost told her.

"Here you go love." She handed Ghost his coffee over the expanse of marble countertop. She sighed and looked me over.

"Glad you're here," she said and I looked her over.

"Why?" I asked startled. Everett and I didn't always get along, she knew about me and Dray... from before, but I don't think that was it, I think I just rubbed her the wrong way for the most part.

"What can I make you first?" she asked with a sigh.

"Um, I'm sorta broke right now," I said, cheeks flaming with a touch of embarrassment.

"Good! This might make things easier!" she said, "Now what can I make yeh?"

I blinked. What a bitch thing to say! But I respected Dray and so I bit my tongue and grated out, "A mocha."

She made my coffee and handed it to me and then came out around from behind the counter, "I was going to beg," she said and led me to one of the little tables in the café section of their shop. I sank into the leather seat and blinked at her.

"Beg for what? Bitch, you can start making sense any second

54

now!" I said and she laughed.

"I can't keep up with the damned books Shelly, I need help," she said and sighed. Mandy joined us.

"*We* need your help," she corrected her friend.

Ghost cleared his throat behind me, "I gotta bounce. I can come back and get you Shells..."

Mandy waved him off, "We can take her home," she said, I nodded slowly.

"Okay," I agreed.

"Kay," Ghost bent and kissed the top of my head and I startled, hard. He locked eyes with me for a second, his expression somber and inclined his head once, slowly, before leaving out the front of the shop. I stared after him for a long few moments, my paper cup of coffee forgotten in my hands.

"Shelly?" I blinked and came back to myself and turned, Mandy and Everett exchanged a look and then looked at me considering.

"What?" I asked. Clearly I had missed something. A variation of the dreaded three words came out,

"Are you okay?" Mandy asked and she was such a timid and quiet thing on a good day that I didn't have it in me to front or be a cow so I simply nodded.

"Yeah I just don't know what's gotten in to him," I said.

"You did. He's liked you for a long time," Everett said. I shook my head as if to clear it.

"What did you want?" I asked.

"The books..." Mandy reminded me.

"I haven't graduated, I don't have my accounting license yet," Everett snorted.

"If it doesn't stop you from doing the club's books..." she trailed off and rose her eyebrows giving me a pointed look. I shifted in my seat uncomfortably.

"Reaver's the club's Treasurer," I started and Mandy and Evy exchanged another look. Everett looked at me like she wasn't impressed.

"Please, Reaver hasn't touched a single damned one of the club's ledgers. Everyone knows he's treasurer in name only, that you're the one that does the books." She sat back in her seat and crossed her arms. Mandy leaned forward.

"Please? Neither one of us has the skill, or know how, when it comes to the numbers like you do. We really don't and we're not asking you to do it for free." She looked so earnest.

"That's right, we'll put you on the books as a barista, I mean it's only a barista's salary to start, but once you're graduated and you're square with your license and all of that then we'll make the switch."

I leaned back and took a sip of my cooling coffee which was just the right temperature to drink. It was phenomenal! I could see the pride in both their faces at my reaction and it made me smile.

"I'm in. Show me to my new brain trust," I said. I couldn't keep living off my cousin and Hayden's charity forever. Mandy yipped and threw her arms around me and hugged. Everett stood up.

"You won't be sorry!" she promised me. Honestly it was almost too good to be true. I loved parsing through numbers and balancing books. It was relaxing to me. Numbers didn't lie or lead you on or break your heart like people did. They brought me a laptop with the software installed that I would need and led me into a back office full of filing cabinets loaded with daily receipts and drop numbers and I think I died and went to heaven. It was warm back here, so I pulled off my sweater and hung it on the back of the office chair before I dove in.

A knock at the door brought me out of my torpor hours later and I looked up and blinked owlishly at my cousin.

"What 'cha doin' Runt?" he asked me. I felt a serene smile paste itself on my face.

"Numbers," I said.

"Yeah and how is that going for you?" he asked searching my face.

"A whole hell of a lot better than waitressing ever did." I made a face. He nodded slowly and sat down in the chair by the desk.

"How are you feeling?" he asked and for once the question didn't piss me off or irritate the crap out of me.

"Good," I ventured and blinked at the time on the laptop screen. The shop had long since closed.

"The girls say you've been in it to win it since you sat down," he said grinning.

"I guess so," I said dubiously.

"Feel like going to the club?" he asked. I looked over the screen a little longingly and he laughed.

"You can't hide under a bunch of numbers all night Runt. Save it, it'll be here waiting in the morning." He stood up and stretched.

"Okay." I nodded and saved everything and put what needed to be put away where it belonged.

"C'mon, I'll buy you a drink," he said, slinging an arm across my shoulders. Mandy was in the kitchen working away when we emerged. She looked up and smiled.

"Hey you! You look refreshed," she looked at me funny as she said it.

"What's that look for?" I asked.

"I'm kind of jealous," she said laughing.

"Oh. Everett leave?" Mandy nodded, "Dray came and got her. I wanted to play with some new recipes in the kitchen, I'll see them at home." She made a face, "If they come home."

I smiled, "Thank you for thinking of me," I said gently and she smiled sweetly in return.

"No problem." She wiped her hands on her apron and picked up a chocolate.

"Try this." She held it out to my mouth and I laughed, opened up and she popped it in. I bit down and the rich chocolate shell cracked and my mouth was flooded with spicy rum. I blinked in surprise. It was a-freaking-mazing!

"What is that?" I asked. Mandy smirked at my big cousin.

"A Kraken rum filled chocolate starfish." Reaver lost it, just howled with laughter and I blinked.

"Why is that funny?" I asked, remembering too late.

"Hayden's been telling stories," Reave said and I blushed kind of hard.

"Ewe gross! Forget I asked, I don't want to hear about you doin' it!" I cried.

I turned to Mandy, "Those are really good but I kind of hate you

57

right now," Mandy grinned, an impish gleam in her eyes. I unfortunately knew the story of Hayden's first threesome, I had been with all the girls when the story came out and I hadn't been *near* drunk enough to hear it. I'd done my best to block it out. Some of the funny of the situation right now lost its edge a bit when I remembered that it was just before the Lake Run that we'd all had that night out.

"Still, I thought you might like to start your night out right, how can you go wrong with booze and chocolate?" she asked. I smiled.

"You can't, you really can't," I said.

"What're these for?" Reaver asked, picking one up and inspecting it.

"Your wife's bachelorette slash birthday party. Your wedding, while romantic, robbed us girls blind of the bachelorette party tradition so we decided to make up for it." Mandy nodded her head once, proudly and almost a little defiantly at my cousin which was cute, really cute because out of all of us Mandy was the meekest right behind Ashton. She didn't really spend that much time with the club despite living with the VP and his Ol' Lady. I think that had more to do with Revelator than anything though.

I looked up at Reaver who smiled down at me even though we weren't that far away in height, just enough for him to be able to do it.

"Ready?" he asked. I nodded.

"Yeah," I agreed, "Night Mandy, I'll see you tomorrow?" she nodded.

"Yeah I'll be leaving in a little bit," she smiled brightly and we went out into the main café. I blinked at Rev who was in the seat the other Sacred Heart man had been in earlier.

"Uhhhh," I started, Reaver grabbed me by my upper arm and towed me towards the front.

"Night Shelly," Rev said with a chuckle. I looked up at Reaver who looked down at me, his blue eyes so like my own gleaming with calculation.

"Not our business Runt," he said simply. I worried my lower lip. I half wanted to go back and give Zander a what for... He'd left

Mandy hanging pretty hard back when Dray and Ev first hooked up. Reaver didn't give me the chance though, he propelled me out through the darkened store front and out into the soft autumn drizzle outside. I shivered.

"I forgot my sweater!" I protested, and he grunted.

"Forget it runt. You're not going back." He pulled off his jacket and cut and pulled his hooded sweatshirt over his head and handed it to me. I pulled it on with a frown and he shrugged back into his jacket.

"You good?" he asked. I scowled back and he laughed.

"Get in the truck," he said and got in on his side and I was startled to realize I'd forgotten to get my own door. Ghost was having an effect on me, so it seemed. I wasn't sure if that was a good thing or a bad thing yet and tried not to think about it too hard. I got in to Reaver's beat up old work truck and we set off.

"Club or home? Speak now," he said as we approached the highway. I thought about Ghost for a split second but he was quickly overtaken by the image of Grinder lasciviously looking me over and I just wasn't up for that.

"Home, if it's okay. It's been a long day and I feel it catching up with me," I yawned just then and realized it was true. I was tired.

"No problem Runt. Hayden and I might stay in my room back at the club, you gonna be cool by yourself?" he cast a side long look filled with worry at me.

"You know better than anyone that you can't run from the things that live inside your head Big Cousin. You can't save me from myself all the time, I need to learn how to cope on my own." I sighed and Reaver's lips pursed in what looked like defeated resignation.

"I'm sorry Shells. I never wanted you to know that kind of burden," he sounded pained when he said it which hurt me, too. I reached out and folded both my hands around one of his larger ones.

"I hear you Cuz, but the big bad is here, and I need to start standing on my own eventually." I swallowed around the hard lump in my throat.

"I love you Shelly," he said and it took me aback. Reaver was a shower not a teller. He didn't say things like that often. He raised my hands up and smacked a kiss on the back of my hand and squeezed it a little.

"I love you too Reaver," I said choking up a little. I turned to gaze out the window so he wouldn't see but he knew.

"You'll call me if you need me. Promise?" he glanced at me. I nodded mutely. Sleeping was the toughest part of my day anymore.

"Promise," I lied. I wouldn't. He and Hayden needed a night off from babysitting me. I smiled in a way that I hoped was reassuring and Reaver smiled back but I could see the mistrust sliding through his gaze.

"I promise!" I cried and he nodded slowly.

"Okay," he said and I was relieved that he sounded like he believed me.

"Okay," I murmured softly.

Okay. I could do this. They were just bad dreams after all, I mean, right?

CHAPTER 6

Ghost

It was cold as fuck and bound to just get colder but I bundled up and rode my bike to the club anyways. I needed the ride to clear my head and it was just the thing. I pulled up into the lot and felt refreshed, energized and I was really looking forward to seeing if Shelly was inside. I pulled off my gloves and undid the Velcro behind my head, pulling off the neoprene-like protective mask from the lower half of my face. It did the job and kept me warm which was all I cared about. Who fucking cared if it made me look like a ninja?

I went into the club and smiled. It was warm and crowded already and the first thing I did was scan the room for that shock of bright, platinum blonde hair. I think my heart sank a little when I didn't see it. Raw disappointment weighing it down. Big hands slapped me on the back of my cut and gripped my shoulders with a near-bruising force. I was shook back and forth a couple of times and it threw me off balance. I scowled but it disappeared when Trigger's smiling face appeared next to mine.

"Hey Sir," I said with a rueful grin. Should have known it was him. He punched me in the shoulder and I frowned, rubbing it.

"Stop calling me that," he said but he was smiling.

"Force of habit man. Fuck!" I frowned harder as my shoulder gave a throb and he laughed.

"Grab a beer and join us."

"Yeah sure, you seen Shelly?" I asked.

"Naw man, just Reaver and Hayden tonight," he said and looked me over.

"Trying?" he asked simply like he was afraid to pry.

"Yeah." I sighed, "She's complicated," I said.

Trig's eyebrows went up and he asked, "What was your first clue?"

"Yeah, I know right?"

I skipped the beer for now and threaded my way over to where he was headed. Ashton smiled up at him beatifically. Once upon a time I'd told her to look me up if she ever wanted to remember what it was like to have a man touch her in a way that was pleasurable. Trig had slammed the door in my face. I'd done it mostly to get his goat, because everyone could see that those two were made for each other… and let's face it, I didn't share. Which had been my biggest issue when it came to Shelly.

I didn't share and she did it with anyone, at any time whenever she wanted. As a man raised a good Christian boy out of Midwest farm country? That just went against my grain so hard and in so many ways… Then there was the whole potential for cheating. I mean fuck, if I wasn't enough for her she'd just go find it somewhere else. Right?

I shoved those thoughts away; pulling out a chair at the table, and dropped into it. Hayden smiled at me from where she was perched in Reaver's lap, his arms wound around her waist, holding her tight against him. I smiled back and gave Reaver a nod.

"Should have seen it today man," I told him.

His eyebrows went up, "Seen what?"

I told him all about Shelly on the highway and Reaver grinned. He rocked Hayden back and forth on his lap idly and nodded.

"Shelly never could stand a bully. She was the same, all growing up. Her mouth would write checks her ass couldn't cash *constantly*. I swear to Christ I got into more fights because of it," he grinned wide, "Which wasn't a bad thing. I liked to fight, she just gave me the excuse to do it." His smile was totally feral at this point and I had to chuckle.

"You two were probably holy terrors growing up," Hayden said flatly.

"You know it, Doll," he said and kissed the side of her neck.

"She stay home?" I asked.

"Yeah, said she was tired. She got her head full of numbers at Soul Fuel. Ev and Mandy hired her on to do their books." Reaver smiled and I was pretty sure he'd planted the initial suggestion in Irish's mind.

"Good deal, she needs something to keep her mind busy."

"I could use help sorting through the mess left behind from the shop," Ashton murmured.

"You should ask her," Reaver said.

"I will." Ashton smiled.

"Shit, we could roll that right into having her sort out the startup costs and budgeting for opening a new place," Trig sighed.

"Any luck finding one?" I asked.

"Rev is looking, I'm looking, and we've both been looking together but not yet. Your last place gets blowed the fuck up terrorist style by a pissed off rival motorcycle gang and the place needs tore down? Well it's not the best thing to have on your rental history," he said ruefully.

"I hear you," I said quietly. The table was uncomfortably silent for a while. All of us thinking the same thing if I had to wager. *Thank God the place was empty and Disney didn't go inside.*

"So what – " Ashton's question was interrupted by Dragon coming to the table.

"Women, find someplace else to be," he grated. Silently Hayden and Ashton rose and met up with Chandra and Everett and disappeared toward the back. Once Dragon was sure the women were out of earshot he cleared his throat and started in.

"Hate to be the bearer of bad news but we got some information," he jerked his head towards Data who pulled up a chair and sat with us.

"Why the cloak and dagger Pres?" Reaver asked, suspicious.

"Data," the name dropped from Dragon's lips like a stone. Data scooted forward and all of us leaned in to listen.

"Dragon set me to the task of figuring out The Suicide King's dynamic a while ago. Specifically, why Grizzly, their Vice President would follow a man like Sparks," he started.

Trigger snorted, "Been wonderin' that myself since I first laid eyes on 'em back at the campground, that first meet and greet," he sniffed and put his hands on his knees, leaning in.

"So what's the story?" he asked.

"Seems this is a lot worse that just killing a President from a rival club," Data winced.

"Spill it man," Reaver demanded.

"Sparks was Grizzly's nephew, Griz raised him," Data said.

"No shit?" I blurted out in surprise. I don't think any of us saw that coming.

"Griz has been around the block a time or two," Dragon sighed, "He's smart, he's feeling us out with these hit and run attacks on our businesses. Seeing how we'll respond. I'm afraid he's planning something."

"I did some more digging, piggy backed some of their wireless carriers, hacked into their email and some of their other shit, bank accounts and that sort of thing trying to establish some patterns and they're smart, really smart. They mostly use burners which is standard operating procedure but one of them fucked up today and sent a text from their personal cell. I'm not sure why..." Data was prattling and the men around him grew tense, me included.

"Get to the fucking point Man!" Dragon snapped, irritated.

"They're watching the girls!" Data blurted. Everyone went still, Reaver and Trigger's mouths set into grim lines. Dray approached and turned a chair so he could straddle it.

"You tell them?" he asked and he looked as pissed off as I had ever seen him.

"Yeah," Dragon said darkly. No one asked what we were going to do. It went without saying: We were going to protect them.

"Jesus Christ these guys are fucking animals, worse than I thought," Trigger muttered.

"Twenty four hour escort," Dragon said judiciously.

"I had guys posted at the businesses already, we need to double it," Trig said.

"They've had us under surveillance since we got back from the lake, from everything I've been able to piece together, Open Road Ink and Garage, those were some enterprising younger members out to impress. Griz is more interested in hurting us where it counts. In his mind that's our women."

Reaver scrubbed his face with his hands, his expression going wintery.

"Should we tell them?" I asked and all of them looked at me blankly, a couple of their expressions turning decisive. It was Dragon who spoke.

"No. Not for now, we don't want to worry 'em. They're spooked enough with having us as a presence while they work, escorting them back and forth is gonna flip some switches and I don't wanna deal. Trig, pick some guys that are better with stealth. Let's keep this on the DL until we know for sure the threat against the girls is real and not just a ruse. They could be trying to misdirect but better safe than sorry. I've never heard of any club going after the women or families intentionally. Shit goes down and they get caught in the crossfire," he paused and the pain was clear. Dray dropped his eyes to the scarred table top. Dragon cleared his throat. "Never heard of it being intentional, that's just not the way we operate and it's just not the way it's supposed to go. Cartel's and shit do that kind of thing." He shook his head.

"You know…" I said carefully, "I'm just not feeling this place tonight. I'd much rather spend some time with Shelly. I thought she was gonna be here," I said, locking eyes with Reaver.

"Why don't you head on over to my place?" he asked and pulled his house key off the ring. "Kick back and relax. Beer is in the fridge," he said and held out the key.

"Sounds like a fine idea. I could use some quiet." I nodded and stood up.

"Hayden and I were planning on staying here tonight anyways. It'd make me feel better knowing my Baby Cuz wasn't alone. She doesn't sleep so well these days," he arched an eyebrow and my heart sank. Shelly was having nightmares, or flashbacks, which I had kind of figured. All you had to do was look at her to see it, still knowing and seeing were two different things and Reaver's reminder was received loud and clear. Quiet might not be on the menu for me this evening. We'd have to see.

"I'll see you guys around," I said, taking the proffered key and shoving it down into the hip pocket of my jeans.

"Good deal," Trigger said, then asked, "You packing?" I lifted the back of my jacket and cut so he could see the handgun I had tucked in the back of my waistband.

"Always," I said.

"Good deal," he repeated, nodding then leveled Reaver with a look, "You should be too," Reaver frowned and lifted the front of his sweatshirt. The handle of his gun dark against his white tee.

"They just aren't as fun but a fat lot of good my knives are going to be if I can't get close enough to use 'em." Everyone at the table lapsed into a thoughtful silence. You knew it was bad news when Reaver started packing heat. The guy just didn't do guns.

"We may be The Sacred Hearts, but our women are the soul of this club," Dray said softly. He was met with a round of grunted agreements.

"I'm gonna call to order in a minute," Dragon said and thrust his chin at me, "Get you gone Ghost. Look after our girl."

I swallowed hard and nodded. He didn't have to tell me twice, even if the phrase he'd chosen to use left a bitter taste in my mouth. *Look after* our *girl*. I left the club and sat astride my bike for a minute. My hands were shaking with a fury born of pure outrage. Not about what Dragon had said about Shelly, I knew she was... loved, by many. No, I was pissed at The Suicide Cunts. *Those motherfucking little cock bites!* I started the gauges on the bike without really seeing them before squaring my shoulders and starting her up.

I rode out to Reaver and Hayden's place. All I kept thinking was, *hadn't they done enough to her?* The more I thought about it, the more I wanted to break someone's face wearing red, white and yellow. I think our Pres. was making the right call keeping this under wraps. Shelly had enough to worry about, trying to put herself back together again. She wouldn't *be able* to pull it together if she was looking over her shoulder every two seconds.

I shut off the bike in the driveway and swung a leg over. The neighborhood was quiet and serene. I silently let myself in to the townhome. There was a lamp on in the living room but the place was quiet. I took the stairs carefully, quietly and cracked the door to Shelly's room to look in on her. She lay still in her bed, pale hair standing out against the darker pillowcase behind her head. I shut the door and retreated back down the stairs with a slight sigh.

I hung my jacket and cut in the hall closet and left my boots in the entryway before heading into the kitchen. I found the beer in the fridge, as promised, and twisted off the top to take a drink.

With nothing left to do I made myself at home on the end of the living room couch. I grabbed the remote and put my feet up on the leather ottoman coffee table thing and turned on the TV, channel surfing until I found something I could watch. My eyes never stayed on the television for long. No, they kept drifting to Shelly's door on the second floor which was visible from my vantage point. I finally switched to the other end of the couch further from the entryway and stairs by just enough that her door was obscured by the ceiling. I was hoping it would help curb the urge I had to go to her.

No such luck, but I did manage to stay in place on the couch.

CHAPTER 7

Shelly

I stared into the fire, back a bit from the throng of people, the dark of the woods behind me. My seething irritation quickly turned to fear when a hand clamped over my nose and mouth and another arm snaked around my waist. I was dragged back into the trees mercilessly. No matter how hard I kicked and screamed nothing would get that hand and that arm to let go! I bit down savagely on the meat of the offending palm over my mouth and heard a muttered curse. I was flung forward, spinning as I collapsed to my knees. I dragged in a hard breath into my air starved lungs when the back of that hand connected with the side of my face.

I pitched over from the force of the blow, white sparks flitting through my vision. I looked up at one very pissed off MC President.

"You're going to suck my cock," he declared and worked the belt and the front of his jeans. I staggered to my feet and tried to run but he caught me by the back of my shirt and my hair. I cried out and he hit me with his fist this time. I tasted blood...

I sat up with a strangled cry, chest heaving like it had that night. I flung the covers off my legs and planted my feet firmly in the carpet beside my bed.

"Floor, Shelly," I told myself, "Floor not pine needles, not ferns... Just a dream Baby. Just a dream," I gasped out in a half mutter half whisper, repeating the words my cousin and his wife used every time I woke screaming. But I hadn't screamed this time. I had woken up before the screaming had begun. Not that anyone had heard my screams. Sparks had kept his hand over my nose and mouth until I had passed out from lack of air.

I scrubbed my face with my hands which was slick with a mixture of tears and sweat and grimaced. I was hot, too hot and as a result thirsty. It was about this time I realized that I could hear the

TV, faint from downstairs. I sighed unhappily. Reaver and Hayden had come home after all. I stood up, still a bit shaky and tugged my robe around me, belting it. I opened my bedroom door and peeked over the railing. I couldn't see Reave, must be at the other end of the living room nearer the fireplace. With a sigh I descended the stairs and paused midway down when I realized the man on the end of the couch wasn't my cousin at all.

"Hey," Ghost said quietly. He sat with his sock covered feet up on the ottoman, a beer in his hand, perched on his thigh. Men's voices came from the television, talking. I blinked.

"What are you doing here?" I asked.

He gave me a half smile, "You weren't at the club."

"I didn't feel like it," I shrugged.

"Get thirsty?" he asked. I nodded. "Go get your glass of water, Princess," he said gently and I found myself wondering vaguely how bad I must have looked. I nodded and went into the kitchen and got some water from the tap. I returned to the entryway.

"Better?" he asked. I nodded, unsure what to say. He smiled.

"You didn't answer my question," I said and he smiled a bit broader.

"Pretty sure I did." He looked me over considering, "Want to keep me company?" he asked and before I could answer I felt my head nodding. I did, I really did. He patted the couch cushion next to him.

"What are you doing here?" I repeated dropping onto the couch a healthy enough distance away to make me comfortable but close enough I wouldn't be considered rude.

"I told you, you weren't at the club," he said and took a drink off his beer.

"I don't understand..." and I didn't, at least I think I didn't. Maybe I just wanted to hear it.

"I had my heart set on spending the evening with my new friend," I closed my eyes, his voice was rich and melodic, pitched a little lower than he usually spoke, his tone soothing.

"I was tired," I said lamely and opened my eyes. His hazel eyes flicked over my face, the brown centers radiating out to a rich green the color of new spring leaves.

"Yeah?" he murmured. I nodded. "Still tired?" he asked. Yes, but I shook my head no. He gave me that one sided tilt of his lips, that half smile I found so endearing and once upon a time, incredibly sexy. Who was I kidding? It was still incredibly sexy, which made me feel incredibly sad. There was no way he'd want me now if he never wanted me before.

"What are you watching?" I asked, if only to turn my mind away from how incredibly intimate the living room space had become. I was pretty sure it was just he and I in the townhouse, and the living room was cast in an intimate pool of light from the single lamp I'd left on in case Reave and Hayden decided to come home.

"Top Gear. You guys have on demand, figured I would catch up while you were sleeping," he reached out a fingertip and I froze, my heart hammering in my chest. He stilled when I tensed.

"It's okay," he soothed and I held very, very still as he brushed some of my too long hair out of my eyes, across my forehead. He sighed, a heavy thing weighted with wistfulness and sorrow. God I must look pitiful. I sank back into the couch and stared fixedly at the television. The show was about two guys walking men through how to fix this or that on different cars. I closed my eyes after a few minutes and just listened, I didn't really need to see. I breathed in deep the outdoorsy smell that Ghost always seemed to carry with him. It was oddly comforting to me, nice, pleasant in the way that a normal person would regard the smell of fresh baked cookies or clean laundry. Safe. It was the smell of safety.

I don't recall falling asleep again but I did. When I woke it was the next morning in an awkward yet comfortable position on the couch, my head and upper body on a pillow on Ghost's lap. The palm of his hand a warm, comforting weight on my back between my shoulder blades. I blinked several times and breathed in deep. His hand disappeared and I used my hands against the couch to push myself into a sitting position. The TV was still on but the house was growing light with the rising sun.

"Hey there," he said and I could hear the hint of smile in his voice before I looked to see it.

"Hi," I murmured and gripped the lapels of my robe together self-consciously. I could feel my cheeks flaming with embarrassment. Way to keep telling a guy not to touch you then sprawl across his lap at the first opportunity. Ghost chuckled.

"You're okay, Princess," he said with good humor, then more seriously asked me, "How did you sleep?" I blinked. I felt more rested than I had in weeks, maybe months.

"Good," I replied, surprised.

"That's all that matters then," and he smiled.

"You couldn't have been comfortable..." my voice was candy coated in guilt, he chuckled.

"Slept in a lot worse places in a lot more uncomfortable ways, and never with a pretty girl in my lap," he promised and I bit my bottom lip.

"Can I make you breakfast?" I asked. He was being so nice, I didn't have the heart to be anything less.

"How about I take you out again?" he asked.

"Afraid I can't cook?"

He laughed. My mouth dropped open in indignation.

"You are!" I cried and he laughed a little harder.

"Well can you?" he asked.

"Yes!" I crossed my arms. "Cooking is just science and in case you haven't figured it out, numbers and science go hand in hand. I'm a math nerd first but science is a close second."

He smiled at me, "Okay." He nodded and pushed up from the couch, stretching hard. I blushed again and averted my eyes from the lean line his body made with the motion. God, he was *everything* I found attractive in a man.

"Besides, the way me and Reave grew up, you learned to cook early and fast purely out of self-defense," I stood, rearranging my robe to ensure I was covered and Ghost looked me over.

"You had it rough coming up didn't you?" he asked softly.

"No worse than the next guy or girl. Reaver saw to that," I said with a one shouldered shrug. Reaver's mom the alchie, my mom the addict. I sighed inwardly. He and I did make quite the pair growing up. Sometimes we were all the other had. I moved into the kitchen and Ghost got up and followed me, making a pit stop in the first floor restroom. By the time he came out I had coffee brewing and a glass of orange juice waiting. I set about fixing bacon and eggs.

"You ever want to talk about things, I'm here. No pressure," he said slipping up onto one of the breakfast bar's stools. I paused and looked at him. Slightly rumpled from his night on the couch, his handsome face sincere.

"Sure, yeah, okay," his offer caught me off guard. It wasn't the first time someone had offered to listen but it was the first time that I really didn't feel pressured, there was no meaningful, long moment of eye contact willing me to spill my guts about my fucked up childhood or my slutty ways. He just had this way of putting it out there on offer and moving right along. Like now, he was talking about what he had going on for the day.

"...so I'll be at the club. Do you want to join me?" I blinked stupidly at him, I hadn't heard anything he'd just said, I'd been lost in the simple pleasure of cooking for someone else and my own machinations.

"You didn't get any of that did you?" he asked and his look became wary, as if he was measuring or gauging my mood trying to decide if something was wrong with me.

"I... I'm sorry Ghost. My mind got away from me. Started chasing a thought down a rabbit hole and got caught up in a whole lot of nothing. I can't even remember what I was thinking about," which was really only partially true.

"It's okay. I said that I was asked last week to help work on some of the rooms at the club, drywall, that sort of thing," I smiled thinly.

"I'll pass. I really want to finish catching Mandy and Everett's books up. I should be able to finish today." I heard the front door open and close and I shifted uncomfortably.

"Yo, Baby Cuz!" Reaver called out from the entry way.

"Kitchen!"

He wandered back and nodded to Ghost, "Hey man," then went right along as if he wasn't even there.

"Ashton was wondering if you could help her slog through the

72

mess left behind from the shop. Numbers, like years of 'em in a disorganized heap and Trig and Rev want to talk budgeting and yet more numbers when it comes to trying to open a new place." He slid onto a stool beside Ghost as I set a plate of bacon out. "Ooo Bacon!" Reaver reached and I slapped his hand.

"Guests first, Jackass," I stated tartly. He laughed and Ghost along with him.

"I wanted to finish catching up Everett and Mandy."

Reaver took a piece of bacon and bit into it and immediately spit it out and blew repeatedly in and out to cool his mouth. I smirked.

"Instant Karma!" I declared and he narrowed his eyes and pointedly ignored me.

"They want to pay you too, Sunshine and the boys," he said as if that would entice me, which it did.

I raised my eyebrows, "Let me make a call."

I plated up breakfast and slid what was supposed to be my plate in front of Reaver. I would make more for myself when I got back down stairs. I went up to my room and picked up my cell and called Everett.

"Hi Shelly," she said by way of greeting. Seemed everyone was up super early today.

"Hey, so um, Ashton wants me to help her get all the paperwork from Open Road Ink in order and get everything sorted out from the explosion. I can do both, I mean your shop and hers and could probably do more, but um, it sounds like she wants me to get started today," I said.

"That's not a problem for me, I saw what you were working on in the office this morning and it looks like you're almost halfway done!" she sounded impressed. I laughed a little.

"You guys haven't been open that long, only like six or seven months," I said.

"Knew you were the right person for the job." Everett sounded a little triumphant.

"So you don't have a problem with me getting started on Ashton's stuff?" I asked.

"Nope. Can you come in Monday?" she asked.

"Actually I was wondering if you wouldn't mind me using the laptop and software to help get Sunshine and the boys' straight," I chewed my lower lip.

"No go right ahead, you want to swing by and get it?" she asked.

"That'd be great." I smiled a genuine smile.

"Okay see you later then."

"Sounds good."

I jumped into a quick shower and got dressed. Jeans, a black tee and I pulled a black cardigan over it all. One with a hood that belted like a robe in case I got cold, but was short like a jacket.

I ran a comb through my hair and pulled on black knee high boots; lacing them up tight in the front. Hayden was in the kitchen when I got back down, freshly showered and in her comfortable around the house clothes which pretty much consisted of yoga pants and a tank top, all though with the turn in the weather she'd added a zip up hoodie to the ensemble. She must have come in with Reave and gone straight upstairs.

"Hi!" she greeted me brightly.

"Hi." I slipped up onto one of the stools across from her and she slid a bowl of fruit across to me. I smiled and took a bite of melon, the sweet juicy flavor bright in my mouth.

"You guys are home early."

"Got rowdy last night," Reaver said, "Couldn't get any sleep for shit decided to come home and crash for a few hours." He was talking with his mouth full and Hayden rolled her eyes.

"*I* slept just fine," she stated. "You know how *he* gets."

Reaver bobbed his head, nodding along with his new wife's assessment. Reave didn't sleep so well around a bunch of strangers. Granted all the new patch-overs were brothers, but some of them were still unknowns to a degree and I could completely understand where my cousin was coming from.

"So what're you going to do?" he asked Ghost.

"Pitching in to finish the clubhouse," he said.

"Mmm," Reaver finished chewing and swallowed, "I'll be there in a few hours. No one is up yet anyways, well except for the girls."

"Um, Hayden?" I ventured.

"Yeah?" she smiled brightly at me.

"Do you think you could, um, make an appointment with your stylist for me? I'll pay you back with my first check I..." Her smile broadened and she cut me off.

"Sure," she picked up her phone and shot off a text and was surprised when it bounced back almost immediately. "She can take you this afternoon if you're up for it."

I smiled, "That would be good. I need to go by Soul Fuel and pick up something and then I can go to Ashton's," I told Reaver.

"Not Sunshine's, all the paperwork and shit is at Revelator's. I'll text her and let her know you're coming." Ghost was leaning on his forearms on the granite countertop watching the whole exchange with inquisitive hazel eyes.

"If you can wait for about an hour for me to run the bike home and get my truck I can take you," he said quietly. I snorted indelicately.

"I'm not the Princess you're forever calling me, I can ride you know." I crossed my arms.

"It's cold Honey," he said and his voice was that kind soothing tone or maybe it was just soothing to me, I nodded.

"If I can ride in February with snow on the ground, I can ride in November when it's dry." I tilted my head, daring him to argue. He smiled instead.

"Okay Princess. Have it your way." I got off my stool and kissed my big cousin on the cheek then went around the counter to hug Hayden who hugged me back fiercely.

"I'll pick you up and get you over to Suzanne at around two."

"Okay," I went upstairs and pulled down my leather jacket off a hanger and a messenger bag off the top shelf. I found my gloves in my sock drawer and brought my gray warm infinity scarf off the hook on the back of my bedroom door. I went back downstairs and encountered Ghost in the entryway, lacing up his boots.

"Bundle up, Princess," he said with a smile. I wrapped my neck and the lower half of my face with the scarf wordlessly and zipped up my coat. I pulled on my gloves after slinging the messenger bag across my chest and I was good to go. My wallet and phone were already where they belonged so I was set. He nodded after looking me over and I pulled a spare helmet down off the top shelf of the hall closet.

Truthfully I was a little giddy inside. I loved to ride and it had been too long for me. I slipped a pair of sunglasses from my outside jacket breast pocket to protect my eyes from the wind and with a last wave at Reaver followed Ghost out to the driveway.

He had a beautiful Triumph America, a deep midnight blue with white accent and buttery soft black leather seats. He took extremely good care of his ride and it showed. The chrome gleaming softly under the overcast sky. I'd ridden with Ghost a time or two before but always with the rest of the MC, never alone like now. He straddled the cruiser and turned her on and I suddenly felt nervous.

"C'mon," he said and held out his hand to me. I went up and obediently threw a leg over the rumbling bike, using Ghosts strong shoulders to steady myself. His gloved hand went over my own, holding it briefly to the shoulder of his cut before patting it twice in reassurance. I let my arms wend around him and wiggled a bit to get comfortable.

"You good?" he called over his shoulder, his voice muffled by the bike and whatever he had over his face. I nodded, realized it was fifty-fifty on if he could see it or not, but he must have because he put the bike in gear and we were moving. It was a brisk ride to Soul Fuel but I loved it anyways. The only awkward bit? The tumultuous feelings I was having where Ghost was concerned.

I got off the bike and he backed it into a parking stall next to another rat bike looking thing with a Sacred Hearts sticker on the gas tank. I pursed my lips. He pulled the thing protecting his face off, which made him look a little badass when he had it on, and sniffed.

"What's the matter?" he asked. I pulled off my sunglasses and pulled my scarf down off my own face.

"Should we be advertising?" I asked gesturing towards the bike next to his. He twisted his lips and looked a little lost in thought for a second.

"I'll mention it to Trig," he said and I nodded. I didn't want anyone else hurt. Andy was already my fault... Trig and Sunshine and Rev losing their jobs, that was all on me too. I couldn't bear it if anything else happened to anyone. A hand gripped my elbow through the leather of my jacket and I jumped.

"Hey, easy Princess. It's just me." Ghost swallowed and his somber expression just piled the guilt higher.

"Sorry. I just don't want to see anything happen to anyone else," I pulled my elbow from his grip and he let me go.

"Is that what you think Honey? That this is all your fault?" he asked. I didn't answer, merely bowed my head and ducked past him into the shop.

"Hi Shelly!" Mandy called as she opened the door for me. They weren't quite open yet.

"Hey Red," Ghost called.

"Hi Ghost! Come on in," we went into the shop and I nodded to the brother in the back. He gave me a chin lift then stood up when Ghost walked up to him. They grasped hands and pulled each other into one another.

"Hey man," the mystery Brother said. He was taller than Ghost who was probably only five foot seven. The brother was probably around my five foot nine, so not that much taller. He had long black hair that curled down his back and I think was some kind of Native American but he had these strange swirling line tattoos over half his face that I'd never seen before and an accent to him that was almost Australian but not, British but not quite that either.

"What is it girly?" he asked me, and grinned his teeth very white in his rich dusky skin.

"Nothing!" I jumped and blushed, ashamed at being caught staring.

Mandy smiled, "Zeb is from New Zealand," she explained, "He was telling me all about it. It sounds beautiful."

"Oh, it's nice to meet you," I nodded and he smiled and again my eyes were drawn to the beautiful swirling patterns on his face.

"I get that look a lot here in America," he said and I flinched. He laughed good naturedly, "Jumpy thing ain'tcha girl?"

"Yes. Sorry," I blushed harder; then a bit emboldened by his good natured attitude, I asked.

"What are they?" indicating the tattoos.

"My people are Māori. It's a way to connect with my past," he said and the look on his face was both proud and tranquil. I nodded.

"It's nice to meet you Zeb," I repeated, "Thank you for telling me. Mandy, the stuff I need..?"

"Right where you left it Honey," she said and I slipped off behind the counter and into the back office. I gathered the laptop and charger and went back out after putting some papers in a better order; away where they wouldn't get jumbled or hurt, seeing as I wouldn't be back until Monday.

"Ready," I told Ghost and he looked up. He stood from where he'd been seated over near Zeb, talking. The laptop was an unfamiliar weight at my hip.

"Make you guys some coffee?" Everett asked.

"No place to keep it on the bike," Ghost flashed her a half smile.

"What you can't get creative?" Dray asked.

"You guys been here the whole time?" I asked skeptical.

"Store room," Mandy said rolling her eyes.

"Hey! Inventory got taken and he only distracted me a little," Everett winked.

"Need things ordered on Monday?" I asked.

"Yeah," Everett nodded.

"Numbers on the desk, I'll run them and if you leave a list of phone numbers I'll make the calls," I said. Mandy beamed at Everett.

"The Lord bless you and keep you Darlin'! I'm glad to be rid of it, I just want to make and sell coffee."

"I just want to make chocolate," Mandy nodded.

"Well I just want to figure out numbers and logistics," I said.

"Match made in nerd heaven," Dray grunted and Everett smacked him. Zeb choked on a laugh. Dray grabbed Everett around the waist and hauled her up tight against his body, cutting off her laughter filled squeal with his mouth as he kissed her. Mandy huffed out a sigh.

"They're like this *constantly!*" she complained but her grin belied any real complaint or admonishment. You could see the redhead was over the moon and ludicrously happy for her childhood friend and truth be told I felt a surge of the very same for Dray in my own heart.

"I'm really happy for you," I murmured and his dark eyes held some softness for me for a split second. He pulled Everett back against his body and looked me over.

"You need to take better care of yourself Baby Girl," he said.

"I'm trying," I promised, even though it was only half true.

"You ready to go?" Ghost asked.

"Yeah," I nodded a little too rapidly and wound my scarf around my face and pulled my gloves on as I went for the door. He got to it first and held it open for me.

"Bye all!" I said with forced cheer, voice muffled by my scarf, sure, but also by my choking up a little.

"You okay Princess?" Ghost asked gently when we were out by his bike.

"Yeah," I lied, when truth be told I wasn't really sure. It was like this a lot lately, one minute I felt like I was back on solid ground and the next the world was tilting violently on its axis.

I know it was a shitty thing to feel, but I was jealous of Dray and Everett, Reaver and Hayden... All I'd ever wanted, from the time I was a child, was to be loved like that and now here I was, all grown up and twenty-two and just as lonely as ever. I was beginning to think that I didn't deserve it. You know? That all that there was for me was some quick enjoyment and then they'd be on to the next. Like I was just a stepping stone before they were on to the next big thing. I felt downtrodden and like a door mat in so many ways and then here was Ghost who didn't want me but was hanging around me out of what? Pity? I felt restless and irritated all of a sudden and I couldn't stop the hurt that had started to ache and burn in my heart and so I asked him...

"Why are you doing this?"

"What?"

"All of this! Any of this? Why?" I asked and sniffed. It was cold, my nose was starting to run. Yeah. That was it.

Ghost's gloved hands slipped from the handlebars and he sat back on the bike and regarded me. He pulled his mask thing off so I could see his face and looked me over.

"I grew the fuck up," he stated as if that explained everything. "Or at least I'm trying to." I looked at him hard.

"What's that supposed to mean?" I crossed my arms, as much to appear a hard ass as it was to hold myself together.

"Let me take you out," he said.

I raised my eyebrows, "What? I'm sorry?" I blinked.

"Let me come to your door, pick you up, take you to dinner, take you out... You know?"

Was he asking me on *a date*?

My shoulders dropped. "You want to go on a date? Now. After everything..?" I closed my eyes and shook my head trying to wrap my brain around it.

"Has to be Tuesday night," he said.

"Why?" I asked suspicious.

"Want to take you someplace special, to see something, but it's only going to happen on Tuesday night." I let my arms fall to my sides.

"Why?" I asked again, and felt like I was starting to sound like a broken record. Ghost flipped off his helmet and ran a hand through his silky looking short brown hair gripping a fistful and bowing his head in frustration before letting it go and giving me his gaze full on. My breath was stolen right out of my lungs with its intensity.

"There's no screwing up with you is there?" he asked harshly and I felt myself take a faltering step back.

"I..."

"Listen to me. I. Fucked. Up. I want nothing more than to go back in time and kill that son of a bitch the moment he laid eyes on you! I can't go back! I can't kill him again! You've gotta realize, I'm not trying to hurt you. I'm not trying to dick you over, I'm trying to be there for you. I'm trying to help you! Now are you going to let me do something nice for you? You going to let me take you out on Tuesday night or not?" he demanded and I blinked, frozen to the spot.

"Yes!" I blurted.

"Fine! Good! I'll pick you up at eight, now get on the fucking bike!" he slammed his helmet back on his head and savagely yanked the chinstrap as he twisted around to face forward. I got onto the bike behind him but not before catching everyone inside staring at us wide eyed and dubious through the front windows of Soul Fuel. I felt my cheeks flame but didn't have time to think too much about it because Ghost had us underway.

We rode in silence all the way to Revelator's house, which, by the way, was an overgrown dump in *severe* need of repair. It was way past needing just a new coat of paint. New roof, new windows, hell, *new* everything was *required* to make this place look habitable. Ghost pulled up to the curb and as soon as I was off the bike nodded once in my direction.

"Tuesday, eight o'clock!" he called over the regular chug of his engine and I nodded. I couldn't be sure through the mask thing he was wearing to protect himself from the cold but I think he was smiling, his hazel eyes definitely holding a triumphant gleam through the clear lenses of his safety glasses.

Son of a bitch.

What had I just agreed to?

CHAPTER 8

Ghost

"How's Shelly?" Trigger asked and I scoffed.

"One giant pain in the ass," I answered, but it wasn't fair of me. I knew it the instant I said it.

"Frustrating as Hell and a total mess?" he asked.

"You interpret me so well, Sir." I handed him another chunk of drywall and he held it against the studs for me to screw into place.

"I said knock it off with that shit!" He scowled at me and I sighed.

"I'm batting a thousand today with my mouth," I said and we were silent for a time, well except for the high pitched whine of the drill as it drove the screws home. Trig sighed.

"We had some good times over there too," he conceded.

"Yeah, you remember that time we got Knack?" I asked. Trig barked a laugh.

"Which time? It was open season on that guy."

"He was always so damned easy! Remember the firecrackers?" Trigger laughed outright.

"Dude we were on the LT's shit list for days for that one, don't even get me started on how pissed the cook was, that was his favorite pot!" I laughed. We'd stolen the cook's pot and set firecrackers off by Knack's head while he'd slept. We were assholes like that.

"Fun times," I stated.

"Hell yeah. Should pull that shit on Dragon or Dray some time."

He grinned and we both howled when Dragon's voice boomed from the next room, "I fuckin' heard that!"

"Seriously though, what's the deal? I see you been spending a lot of time the last few days with wounded bird."

I nodded, "Dude, I was a fuckin' asshole," I groused. Trig raised his eyebrows.

"How so?" he demanded. I sighed again.

"I got it into my fuckin' head how it was supposed to be. You know? You're raised with these ideas that chicks are supposed to be all cuddly and soft and shit and then here comes this smokin' hot chick and…" I shook my head.

"Seriously man. Spill it. No bullshit. What was the deal? She tried six ways to Sunday to get your attention and we all knew you had the hots for her…" I nodded.

"Yeah, for her, not for every other guy in the fuckin' MC." I shuddered. Triggers eyebrows went up.

"Can't deal with the fact that women like sex too?" he asked and sounded almost disappointed.

"No! No… wait… uh, what?"

"Derek sometimes you are the biggest dipshit!" Trig sighed.

"Don't I know it?" I set down the drill and faced my old CO and friend.

"I wanted her. I still want her, I just want her to want me. Just me." I crossed my arms.

"Ah ha. So this is less about Shelly's being…" he groped for the right words.

I winced and supplied, "A slut?"

"Watch it asshole! That's my baby cousin I'm pretty sure you're talking about over here." Reaver walked some more drywall through the door, Data on the other end of the panels.

"Sorry man," I said. Reaver shrugged.

"Can't really argue with the label but look at it this way, a guy goes out and nails whatever pussy he wants and he's a fucking stud. My baby cuz does it, you call her a Ho, or a slut or all sorts of other shitty things. Who's the fucking dick out of that scenario? Sure as hell isn't Shelly." He gave me that icy stare of his and Trig stepped between us.

"As I was saying, so this is less about Shelly; it's more about *you*." I looked up at Trig and frowned.

"Me?" I asked. Trigger nodded and Reaver was still pinning me with an unfriendly look.

"I'm out of here, too Dr. Phil for me," Data muttered and he left the room.

"Insecure much dude?" Reaver asked me, eyebrows going up. My mouth dropped open and I wound up, about to smart back, when Trigger stopped me with a hand on my chest.

"Seriously, think before you speak right here Ghost," he said and I shut my gob and thought about it.

I'd been with a grand total of two girls and my right hand, sometimes my left if I was feeling adventurous. I stared off into space. The military had kept me seriously fucking busy and both of those relationships had ended because the girls had cheated while I was on deployment. Trig knew that. It was the last one back in Kansas who'd really busted my heart. I'd come back from my last tour to find her seven months pregnant when I'd left over nine months before.

"Fuck me," I said and hung my head. I'd been crucifying Shelly for the sins of my ex's.

"Just because my cousin gets around doesn't mean she's unfaithful," Reaver said quietly, "Just the opposite, she's fiercely loyal. She's just given up. If you'd ever bothered to really *talk* to her, to get her to open up you might know that about her." Reaver looked aside.

"What're you saying bro?" I asked him.

"I've already said too much. You should get the rest from Shells." I nodded, Reaver didn't know it but Shelly *had* opened up about it. I guess I was just wanting to hear it from multiple sources, but you know what? People in Hell wanted ice water and as far as I knew it, Shelly didn't lie about the big stuff, the exception to that being to say that she was fine when she wasn't.

"I really like your cousin," I told Reaver.

"I know you do, and she's done a lot better than I've seen her lately, the last couple of days. I don't know what you're doing, but keep it up please?" he said.

"I don't know exactly what I'm doing either, man. I'm just trying to be what she needs rather than just what she wants. Thought maybe it might do something for her. Something good. Still trying to figure it all out though," I shrugged a shoulder.

"What she needs is someone to stick it out. She gets scared, she starts pushing, testing limits until she breaks it so she can say 'see, it wasn't meant to be' or some shit like that. She's too used to being alone. She needs someone strong to show her she doesn't have to be. I really don't know what to do about the rest. She hasn't talked about it to anyone. Hasn't opened up," He lowered his voice and glanced over his shoulder towards the open door, as if afraid to be overheard.

"Shelly hasn't slept with anyone in a long time, since before what happened either. She started holding out for you man," I bowed my head a little, shamed by a lot and nodded.

"Zander told me, that night, right before…" Reaver gripped my shoulder.

"Look, we're more civilized than most of the other MC's out there but rules are rules and these new cats in town… it's a double edged sword and Shelly knows that. She loves this club. She loves the people in it and being a part of something bigger than herself. This is the family she never had but always wanted, if it comes out that she's not puttin' out? Then she's done. We can't afford to alienate any more of these guys. We already lost three interested in patching over back to their home chapters. Shelly needs to put on a good show. Man or woman you pull your weight. Everyone knows she's no one's old lady, now please tell me you're picking up what I'm putting down?" I nodded but he went on, "Shelly loses this club I'm afraid she'd lose one of the last threads holding her together." He gripped my shoulder tight and let me go.

"You need me to be cool," I said, understanding.

"You got it. Shelly flirts with the best of 'em but there is going to come a point when flirting is just not enough. She hasn't gotten painted into that particular corner yet but it's bound to happen. Dragon can't give her a free pass forever though lord knows he would if he could," Trigger said.

I nodded and sighed inwardly. I hadn't thought about any of that and I berated myself for it. I needed to pay more attention to the bigger picture. With nothing left to say we three got back to work. I didn't do much talking, I was thinking too hard instead.

The whole dynamic in the club had pretty much changed

overnight because of these Suicide Cocksuckers. We were still feeling a lot of these patch-over guys out. Especially the ones that had ridden in from the North East where some of the SHMC were still running drugs and guns. Dragon and Dray had been selective when they'd put out the call but still… word gets around and some of the guys that had turned up were rougher around the edges than we would have liked. One dude having just gotten out of the penitentiary. Although to be honest, the guy who'd shown up like that we had the least to worry about. He was all for going on the straight and narrow.

We worked hard and late into the evening, showering and redressing in our designated rooms. I still found myself shaking my head when it came to how damned big the club compound was. You'd never realize it from the front, but if you went out the back and across the expansive 'back yard' past the corrugated steel garage/storage building, there was another outbuilding that was just as big as the main clubhouse. It had pretty much been framed on the inside, it just needed electrical and to be insulated and dry walled. Now after some weeks of work, we were in the final phases of completing what turned out to be almost a dozen separate rooms and two communal bathrooms, on at either end of the long one story out building.

The entire property was wooded, but still, an eight foot chain link fence topped with razor wire surrounded the entire perimeter. I'd once asked Dragon what the hell this place used to be and he'd grunted and told me it was an old juvie facility that had been mothballed due to its small size. It had been completely gutted when Dragon had bought it with his ill-gotten, but laundered, gains and the rest of that money and then some went into getting the front building up to code and livable for at least the officers of the club and a couple of guests. It had just taken this long for there to have been a need to finish the rest and I could tell by the gleam of pride in his eyes that he was fiercely proud that we'd pulled the rest of it together this quickly.

I was proud too. To be a part of something bigger than myself but also, because my presence here was not only welcome, but appreciated. I hadn't felt right when I was honorably discharged from the Marine Corps. I felt cast adrift, like I didn't have a home and I'd had a *plan* then. I was going to marry the girl that I'd thought had waited for me. We were going to have kids, I would start my own tow company... Then I'd walked into my fucking kitchen with that damned bouquet and all those plans turned to one big steaming pile of shit.

I was pretty much desperate to get the structure, that sense of family and brotherhood back that I'd had in the corps, and so I'd called Sgt. Howard and he'd told me to pull up stakes and try it out here for a minute to see how I liked it. I threw my shit in storage and I rode out on my bike with a duffel full of clothes. That was it.

When I got here, the first thing I thought was that the countryside was beautiful. Hilly and green with plenty of hunting. I used the money I'd had saved from my time in the corps to buy my truck and to start up my business, to put the down payment on my house. The rest, furniture and the like, had come later. Trig and I both had flown out to pick my shit up out of storage and haul it out here. He'd even paid for his own ticket. When I'd been at my lowest after coming home to find my girl barefoot and pregnant with another man's child, Trigger had been the one to throw me a damned rope. As far as I was concerned, he'd saved my life twice now. Once over there and once over here.

There wasn't a God damned thing, come Hell or high water or anything else that would test my loyalty when it came to him as a result and by extension my loyalty to this club and the other men in it, being as they were so important to him. Hands descended on me, slapping the back of my cut as I sat at the bar nursing a beer, turning all these thoughts over and over in my head.

"Ghosty! What you thinking about man?" Revelator asked.

"The usual. The past, women..." he let out a hissing breath.

"You need to think about something else," he said.

"Got a lot on my plate at the moment. Life is at another crossroads."

"This about Shelly?" he asked.

"Some of it, some of it's about me too."

"Shit, you're doing some deep thinking over here ain't you?"

"Uh yeah," I agreed.

"Lay it on me," he grinned, the chip in his tooth making it almost comical.

"Was gonna take Shelly up into the hills to do something special for her. Take her to see something I know she'll like," I said.

"What that meteor shower thing?" he asked.

"Yeah, but I'm thinking I need to do something on a bit of a grander scale."

"Oh yeah? What did you have in mind?" he asked.

Good question. I searched my buddy's face and felt a slow grin overtake mine.

"I have an idea, but I'm going to need some help and maybe a woman's touch."

"You can count me in on the heavy lifting but if it's a woman's touch you're wanting you should try one of them hookers over there," he gestured with his bottle of water at some of the chicks that hung around the club... chicks like Shelly, but not like her at the same time... everything that Reaver had told me came flooding back to swirl around inside my noggin.

"I think I'll ask Hayden but I'm still going to need your help," I said.

"As long as it doesn't cut into my training," he shrugged.

"Got a fight coming up?" I asked.

"Next month, bottom tier but I should work my way up fast," his grin turned into a wicked, dangerous thing and I felt an answering smile of my own.

"Feel sorry for the poor bastard," I said and Rev clapped me on the back hard enough to rattle my ribs like a demented wind chime. I coughed.

"Real sorry," I wheezed.

CHAPTER 9

Shelly

I smoothed my hair and blinked into the mirror at my dressing table. Ghost had been busy, and truthfully, so had I since Saturday. The mess Ashton pulled me into was going to take much longer than I anticipated to sort out. Half the pages in the boxes were waterlogged and barely legible let alone readable at all in some cases. Some of the pages were lost all together, some of them had burned and by the time we'd gotten a quarter of the way through the first box Ashton was in tears thinking about 'what if's'.

It was grim work, and she and I both kept exchanging grateful looks that none of the boys had been there or were seriously hurt. We'd both gone to Disney the moment he'd stepped into the garage and smooshed his fairy ass in a girl sandwich. Aaron had been nearly hysterical at the look on his boyfriend's face and then they had both pitched in to help in whatever way they could.

We'd been at it both Saturday and Sunday when I finally got to go back to the easy stuff on Monday at Soul Fuel. I'd finished the last little bit of catching Mandy and Everett up this morning but they really hadn't been behind. I'd found one or two discrepancies in the whole lot of it which didn't really amount to any real losses. The girls were doing awesome.

"Hey Runt, you about ready?" I raised my eyes in the silver glass to meet my cousin's behind me. He stood with his back against the doorframe, arms crossed over his chest, face carefully neutral.

"Is he here already?" I asked.

"Not yet. I came up here more to see how you were doing," I rubbed my hands together.

"Would you believe I'm nervous as hell?" I asked with a shaky laugh.

"Yeah," he made no move. Didn't push off the door frame, didn't come across the carpet at me. He knew better. Sometimes I needed my space, I wasn't one hundred percent sure this was one of them though.

"You look good," he said and his lips quirked in a twitch of a smile. I looked back at my reflection rather than his. My hair was back in its short pixie cut, white-blonde bangs sweeping sideways over my forehead. I'd done my makeup, albeit lighter than I usually did. Just a little powder and some mascara, a bit of natural lip gloss.

Ghost had passed a message through Reaver at one point in the last couple of days to dress warm for tonight, but not to expect a ride. I wondered what that was about but wasn't getting any answers. Normally surprises were fun and exciting but lately they were nerve wracking. I sat in a pair of fitted jeans and knee high riding boots with a plush gray sweater with a high neck that clung in all the right places which unfortunately for the girl I was now, were all the wrong ones.

"You look like you're about to shit yourself Baby Cousin," I frowned at Reaver's reflection.

"I don't know if I'm ready for this Reave," I said.

"I know Babe," he said and his eyes thawed with compassion.

"What if I... What if *he*?" I swallowed past the lump in my throat and shivered, but not from cold.

"Baby Cuz, it's *Ghost*," he reminded me gently, "One of my brothers, a guy Trig trusts with his life and you know how I feel about the big man." He smiled and left himself wide open for one of my usual jokes.

"Someone should write a bromance novel about you two," I cracked and he smiled wider.

"It's gonna be fine. I promise, and if it isn't..." his eyes went glacial. He didn't need to finish that sentence. I knew full well what he meant. The doorbell rang and I stood up.

"Reaver?" I asked as I went to go past him.

"Yeah Runt?"

"If, one day I asked... If I needed to know... would you tell me?" I looked at him and his expression looked both sorrowful and afraid.

"What I did to him?"

90

I nodded.

"If you really wanted to know, *needed* to know, then yes, but I'd rather you get it from one of the other guys." I searched his face.

"Why?" I asked. He lifted his shoulder in a shrug.

"It's different hearing about it from one of them. I want you to still like me Shells. It'd kill me if you didn't." He backed out of the doorway and I thought about what he was saying and it made sense.

Hearing it from someone else would be less awful somehow, because from someone else, even Ghost, I wouldn't really wholly believe what they were saying. Reaver though, I believed everything that came out of my cousin's mouth as if it were gospel. Reaver would never lie to me. Never pretty it up just to make me feel better. We'd made a pact when I was ten that it would always be the truth between us no matter what and we stuck to that like glue. Reaver I could always count on, would *always* count on him. No matter what.

"Okay Reave, I get you," I said and I swear his whole posture eased with relief.

"I'm a monster Cuz," he said softly and sounded sad.

"I know Reaver," I hugged him. "But I love you anyways and I always will." He hugged me back and lingered a bit.

"I know I don't say it enough Shelly but I love you," he said and I felt my eyes get a little misted. I shoved him back and swallowed back the tears.

"Okay that's enough. I fucking hate getting all emo and shit." He laughed and we turned for the stairs and that's when I looked over the railing and saw him.

Ghost looked good. Really good, in dark new jeans that rode over clean brown sturdy boots with red laces. He wore a long sleeved flannel shirt in greens and blues and whites that brought out the green at the edges of his eyes. He'd actually done something with his hair other than cram it under one of his hats and it looked a bit stiff and unnatural with the product that held it in place in the front but the look suited him.

"Hi," he said and smiled.

"Hi," I echoed.

"You look good, Princess." I smiled and shook my head.

"I'm not a princess," I told him.

"Yeah, well, maybe tonight you are," his retort surprised me and made me blush. I went down the stairs before he could say anything else and brushed past him, grabbing my coat from the closet.

"Don't wait up," he said with a grin to Reaver and I stiffened, swallowing down some panic. I kept my cool. This was Ghost. *Ghost didn't want me like that*, I had to remind myself.

I swung my coat over my shoulders and slid my arms into the sleeves as I stepped out onto the small front stoop. He closed the door behind us. His truck waited at the curb and, of course, he got my door for me, which made the panic at his earlier presumptive joke dissipate further.

"Where are we going?" I asked when he climbed up into the driver's seat.

"Dinner then I'm taking you someplace special," he declared.

"Okay," I fastened my seatbelt and he pulled away from the curb. We rode in silence to a steak house off the highway. Not like a Roadhouse kind of joint, no this was fairly classy. A nice place.

We were seated in a quiet two person booth, a little oil lamp burning next to a slender vase with a fresh cut white carnation and some baby's breath in it. The menu was a heavy leather bound affair and we spent several minutes in quiet contemplation over it. We gave the waitress our orders and were suddenly left without anything to do or say. I took my time looking him over and he did the same to me.

"Why?" I echoed my question from days ago and it made Ghost smile.

"I told you, I grew up," he said shifting uncomfortably.

"You're like 30 something, you're already grown up." He laughed.

"In some ways, not others," he said. We sat in silence for a long time, regarding each other.

"I don't understand."

Ghost sighed, and folded his hands on top of the table, "I enlisted when I was eighteen. Proposed to the girl I fell in love with in high school and went straight into boot camp. By the time I got out she was with my best friend and I was being deployed," he twisted his lips.

"I'm sorry," I murmured.

"Came back, met another girl. Thought she was my end all of be all's. Talked to her every chance I got through the second deployment, came home; was stupid in love... Last tour, everything was great. Everything was awesome... got off the plane and raced home to find her barefoot and pregnant with another man's child." He scrubbed his face with his hands.

"I'd already put in my papers, was honorably discharged and was ready to make a life with her. Put the sand behind me. All of it shot to hell worse than anything I encountered over there the second I rounded that doorway." He shrugged.

"What did you do?" I asked.

"Called Sergeant Howard. Packed a duffel, shoved the rest of my shit in storage and moved out here. I mean sure, other shit happened and that's the super condensed version..."

"Why are you telling me this?" I asked. My heart ached for him. I knew what it was like to be cheated on, though I had never cheated. Not once. When I started up with the club and the guys, they all knew it was strictly no strings. No one ever knew my secret; that my dumb ass was hoping one of them would sweep me off my feet or some shit. I wanted it to happen because it was *meant* to happen.

Ghost regarded me for a while. Our food was set in front of us but we ignored it for the time being. Finally he spoke, "Because I fucked up with you Shelly. I took you at face value and pretty much crucified you in my mind for the sins of my ex's and it was bullshit, and now I'm looking at you all tattered and broken inside because I was a stubborn close-minded Midwestern hick. And if I'd given you the time of day," he turned his face and looked away, sniffing. My eyes welled with tears which matched the ones in his eyes that sparkled in the little candle flame. It hit me then, hard in the center of my chest, radiating out along my nerves in a prickling rush... Ghost was really torn up over what happened to me. He really did think he was responsible.

"It's not your fault," I whispered, the revelation leaving me barely able to draw breath let alone speak.

"It's not yours either, Honey," he said and swallowed hard. I stared at my plate and clutched my shaking hands beneath the table. We sat for a few more moments and finally began to eat before our food grew too cool to be palatable. Neither one of us could think of anything to say. I know I couldn't. So much of what Ghost said hurt to hear. I hurt for him, I hurt for me and it was just... all of it so incredibly tragic and at the same time just so *stupid*. If only we'd *talked* to one another.

We finished our meal in silence. He held my coat for me and I shrugged into it.

"We have a bit of a drive ahead of us," he said quietly when he opened my door to his pewter gray pickup for me.

"Where are we going?" I asked.

He smiled and it was tinged with a deep melancholy, "You'll see."

I got into the truck. Truthfully, I was tired and emotional and I just wanted to go home and to bed but Ghost looked like he needed this and so I sat and watched the scenery pass as he drove us out on the highways and finally wound us along back roads up into the hills. We must have driven for over an hour before we finally turned off the paved road and went deeper into the trees. I swallowed hard, my anxiety rising, before finally the trees broke and he pulled off to the side into a clearing beside this great big canvas covered thing. We sat high on a bluff overlooking darkness, lights twinkled far below and far off into the distance.

"Wait here," he got out of the truck and went into the dark and pulled the canvas up at the back. He knelt and did something or other and then came to the truck and opened my door. I got down.

"What is it?" I asked. He went to the thing and folded the canvas off it revealing an old fashioned brass bed, made with thick blankets and an army of pillows like something out of a magazine, in the middle of the woods on a cliff under a star shot sky.

"Ghost..." my voice was hollow with fear. I wasn't ready for anything intimate.

"Shhhh, it's okay Shelly, it's not what you think. Tonight is the Zephyr meteor shower. I was just going to bring you up here with a blanket but decided that wasn't good enough." There was a sound like fans running and I looked to him.

"What's that noise?" I asked, stalling for time, trying to think... Ghost had brought a bed, out onto a cliff in the middle of the woods just so I could watch a *meteor shower?*

"Rigged up some car batteries to run some electric blankets to keep us warm." He held out a hand to me and waved me forward. I took a halting step and he drew back the blankets.

"You did this all for me?" my voice was hollow with disbelief.

"Come on, sit," I sat on the edge of the bed which was plush and comfortable. He had really hauled an entire bed, mattress, box spring, frame and all up a mountainside. Ghost knelt and unzipped first one boot then the other, sliding each from my feet.

"You want to keep your coat?" it was cold up here but the coat would be too bulky. I gave it up. He got into the bed on the other side after taking off his boots and covered us up. Our breath fogged the icy air and I turned my eyes to the heavens.

"Shelly?" he asked after a moment.

"Yeah?"

"Can I hold you? Please?" I nodded after a brief moment of contemplation and sat up, scooting closer. His arm went around me and I laid my head on his shoulder. It was warm under the blankets. Heat radiating from the bottom as well as down from the top. I gasped as the first glimmer of white streaked across the sky.

"Make a wish Princess," he murmured.

I didn't have it in me to smart off, to tell him I wished he would stop calling me 'Princess', so I settled for the truth.

"I don't know what to wish for."

"You can wish for anything."

"I wished for you for a long time," I admitted.

"I know. I'm sorry. I had it in my head for a real long time that you were a smart girl, that you would figure it out and ditch those other guys and just want me and only me. But that wasn't fair. You weren't and aren't a mind reader." I laughed a bit brokenly. No. I wasn't. But neither was Ghost.

"I stopped... you know? I kept hoping that you would see it, I didn't exactly make it easy on you, I wanted you to see the real me but I didn't exactly go out of my way to show you." I gasped as three more glittering arcs made their way across the sky.

"Now you wish," I said.

"I wish I'd paid better attention," he murmured.

"Are you now?"

"I think so." His arm tightened around me and I rolled my head back against his shoulder to look at him in the dark. I caught a slight glimmer out of the corner of my eye and smiled a little.

"Stars are up there, Beautiful," he said gently and I turned my attention back to the sky. A moment later his voice came again, softly inquisitive, "Tell me something about yourself? Something no one else knows..."

"What like a secret?"

"Yeah something like that."

I chewed my bottom lip thoughtfully for a moment or two, then sighed... I didn't know what to say. I was almost afraid to open up like that, I'd kept myself closed off for so long so I wouldn't get hurt that opening up was almost unheard of. Like the door was rusted shut on me and I really had to work at it.

Ghost shook me a little and as if he'd read my mind said to me, "Come on Princess. I showed you mine now you show me just a little something of yours. Be brave, I swear to you on my honor, I won't tell a soul." I could hear the sly grin in his voice and it was so like something I would have said to him in the time before that I laughed a little. I pursed my lips, took a deep breath and took the leap of faith deciding that I had to at least try to do *something* different... Didn't I?

CHAPTER 10

Ghost

"No one really knows what happened that night," she said softly and I tried not to freeze up. She was right, I mean no one really did. We knew she'd been attacked. Knew she'd been... hurt... but she'd remained silent on the details. She hadn't even been the one to tell us who. That had been one of the Suicide's girls. I lay patiently beneath her, eyes fixed on the star spattered sky, and watched a couple streak across the midnight blue while she gathered her thoughts.

"I left you and Rev by the fire and went to a different one. I was standing with the woods behind me, just a little apart from everyone when he grabbed me. Sparks, I mean. He dragged me back into the woods and I bit him..." her story spilled from her lips in a rush of agony, her voice raw with fear and pain. I held her warm and close and listened and tried to let the rising tide of anger go. She needed me here, to listen to her, to hold her and be here for her. Not to fix this. There was no fixing this, but by hearing her out maybe she would start to heal some.

Her story took a while, and the more she spoke, the more my heart sank with the weight of her sadness. She spoke in sensations and emotions and used words no one should ever have to apply to themselves or to describe anything that had happened to them. She fell silent for a moment or two and I realized that she wept, only when she raised a hand to wipe the tears away.

"The worst part was knowing..." she took a halting, hitching breath and pressed on, the words spilling from her in a rush as if she were terrified to speak them, that once spoken aloud that everything would change violently and irrevocably.

"Knowing that if you didn't want me before, that there was no way you were going to want me after... after what he did to me."

She shuddered in my grasp and I stared hard at the glimmering lights above us and I felt so incredibly small and it had absolutely nothing to do with the vastness of the universe pressing down on us. No, it had everything to do with the fact that I had presented myself in such a way to her that she would or could ever think such a thing of me.

"Oh Honey, oh Baby no," I reached across her with the arm that wasn't pinned beneath her and grazed a thumb along the soft skin of her cheek. She looked up at me startled, her sapphire eyes luminous and filled with the reflected stars above us. She was so lovely, so beautiful in that moment I couldn't not…

I wasn't sure it was the best thing to do right then, or if it was the right thing to do but it *felt* right, so I tentatively brought my lips to hers. The touch was so soft it was barely there and I couldn't help but feel a slight surge of triumph. I'd been right. Absolutely one hundred percent right. Shelly's lips were softer than rose petals beneath my own. When she didn't flinch, when she didn't jerk away I allowed my eyes to slip shut so that I could revel in the sensation of her soft mouth against my own.

I kissed her upper lip and then her lower, chaste little presses, my tongue kept firmly out of the mix. Shelly let me kiss her, relaxing into my hold like she'd finally come home and I couldn't exactly deny that it was how I felt too. I drew back from the gentle kiss slowly and searched her face which was filled with surprise and wonder.

"Princess, I've wanted you from the moment I first saw you. I just let my own hang ups get in the way. I am so sorry for that, for what happened to you," she closed her eyes and looked pained for a fraction of a moment before she opened them, her gaze pleading for me to go on. To finish what I had to say in hopes that it would somehow make things better. I hoped it did, but words weren't going to be enough alone for this, this would take time and care and commitment to be healed and I was startled to realize that I could do all of those things, that I wanted to.

"I'm here now. I'm not sure how things are gonna work, or when or how things are gonna happen but I wanna try. Are you okay with that?" Shelly took her eyes from mine and lifted them towards the Heavens. She quirked her beautiful smart assed half smile that I hadn't seen in months and dropped her eyes back to mine.

"I guess wishes do come true," she smarted and I laughed. The air lightened between us, some of the tension was gone and it felt as if a fragile truce had been declared that was strengthening by the moment. We watched the stars cascade across the skies for hours, comfortable in my grand gesture of truce and I was very glad for the random stroke of genius that'd made me think of it.

I held her under that canopy of stars as we watched them glitter and streak across the sky. Sometimes there were long spates of time between star falls and we murmured softly to one another, telling stories and truths about ourselves. Learning about one another.

"What is it that made you decide to be an *accountant*?" I'd asked her at one point. She was quiet for a little bit and finally asked me:

"Do you really want to know?"

"I wouldn't have asked you if I didn't Honey," I'd smiled as I said it and she heard it, because she chuckled.

"When I was introduced to numbers and logic it was a revolution to me. I remember thinking to myself, *you mean if I do this and that that it will always equal that?* It was unbelievably exciting to have something there that I could always count on. Numbers don't lie. They're a constant thing that tells a story in a very precise and chronological order. I *love* that. So simple, so useful and I don't know... It just appealed to me so strongly," she rolled her head back to look at me and met my lips with her forehead. I pressed a lingering kiss there.

"What was that for?" she asked softly, and I could hear the confusion in her tone.

"Let me ask you something," I said, changing the subject.

"Okay," she smiled and it made her beautiful.

"If you could be anything, do anything at all, what would you want?" she turned her attention skyward and thought about it. I mean really thought about it, which I appreciated about her.

"Honestly I'm sort of doing it. I mean, I love this club and all of the people in it. I love my cousin and having a big family. I always wanted a big family. Growing up it was just me and my mom and Reaver and sometimes Aunt Candy, that's Reaver's mom," she gasped at a streak of starlight that was exceptionally bright and even I oohed with her when it seemed to come so close that you could actually *hear* it fizzle through the atmosphere.

We were quiet for a time, simply watching the stars fall across the sky. She cuddled closer into my side and it made me smile to myself. I once read somewhere that it took a man 8.75 seconds to fall in love but it took a woman 15 days. I wasn't entirely sure I believed in all of that, but here, right now with the vulnerable and open version of Shelly Jordan in my arms. It seemed plausible. At least a little.

"What was I saying?" she asked, voice still distant and tinged with wonder.

"Big family," I prompted.

"That's what the MC is for me. You wanted a secret?" she swallowed hard.

"Only if you want to tell me," I said gently.

"I stopped but I couldn't exactly *stop* you know? Everyone earns their keep in the club, if you're not someone's Ol' Lady then you're fair game. I can't hold out forever Ghost and losing the MC... I don't want to think about that. I don't want to lose my family. It may put the 'fun' back in dysfunctional but it's the only true family I've ever known and..."

"Shhhh, I know that now. I guess I'd never really thought about what it was to be a woman in the MC. We're a bunch of cavemen." She laughed abruptly.

"Yeah, a bunch of really hot cavemen. It's not bad with the Sacred Hearts though. It was something to do, you know? It was better than being alone and I know it's stupid but I kept hoping," she stopped and huffed out a nervous laugh. I closed my eyes and sighed out.

"You kept hoping one of them would see you and want you enough to make it just about you," I finished which was exactly what I'd wanted from *her*. I silently cursed myself in every language I knew how to swear in for being just so damned blind and stupid. If only I'd hung up my hang ups and communicated like a fucking grown up... I mean shit! Shelly was barely into her twenties, she was young, I didn't have a fucking excuse.

"Yeah," she admitted softly and the fans clicked off. The batteries powering the blankets had run dry. I shifted slightly.

"It's still warm!" she protested and I stilled, "Can we stay just a little while longer?" I smiled to myself and nodded.

"Yeah Shelly, we can stay just tell me if you start to get cold. I want to make sure you're good, that you're taken care of."

She sat up and leaned on my chest and searched my face. I couldn't see hers as dark as it was and with the backdrop of stars behind her. I wondered how much she could see mine but she must have been able to pick out my features well enough because *she* kissed *me*, a timid thing at first which grew into a beautiful meeting of the souls.

Her mouth was soft and sweet against my own. Asking for permission in tentative touches for more. I gave her everything she wanted, slowly, patiently following her cues. I cradled her face in the palms of my hands and opened to her at the first flick of her tongue against my lower lip. She tasted sweet and pure and like everything I'd imagined. Sweeter than honey, decadent and rich. I let her set the pace and Lord knows, that was really hard for me. I wanted so badly to press her back into the mattress, to control the kiss to mark her and make her mine but I couldn't. I'd spook her and I didn't want to do that. I wanted her to be comfortable. I wanted her to be all right and to trust me and things were so fragile, so new as it was... She whimpered softly into my mouth and I drew back.

"You okay Babe?" I asked, breathlessly.

"Yes," but her voice was strained.

"Talk to me Honey," I stroked my thumbs across the so soft skin of her cheeks and she laughed a bit bitterly, a wounded, broken sound that hurt to hear.

"I want so badly to be normal again. To be the girl I was before and to... I can't," she sounded strained.

"Okay, okay, shhhh it's okay. Baby I'm way passed any of that right now. I will take what you give me and be grateful for it. You go at your pace Baby Girl, not mine, not anyone else's. Okay?" she laughed and it was a lighter but derisive sound.

"This is so backwards and confusing," she said, tone much sobered.

"Yeah I guess it is," I agreed wryly.

"How did we go from one extreme to another?" she asked.

"We both know the answer to that," I said and pulled her back down into a light embrace. She felt so good in my arms.

"Yeah. I guess we do," and the sadness was back again. I sighed softly and kissed her forehead and we both turned our eyes to the sky until it became too cold to stay any longer.

CHAPTER 11
Shelly

"Awww! It sounds so romantic!" Chandra gently teased me. I bowed my head and continued arranging these roll things Ashton called pop-overs on a tray and nodded.

"I guess it kind of was," I admitted. Ashton smiled at me from over at the oven.

"I didn't know Derek had it in him," she murmured and Chandra laughed.

It was Thursday and Thanksgiving and the women folk were all in the club house kitchen while the men sat around the lined up tables drinking, the football game projected on a sheet duct taped to the wall behind the stage. Some setup Data had pulled off. I smiled a little wryly to myself. No one knew it but Data was a gentle lover with a soft touch behind closed doors. It had surprised the hell out of me. I figured he would be as impersonal about fucking as he was when it came to everything else he did. I sighed at the memory and was startled by Reaver who swept into the kitchen and hugged me from behind.

"Jesus Reave!" I cried. He laughed and I rolled my eyes. Damn it. Shouldn't have let him know he'd scared me. I slapped at his arms and he let me go.

"*Asshole*," I muttered with feeling.

"Never said any different Baby Cuz," he went to his wife who was using a stick blender in a vat of potatoes. She leaned her head way back for a kiss and Reaver laid one on her that was mellow by their standards.

"Come in the kitchen, get put to work," Ashton said and she held out a knife. Reaver grinned like the maniac he was and took it and set to work carving turkey and ham. Ashton had fixed both.

"At least you found something suited to him." I stuck my tongue out at my cousin and he winked at me. Trigger came in and pulled his little woman close and she giggled pushing against his chest.

"Out! And take something with you for the table," she cried. Everett laughed and handed a tray to Dray before he could get to her.

"You are gonna get it so fucking hard," he growled at her.

"Don't you be threatening me with a good time!" she bantered back and I smiled.

"Can I take something for you?" Ghost asked softly and I felt myself melt a little on the inside. I turned and smiled and handed him the tray of pop-over rolls.

"Thanks," I said just as softly in return.

We were cautious of one another. I hadn't seen him since he'd dropped me off at my cousin's door the night of the meteor shower. He'd called and we'd texted a bit but both of us were busy the last couple of days. The weather was bad which meant business was good for him.

He'd gently asked if he could kiss me again at my cousin's door and I'd nodded. I liked kissing Ghost. His mouth was so gentle but sure against mine. His posture tense as if he were holding himself back, every time our lips met, our tongues touched. He was trying so hard and truthfully I was too. This was so different from anything I was used to. I wasn't used to going on dates and taking things slow and truthfully... It was both something I liked and something I needed.

We loaded up the long table, which was really just all the tables pushed together to form one big one, out in the common room. Most of the MC was here and a few displaced club girls without family. Hayden's father was here, which was a little bit strange but he didn't have any place to be other than with his only daughter and this was me and Reave's family. Had been for a very long time. When Reave had asked Dragon and the club if his father-in-law could join it was widely agreed that it was fucking weird but what the hell? It was the holidays.

Ashton had rounded up the Ol' Ladies and Club Bunnies, which still made me damn near hysterical with giggles to hear us called *that,* but Ashton just wasn't a swearer and for some reason that's what she and Hayden had come up with while drunk and stupid one night. Anyways, Ashton rounded up everything at the club Thanksgiving with a vagina and put them to work in the kitchen helping her fix dinner and it was kind of perfect. Chandra sure wasn't letting it go to us 'Club Bunnies' heads though.

"Hey! Hey you! Yeah you!" she called out to one of the newer girls that had started coming around when the new guys had hit town and started bringing in bitches from the bars or Sugar's.

"Me?" the fake blonde with fake titties asked. I think her name was Sable or some shit stripper name.

"Yeah, you hooker! Take this out to the table and keep your dirty snatch away from my man," Chandra said sweetly. Everett and Hayden burst into a fit of laughter. Ashton looked on with a frown but even I'd seen her hold her ground with these new snatches when it came to her Trigger. She was polite about it but sometimes the *way* she was polite about it sank the claws deeper. Ashton knew how to hold her own and I'd already decided if it came to blows and I was around, I'd do the ass kicking for the smaller woman. Ashton just wasn't big enough to land a punch on another bitch that would count for anything.

Sable gave Chandra a dirty look. "Which one is yours?" she asked looking her over.

"Doc. Now hurry the fuck up Princess." She handed Sable a green bean casserole carefully and Sable scowled at her but didn't say shit. We knew how it went. As a slut, you didn't say shit or you could and would get your ass beat by the Ol' Ladies and your happy ass bounced from the club for starting drama. Even I had been put on time out a time or two for the drama clause. Reave had always sweet talked my way back in though.

Sometimes I wasn't sure that was a good thing but at the same time I think he knew just how much being a part of this world meant to me. The club was my family just as much as it was his, even with how fucked up and dysfunctional it got, how chaotic and sometimes violent it could be... It was more family than he or I had ever grown up with and was such an integral part of our identity I was terrified of losing it.

We brought the food out to noises and whistles of approval and took seats around the table. I sat between Reave and Data. Ghost was across and down two seats from me and we traded a smile before Dragon stood up at the head of the table. Dray at his right hand as always.

"Now I'm not sure how you boys did this when you were Nomad, or in your other Chapters but here, we do Thanksgiving as a family even when some of us have families we could otherwise be with," he looked around.

"Truthfully this table is the fullest we've had in a real long time," Dragon swallowed hard. We all pretty much knew it was because a lot of us were displaced with nowhere else to go.

"My boy Dray, yer VP made a pretty hardcore observation the other night and it stuck with me. I'd like to share that with you all tonight. He said, 'The men may be the Heart of The Sacred Hearts, but the women, they're our soul.'" There was clapping and some cheering and whistling and Dragon waited for the noise to die down. The girls all exchanged looks some blushing, some looking thoughtful.

"He's right, and I don't think that could be more evident than by this fine spread here," he gestured at the gargantuan mountain of food spread all across the expanse of table. What couldn't fit on the table sat up on the bar behind Ghost and the lot of them on that side of the table, "So I'm going to say, that we are all pretty much thankful for our brothers and our women and for this fine feast prepared for us *by* our women. Sacred Hearts Forever, Forever Sacred Hearts." The men all chorused the last together and Dragon nodded. "Let's eat!" he declared and with a last, loud and rowdy cheer we tucked in to the food.

It was one of the most heartfelt and sappiest speeches ever given by our Pres., but at the same time, it was perfect and just right. I'd been here, with The Sacred Hearts for more than a couple of minutes by now and I could honestly say, some of these guys could be the biggest fucking assholes, but at the same time, most, if not all of them, had a heart of solid gold in there somewhere. Dragon was no exception to that rule. Not by a long flat mile.

I looked around the table at the swollen ranks of Sacred Hearts men. I recognized all the original crew. Disney looking a little more somber than usual, probably because Aaron was at his parents instead of here. I recognized Zeb with his strange facial tats, and Grinder winked at me up the table which made me blush and check Ghost, who was sizing the man up, chewing thoughtfully. There were still a lot and I mean *a lot* of guys I didn't know yet.

There was a guy they called Blue, couldn't tell you why though, and another dude they called Duracell who was this smokin' hot Ginger. I'm assuming he was called Duracell after being a 'copper top' but you just didn't really ask those things, it was considered rude... I tried to give the man candy at the table smiles and equal looks to maintain what had become a cover to stay with my chosen family, but my eyes always drifted back to Ghost who would smile softly at me or give me a slight reassuring nod, although I would have to be blind to not see how it strained him.

I wasn't sure how I felt about his possessiveness. The girl I'd been would have been pissed about him being a fucking caveman when he didn't have a god damned right to be but the girl I was now... I don't know. I kind of liked it, it didn't feel oppressive; it felt comfortable. Safe even. I ate quietly and listened to the stories flying across the table about this run or that and tried to sort out my feelings.

I guess what it really boiled down to was how I was feeling versus how I thought I was supposed to feel given what had happened to me, which was crazy and ridiculous but it was there just the same. I leaned back in my seat at my epiphany...

Holy shit. That was it. I was tying myself up in knots about not feeling or feeling this or that because of what had happened to me, not because it happened but because I was afraid that by wanting Ghost that I was somehow betraying my gender and all other women who'd... I scrubbed my face with my hands and took a deep breath and let it out slowly.

"Shelly?" Ashton's soft murmured voice at my elbow. I looked up startled into her golden eyes which were concerned above her smiling mouth. "Could you help me in the kitchen?" she asked and I leapt on it.

"Yes! Yes absolutely." I shoved back from the table and followed the slight woman into the kitchen behind the bar.

"What's wrong?" she asked gently when we were out of earshot away from the table.

"That obvious huh?" I asked.

"You looked like you'd…"

I put up a hand and laughed, "No puns, accidental or not." She smiled at that but inclined her head, a gesture that told me to go on with whatever it was I had to say.

"No, I was thinking about my place here and um," I raised my eyes from the floor to meet hers and she cocked her head to the side and searched my face. The light bulb went off pretty quickly.

"Sex?" she asked.

"Sounds good to me!" Grinder came through the kitchen door and pulled me into his side. I put up my hands and stopped him from pulling me closer. I laughed and hoped it sounded light hearted.

"Maybe I have a date for tonight," I tried.

"Yep! Me," he said and his tone wasn't something that you could, would or should argue with. I laughed again but it was really strained now and I pushed a little harder against his broad chest and cut as he walked us back out into the common room, making for the back rooms of the club. I cursed in my head. He'd tied one on pretty good and the old me would have just shrugged and said fuck it. She would have gone with him, got on him, gotten off, gotten *off* of him and called it good.

But I didn't want that anymore. I wanted Ghost… but I also wanted to keep my family. I pushed against Grinder harder and his hold on me tightened. Ashton was furiously whispering into Trigger's ear, everyone else was engaged in conversation, I desperately cast my eyes for Ghost but he was at a bad angle, his back to me. Trigger coughed, I gave him a look and tried to telegraph with my eyes that I wanted one more shot at talking Grinder down. Trig nodded, I looked up into Grinder's muddy hazel gaze and bit my lower lip and smiled. A coy flirtatious look I'd mastered.

"Slow your roll there big boy!" I tried, again, for a light hearted tone.

"I have to help clean up," I was grasping at straws. Hell. He stilled and smiled back at me.

"You can when we're done," Fuck. Which was so what I *didn't* want to do for a change. I frowned and pouted a little.

"Come on, let me help the girls clean up," I pushed against him more insistently this time and twisted in his grasp.

"What I'm not good enough for you?" he asked.

"Not what I said!" I laughed.

"Good," He tried to kiss me and I turned my head. I saw Trigger stand up sharply out of the corner of my eye and Reaver pop up a half second later. The conversation halved but didn't die.

"Come on, let me go, please?" I said and he glared down at me.

"Never met a choosy whore before. What the fuck?" he demanded loudly and the conversation died, like a switch had been flipped. The jig, as they say, was up. I felt my shoulders drop in defeat.

"She's not a whore," I turned and blinked at Ghost who stood just outside arm's reach, his thumbs casually hooked in his belt loops. His hazel eyes soft when they fell on my face.

"You're not going to lose your family Baby. I'm not going to let that happen," he said low and gentle. I blinked at him. Grinder had stilled and I looked up at him. He was glaring at me.

"Ghost?" my voice was confused which matched what was going on inside my head perfectly.

"Let her go man. She's mine. She's my Old Lady," Ghost said and I blinked.

"She said she didn't belong to anybody," Grinder frowned, his alcohol fogged brain trying to catch up.

"She told you that on Friday man, she didn't belong to anybody then. I made her mine on Tuesday," Grinder looked down at me.

"That true?" he demanded. I stared at Ghost and nodded dumbly. Grinder let me go, thrusting me back like I'd burned him.

"Shit man! I had no idea. She didn't say anything." I blinked stupidly.

"You didn't really give me the chance," I said defensively.

"Mouthy bitch! You might want to look to that brother," Grinder said to Ghost and sniffed. Ghost looked at me, his lips thinning.

"Yep. I'll do that now," he said and grabbed me by the arm. Firmly, but not hurting. He towed me toward the back and I went right along still trying to figure out exactly what just happened. He opened the door to his room and thrust me inside and quickly followed me in, closing the door tightly behind us. I stood stunned and turned and Ghost was there, hands gently checking me over.

"Baby you okay?" he asked me. He stripped off my cardigan and I startled hard at that. "Easy, easy Princess, I'm just checking you out making sure he didn't hurt you, leave any bruises." I blinked.

"What did you just do?" I asked in a strained whisper. He smiled that one sided boyish smile that made my heart melt every time I saw it.

"I wanted to do things right, wanted to take things nice and slow and build up to it and ask you proper but... Oh Shelly." My eyes welled up, I couldn't help it. He gently cupped my face and smoothed his thumbs over my cheeks.

"When you told me about keeping up appearances? There was no way I was gonna let you lose your family on Thanksgiving. No way. You don't have to do anything. I don't expect-" I kissed him. I grabbed him by his shoulders and kissed him fiercely and put every ounce of what I was feeling behind it.

His hands dropped to my waist and stayed where it was respectful and he kissed me back. Slowly and carefully. Like I was fragile, like I might break, and I don't think he was far off the mark. I broke the kiss, my hands holding his face like his had held mine just a moment before and I rested my forehead against his.

"I don't understand! Why would you do that?" I cried.

"Well... because," he said as if it explained everything.

"Because! Because why?" I sniffed and realized I was full on crying and didn't even care. I was just so shocked and so grateful and confused and scared and elated and so many things were going on inside my head I couldn't keep any of it straight.

"Breathe, Princess," he said and I did, mimicking his movements like I had on the road, God was it only a week ago?

"I don't understand Ghost! Why would you do that?" I demanded again and he smiled and let his hands slide from either side of my waist to my back, pulling me closer to him and something in my chest eased, an anxiety or stress or something I didn't even have a word for. It just loosened and I felt myself relax because being like this, with Ghost... It was all I had ever wanted and I could see it in his eyes before he said anything...

"I did it because it's true Princess, I want you. I want you as my Old Lady, in my bed, in *only* my bed. I want you because maybe it is true what they say. Maybe it only takes 8.75 seconds for a dude to fall in love because I'm pretty fucking sure it took me less than that to fall in love with you."

I stared at him, chest heaving. Wait, what?

CHAPTER 12

Ghost...

She was panicking, overwhelmed or something, and so I switched tactics ever so slightly.

"Shelly, Shelly, look at me." I needed her to look me in the eye, I needed for us to be clear on this. I put my hands to either side of her head and those sapphire eyes darted to mine, she was on the verge of really freaking out. I rested my forehead against hers and made soothing sounds until the fear left her body, muscle groups losing their tension one by one, until her eyes closed and her breathing slowed. Her eyes opened and she did what I needed her to do, she looked at me.

"I'm only going to say this once, so you'd better listen and you'd better listen good. I am not a onetime thing Honey. You have to understand, there is no one and done here. I don't care if I'm the best you've ever had or the worst... This is it. You sleep with me and you belong to me and that means all of you, the broken bits, the jagged bits all of it. You on a good day, you on a bad day, it doesn't matter. I'm not like those other guys. I don't do casual, there has never been one and done here and there never will be. You do this... We do this... It's forever. You get what I'm saying?" I stared into her eyes from bare inches away and they became luminous with her tears. She sniffed and she trembled in my hands, I smoothed my thumbs beneath her eyes and wiped away the tears. It killed me when she cried. What I'd said needed to be said but I was also hoping it would piss her off just a little. She seemed to center out a little better when she was angry, but anger isn't what I got from her on this, which surprised me.

"I don't understand!" She said helplessly, "Why would you want to tie yourself to someone like me someone who's... Who's..."

"Who's what? Beautiful? Smart? Funny? Caring? A total fireball who makes me smile? Who makes me laugh outright when it feels like the whole damned world has gone to Hell around me?" I smiled a little sadly, knowing she saw none of those things in herself and was a little surprised when she ventured with,

"Is that what you see when you look at me?" I felt a small surge of triumph.

"That and a whole lot more just waiting to be discovered if you'd let me," I told her. She sniffed and pulled her face from between my hands, rubbing the tip of her nose with the back of her hand.

"You think about it," I told her gently, and blinked in surprise when she scoffed.

"I don't have to think about it Ghost!" she cried, "It's all I've ever wanted." She dropped her hands from my shoulders and sighed out, her eyes closing.

"What Honey?" I asked her.

"Just promise me that this isn't because of what I said on the mountain." I laughed a little.

"No, I've felt this way for a while. Why else would I get so butt-twisted when you were with other guys?" I headed her off at the pass, I could see right where she was going. "I know! I know, you weren't actually with them but you played a convincing game Princess you had to, I understand that now. I was a dense mother fucker but I'm paying attention now." I pulled her in and her resistance was fading. I held her close and her arms went around my shoulders and she held me too, gasping when she got a look at the bed. I chuckled.

"Yeah, same one," I said and leaned back to look at her. I opened my mouth to ask her what she was thinking but a knock fell at the door. I reached out and twisted the handle and it popped open. Ashton and Reaver stood outside. Ashton looking worried, Reaver's eyes sparkling with a wicked good humor.

"How you doin' Baby Cuz?" he asked with a wink.

"Did you know about this?" she asked him and he opened his mouth, "Don't fuck with me Reaver, I don't think I could take you fucking with me right now. So please don't. Please don't fuck with me!" her face collapsed and Ashton rushed in and hugged us both.

"No Runt, I didn't know but I'm glad. I'm happy for you," Reaver looked solemn as he said it and Shelly reached out. Reaver came in and pretty soon I was part of a very awkward group hug which I didn't really mind. Shelly seemed to need it.

"Pretty sure you made an enemy for life outta Grinder," Reaver said dispassionately.

"Fuck that fucking fuck," Shelly said, voice muffled where her face was pressed into my shoulder. Reaver, Ashton and I laughed.

"That's my Baby Cousin!" Reaver declared.

"Right," Ashton said dubiously, "Now both of you get out. Shelly and I need to talk about something." I blinked.

"What did Trig do to you?" I blurted, remembering the shy as fuck, meek girl I helped move in to her first apartment.

"C'mere, I'll show you," Trig said from the door and Reave pulled back from our little knot of three and went for his best friend. I shook my head. Shelly sniffed and pushed back from me.

"Go on, Ashton's right. I wanted to talk to her but Grinder interrupted us."

"You sure you're okay?" I asked her, she gave me a baleful look, I laughed softly, "See, fireball." I joined the boys in the hall and Ashton shut the door on us.

"I need a fucking beer," Reaver said and hung his head.

"Me too," I said.

"Fuck, I need something stronger than that," Trig said and put his e-cig in his mouth.

"Can we go shoot something?" I asked. Trigger raised an eyebrow.

"Next best thing?" he queried. I wanted to beat Grinder's ass but I couldn't.

"You read me so well Sir," I said and Trig grunted, letting it slide.

CHAPTER 13
Shelly

"He says he's in love with me." I scrubbed my face with my hands. Ashton smiled.

"I can believe it." She popped up onto the side of the bed and swung her feet a little patting the quilt beside her. I sank down and trailed fingers over the material and remembered our night under the stars. It made me smile and Ashton laughed.

"I don't think you have much to worry about Shelly, but you were trying to ask me something in the kitchen..?"

"Yeah. How did you do it?" I asked and looked at her.

"Do what?" she frowned confused and I bobbed my head, lips pursed trying to think of a way to ask that wasn't totally epically rude and finally just settled on...

"Trigger."

Ashton blinked and laughed.

"Um, you're experienced in the birds and the bees. How do you think?" she blushed a furious shade of crimson and I scrubbed my face with my hands again, pressing my fingertips into my eyes.

"Wow. Okay, I really hate bringing the douchebag up but I mean..." I decided to just stop beating around the bush. "Your ex-husband raped you, right?" I winced. Ashton nodded silently and understanding crossed her delicate features. She swept her long auburn hair over her shoulder and ran it through her hands. Taking a moment.

"You want to know how I could be with Ethan after what Chadwick did to me." She smiled at me and it was a little sad.

"Yeah, I mean... I don't know, is it too soon?" I asked and bit my lip.

"Shelly, I know we aren't the best of friends and we aren't super close. I'd like for that to change."

I rolled my eyes, "I guess it will now!" I laughed a little. There were some very real dividing lines between a club slut and the Old Ladies and while I was generally more accepted by the Ol' Ladies of the Sacred Hearts, I knew my place and which side of the dividing line I lived on. The only reason I'd even been more accepted was because they knew, and I made it clear, I stayed away from their men unless their men didn't really make it an option to.

I wasn't like a lot of the fuckin' hoochies that hung around. I had more self-respect, or so I'd thought, but no matter my slightly elevated status, because of my morals, or my cousin, I was still set apart as 'other' and so I kept my distance and never got too close. Ghost's proclamation had changed a lot of shit for me in just a few seconds time. I took a leap of faith with Ashton here, but truthfully, she made it so easy just by being the fucking ray of Sunshine she always was.

"I'm afraid of what the Old Ladies, hell, *any woman* would think if I did Ghost this soon after what happened. I mean, I was a slut. I get that, and I was even okay with that! Before... I mean I never felt gross, or dirty or any of those things but then he made me and I didn't want to and..." I slammed my lips shut and tried hard to force the angry tears down but they forced their way out anyways.

"He took something from you, but he's dead now and he can't keep it. Not if you don't let him. Shelly you are one of the bravest women I know and he hurt you but you *survived*. It's not up to this woman or that woman on if you've healed enough or on if enough time has gone by for you to try again. That's up to *you*." She rubbed my back, a fierce look of empathy in her eyes.

"Did you worry about this stuff, you know, with Trig?" I asked. She smiled and lit up from the inside at his name.

"Oh boy! Did I ever! I was so afraid I was replacing Chadwick with Ethan and I didn't want that, I didn't want that at all. I know it sounds strange or unreal but everything with Ethan was so *natural*, it felt right. In here." She folded her hands above her heart, pressing against the chest of her light pink tee shirt.

"No one but you can say if and when you're ready. Or if and when you're..." she made air quotes with her fingers, "Over it.

Truthfully, you never fully get over something like that, you adapt and move around it. It's this big boulder of ugly that drops from the sky and remains firmly lodged in your path for a minute and then you walk around it and keep going on your way, but that doesn't move it, or remove it. It'll always be *on* your path you just have to learn to go around it or over it and put it *behind you*. If you feel comfortable, if you want to sleep with Ghost or you want him to touch you or to love you, then I am so very happy for you!" she said and I felt my eyes well up again.

"Do you ever… Are there things you still can't…" she smiled.

"Yes, but Ethan and I *talk* about those things, candidly. We are honest with each other and we face those things head on. Some of them I am able to do again, some of them I am still working on. The thing to remember is that I *trust* Ethan. If you *trust* Ghost and you know you can trust him. That makes a huge difference." I nodded and bit my lips together, thinking about these things. Ashton smiled and sighed.

"You're still so very young Shelly and life doesn't come with an instruction manual. These things worked for me and I hope that my insight helps you but ultimately you have to find out what works best for *you* Sweetie. No one else can dictate how you feel or what time is right to do what. There are some generally accepted standards out there, guidelines if you will, made up of a bunch of different people's experiences but you are uniquely you. Just like I am uniquely me. There is no one and I mean *no one* who should be judging you based on those standards because they don't know you like you know you." I blinked at Ashton and wondered how the hell I had missed her being such an insightful and intelligent woman. I hugged her and nodded.

I had a lot to think about. A lot to do to work on myself and I didn't exactly know where to start but I figured, here and now was as good as any. I pulled back from Ashton just as the door burst open. Everett and Chandra barged in with plates, Hayden right behind them. She kicked the door shut. Chandra lit a birthday candle in the middle of a slice of pumpkin pie.

"Congratulations Baby! You've graduated!" she cried and I

laughed. Everett grinned at me and they all started settling in around Ghost's room with their pie.

"What are you doing?" I asked.

"The guys are all watching football or going out back to shoot. Figured we could use a break from the kitchen and from the ho's out there," Everett rolled her eyes. I shifted a bit uncomfortably.

"Oh please?" Chandra cried. "You ain't been one of them in a long damn time, Darlin'," she took a bite of her pie and said with her mouth full, "Pretty soon you're going to have to kick some bimbo's ass the way I kicked yours." I blushed at the old memory which wasn't quite old enough. Hayden and Everett burst out laughing.

"This I have to know," Everett said and winked at me.

"Nothin' really to say," Chandra said and kept the story blessedly short, "She got mouthy, I whopped her ass and we've been straight ever since," which was true. I'd smarted off at Chandra when I was green as grass and she'd let me have it verbally but I didn't get the hint and smarted back so she'd grabbed me by the back of the head and had slammed my face into the bar. It'd hurt. A lot. Had bloodied my nose and I'd had raccoon eyes for what felt like weeks but I never made that mistake twice. Oh, I smarted off plenty, just never to Chandra again. I was lucky she hadn't broken my nose. By the time I finished telling the full story Everett was in stitches and Hayden and Ashton were wide eyed. I smirked at them.

"Not worried about you Hayden, I think you can handle it, but no worries Sunshine, I already decided if some bitch gets too handsy with Trig and doesn't want to listen to you, I'll kick her ass for you." I licked some whipped cream off the back of my fork. Hayden dissolved into laughter with Chandra and Everett.

I was feeling markedly more human, more like my kick ass old self, by the minute. I decided then, that I had a lot to be thankful for this Thanksgiving. My cousin, his wife, this club, my girls but also... even though I wasn't sure what the hell we were doing yet, I was really thankful for my man, for Ghost.

CHAPTER 14

Ghost

"Here comes trouble," Grinder muttered under his breath and I looked up from the magazine for a Glock 23 in my hands.

Shelly was striding across the grass towards our shooting range we'd built over the summer, huddled in her cardigan which she had pulled tightly across her body, hands hidden by the crook of either elbow. She stopped in the midst of us. Looked up at Grinder, looked at me and held out her hand. I wordlessly passed her the mag having no fucking idea what she was going to do with it. Reaver bounced a little on the balls of his feet and grinned like a lunatic.

Shelly stepped up to the table, picked up the Glock and ran the magazine home. She pulled back the slide, checked the safety and like a pro, raised the weapon, sighted and fired. She emptied the thing quickly and efficiently at the paper down the end of the range tacked to some plywood. She looked at her handiwork, lifted one shoulder in a shrug, gave Grinder a pointed look and raised one eyebrow. Then she turned to me and her look softened.

"Talk to you?" she asked me. I peered down the range at her impressive cluster and felt a slow grin spread across my lips.

"Yeah." I put an arm around her and pulled her into my side, kissing the side of her neck.

"I got your weapon. Go on," Trig said and he was smiling too. Reaver laughed and knocked Grinder in the shoulder who was looking at Shelly like he'd never seen her before. His eyes flicked to me.

"Did you know she could do that?" he asked. I looked down the range at the cluster in the crotch of the silhouette and the corners of my mouth drew down to crush the grin. I raised my eyebrows and shook my head.

"Nope," and it was true, I'd had no clue my girl was good with a gun and I have to say I thought it was sexy as hell.

I walked with Shelly back towards the clubhouse and heard Reaver say, "She's just as good with a knife. I taught her myself. Just in case, you know, you get any ideas," then he laughed, probably at the look on the dude's face.

Grinder had come out and had actually apologized. I'd kind of expected him to start some shit, but he didn't. It had given me hope for some of these new guys from out of town but then I figured, Dragon and Dray knew what they were about. If they didn't think a dude was going to be a good fit, they probably had talked to them about it quiet like and those dudes had probably moved on.

"What's up Princess?" I asked Shelly when we were good and out of earshot.

"I'm a little lost Ghost," she said and her voice, her tone, it was so frank and so surprisingly open and honest, I changed trajectory and moved for my club room instead of the media or common room where I'd been going.

"Lost how Honey?" I asked.

"I've never exactly gotten to do the whole relationship thing where I could be absolutely sure I was the only one. Where things were pretty exclusive; while I know how things work in *theory...*" she pursed her lips.

"Hey," I stopped her and put my hands on her shoulders, caressing over her collarbones through her thin white tee shirt with my thumbs. Thrilled that she so easily let me touch her now. That she trusted me to the point she didn't think about it anymore.

"What?" she asked. I shook her a little bit, playfully.

"Stop over thinking things," I said and she gave me a sad little watery version of her typically fiery smart assed half smile.

"Have you *met* me?" she asked and I laughed a little. We kept walking and I ushered her into my room. She stood for a long minute staring at the old brass bed from the mountainside. It'd been a bitch and a half dragging that thing up and down the mountain but it'd been so worth it.

"I'm scared," she confessed, and turned to face me.

"Okay."

"Not of you, or that you're gonna hurt me but more that, you know, I won't be able to… That I won't or can't without," she closed her mouth and dropped her eyes to the floor, shifting from foot to foot.

"That you'll be thinking of what he did?" I asked. She bit her lips together and nodded. I went to her and pulled her lips down to mine, softly, gently, kissing her. Some tension eased from her and she kissed me back, cautiously, sweetly. I had another bright idea.

"You want to try and find out Princess?" I asked against her lips. She nodded and I went to my sock drawer and pulled out a couple of my ties.

"I don't know Ghost, I've never much liked the idea of being tied up." She looked really troubled and I chuckled.

"They're not for you Princess," I tossed the ties on the bed. I toed off my running shoes and shrugged out of my jacket and cut. I hung them on the hook that went over the door lining the back of the wood for coats and shit. I stripped my tee over my head and let it fall to the floor. Shelly sucked in a sharp breath and it made me smirk.

This so wasn't my usual bag. I liked to be in control, but I could give it up if it meant making her more comfortable. I was getting painfully hard in my boxers and jeans thinking about her hands on me. Her mouth on me… I stripped off my socks but left my jeans in place. I went to the bed and rigged up the ties to the old brass headboard. I fashioned some slip knots and with a deep breath laid down and put my hands through the loops and pulled tight. I would need her help to get out of this so I was trusting her here. I looked at her, standing so still in the middle of the midnight blue area rug on the lighter carpet and smiled.

"Your move Princess," I said and settled back, content to just let things happen. Her sapphire eyes swept me from head to toe and she stood stalk still, hugging herself, fingers curled into each opposite sleeve of her comfortable if tired and shabby black cardigan. She licked her lips and swallowed. For a minute I thought she was going to walk out but then the tension in her posture eased slightly and her arms uncurled from around herself.

"What if I want you to touch me?" she asked softly.

"I'd like that Baby, I really would, but you decide what happens when here."

She nodded slowly and slipped the old sweater from her shoulders and let it fall. I watched her as she meticulously slipped first one black and white Chuck Taylor, then the other, off her feet. Lining them up neatly in front of the closet door. It was cool. It was fine. I was in no rush. I just wish that someone would tell that to the raging hard on I was sporting.

She tucked her socks into the shoes and straightened. Her back was to me and I couldn't see her expression but her body language was tense, her back rising and falling a little too quickly with short breaths. She slid her jeans from her hips and pushed them all the way down her long shapely legs to the floor and Oh. My. God. I know she didn't intend it to be but it was probably the hottest thing I'd seen her do. So fucking erotic! I knew I'd be replaying it in my mind in those quiet hours in the deep of night while I was in the truck alone and the world slept on oblivious.

She straightened, and gripped the hem of her close fitting tee, lifting it over her head, revealing the long lean line of her back in one swift movement and it was like a magician with a magic trick. I licked suddenly dry lips and felt the pace of my breaths quicken.

"God! You're fucking gorgeous," I uttered and she looked back over her shoulder startled as if she'd forgotten I was here. She blushed, a faint pink painting her cheeks and across the bridge of her nose. She wore a simple matching white cotton bra and panty set and while I was sure she had lacier and racier underthings, the simple set of bikini briefs and white bra against her smooth creamy skin was enough to drive me fucking wild.

She came over to the bed and stood over me, her jewel bright eyes wandering over my face, my chest, my stomach…

"Like what you see?" I asked, voice gone husky with desire. She quirked that little smart assed half smile of hers, and I felt an answering smile of my own. She reached up behind her and unhooked her bra and let it fall. I took in a sharp breath. *Jesus Christ!* She had the most perfect pair of tits I had ever seen, high and tight and how the hell she managed to be as thin as she was and still have a good C cup going on was beyond me but damn! I felt my hands jerk reflexively at my bonds. I wanted to touch her so badly. Run my hands over all that smooth skin to see if it was as soft as I thought it would be...

"You're killing me," I told her and it won me a genuine full on smile. She reached out tentatively and slid the leather of my belt through the buckle. I raised my hips off the quilt under me after she'd unbuttoned my fly and let her strip me of the denim. She looked her fill, trailing fingertips down the center of my chest, off to the side, down my ribs in a feather light touch that had me jerking sideways to get away from it. She laughed and the sound was high and bright and perfect.

"You're ticklish?" she asked and I smiled up at her.

"Yeah, you?"

"You crazy? I'm not telling you!" she said and sat down carefully by my hip on the edge of the bed.

"If I'm lucky, maybe you'll let me find out later," I said and she nodded, face gone serious again.

"You're amazing," she told me, and her eyes were back to wandering. "I could look at you all day." I was letting my gaze do some unabashed and appreciative roaming of its own.

"You're probably one of the most beautiful women I have ever laid eyes on," I said honestly. She stood up so abruptly I thought I'd said something wrong but then she skimmed her panties down her legs and my brain went out to lunch without me. She laughed, that high wild peal of laughter that reminded me of summer time and all the damned good things in life.

"I showed you mine, now time for you to show me yours farm boy," she teased, and hooked her fingers in the elastic waistband of my boxers. I gripped the bars of the headboard and obediently lifted my hips. I'd be straight up lying if I said I wasn't nervous about what she'd think. I wasn't small by any means but I wasn't huge either. If anything I thought of myself as square in the middle of average. I don't think I needed to worry though. Her lips curved in a secret little appreciative smile and her so blue, crystalline eyes danced with a glimmer of, if I had to guess, victory.

"Like what you see?" I asked her again and skimmed her expression. She got up onto the bed next to me on her knees, folding those beautiful long legs underneath her.

"More than you could possibly ever know." She said and eyes locked to mine she brought her lips to my chest and kissed me, a soft press of lips, followed by another, slightly lower down on my body than the first and then another, torturously slow. I groaned and closed my eyes, reveling in the sensation of her petal soft lips on my skin, jolting when her hot silk mouth wrapped around the head of my cock.

"Oh God!" I swallowed convulsively and felt her lips smile around me. She was really, and I do mean *really* good at that.

CHAPTER 15

Shelly

I was nervous about getting naked, for the first time that I could ever remember but with him tied to the bed like that, it gave me the courage I needed to follow through. I wanted to see him, all of him but it seemed only fair that I take the plunge first. I was so fucking grateful that he wasn't too big. I didn't want to compare him to anyone, and to be honest, I couldn't, because he was *Ghost,* and no one I had ever been with was, but there was something to be said for an average sized penis. I loved it. I loved that I would be able to take all of him, too big and you couldn't do that and there was discomfort if the sex got rough. Not big enough and yes, you could make up for it but it wasn't always as satisfying.

Ghost though… Ghost was perfect. I knew it the moment I took him into my mouth. I loved sucking cock. It turned me on faster than anything and having Ghost in my mouth put me up and over the moon and launched me into the far reaches of space, never mind the stratosphere. He was so hot to the touch and I don't think a man could get any harder. He tasted amazing, salty and masculine and I could take all of him which was just awesome. I took him all the way down and just had to relax my throat a little bit, be conscious of the gag reflex.

I loved the sounds I was bringing out of him. The short strangled cry, the sharp panting breaths, his reactions made me incredibly hot, my core throbbed with want, my nipples pebbled in the cool air of the room. He had his eyes squeezed shut, head tilted back, knuckles mottled white where he gripped the bars of the old brass headboard. He was so beautifully responsive and it made my heart glad that I could make him feel so good.

"Oh my God Princess stop! Stop or I'm gonna go!" he panted and I drew back off of him, climbing his body the same way I'd descended, with one soft, gentle kiss after another. His skin pebbled, awash in goose flesh. I laid a kiss on each ridge of his washboard abs and threw one leg over both of his until I ended at his throat. I nipped his collarbone and he gasped, I sucked that place on the side of his neck that I knew drove *me* wild and the bed jerked, he'd reached for me but his hands were kept fast by the ties he'd done on himself. The neck ties cutting into his wrists. He couldn't reach me. I swallowed down my fluttering heartbeat and kissed his chin and looked into those amazing hazel eyes of his.

"You're killing me," he said, breathing uneven.

"Not yet," I murmured then pursed my lips.

"What? What is it Princess?" he asked softly.

"I'm clean," I said, "But do you want me to get a condom anyways?" I swallowed hard.

"You on birth control?" he asked.

"No," I answered truthfully, "You have to have sex to get pregnant and I stopped that along with everything else so…"

"Hey, stop," he captured my gaze with his. "Up to you Princess. I told you this was forever and I meant it." I blinked.

"Where do you keep them?" I asked. He gave me a one sided grin.

"Sock drawer," he said and I let out a breath I hadn't known I was holding. I slapped him on the chest.

"If you'd said you didn't have any I would have marched out there bare assed and gotten one from my cousin," I said.

"The hell you would've!" he cried and I laughed. I moved off of him and went and got a spate of condoms from his sock drawer and put them inside easy reach on the bedside table. He was no less hard from the conversation. I rolled one down his length and resumed my earlier position, straddling his hips. I *burned*, I wanted him inside me so bad.

"You seriously would have let me…" I didn't want to say 'fuck you' because I had no intentions of something so impersonal with Ghost so I let the air hang empty of the words, let him put whatever label on it that he wanted inside his head. "…without one, knowing I could get pregnant?"

"You want a big family," he reminded me. I reached between us and raised him off his stomach, slipping him inside of me. Oh God was he ever perfect. Filling me but not over stretching me, I ground down on him and he touched that spot deep inside of me. I closed my eyes and turned my head. Oh he felt so good!

"Oh Baby, oh Honey, oh God!" I felt the bed jerk beneath my knees, he'd pulled on his restraints again. I opened my eyes and met his, hands splayed across his ribs I leaned forward and used my legs to lift me a little so I could ride him.

"Oh fuck Shelly! I want to touch you," his voice was strained and passionate and I felt some of the constriction around my heart ease, the bands of sorrow loosening. Truthfully, I wanted him to touch me, I wanted his warm hands on my skin. I rolled my hips a few more times, he felt so good I didn't want to stop but I needed him to touch me and so I fell onto his restraints, picking at the knots with my fingers until I could slide them loose. He slipped his right wrist free and his hand fell on my hip, where he patiently rested it while I freed his other one. I swallowed hard, his body was corded with restraint. Restraint, that when his other hand was freed, he lost a bit. He sat up abruptly, his arms curving behind my back holding me upright.

I wrapped my arms around his powerful shoulders and buried my hands in his short, professionally cut hair. It was as soft as it looked, like satin between my fingers. There wasn't much thrusting going on but he was seated as deeply as he could get in my body and felt so fucking amazing there. I was taller than him, riding his body as I was and I looked down into eyes the color of winter, so brown, being swallowed by life at the edges, the color of new spring leaves, new life beating back the cold.

I kissed him and he held my body to his and claimed my mouth, my heart, and my soul with his kiss right back. He moved, somehow, twitched inside of me and swallowed my gasp and then I was tumbling, off to the side but Ghost had me, held me fast as he turned us so he was on top, between my thighs and then he *moved*, withdrawing from me, until he was barely there before surging forward in a powerful thrust that for a moment I thought he may cleave me in two. Heat sparked to life in my womb and I held his face fast to mine.

This was unlike anything I had *ever* done before and I realized it was because I loved him too. I loved him for trying, for sticking with me, for being there for me, for doing the amazing things he'd done for me to try and get me to open up; to heal despite what a stubborn shit I was being. I wound my legs around his hips and cried out into his mouth. Breath panting, body melting, I was wetter than I could *ever* remember being before, Ghost gave me no quarter, his thrusts, measured and sure, firm but not rough, not demanding just enough to tell me with his body rather than his voice that I unequivocally belonged to him.

His mouth broke from mine and he reared up just enough to get a hand between us. He slid that hand down my body, between my breasts, through the light dew of sweat on my skin. I didn't know how long we had been at this, time was irrelevant and truthfully, I felt so good after so long I didn't really care how long, all I knew was that I didn't want it to ever stop. Ghost dipped his thumb at the top of my sex, teasing just below the top of my mound and I arched crying out when he found his prize, he smiled, his expression exquisite concentration as he teased that bundle of nerves. It was too much, he was hitting me perfectly from the inside and my cup was already full, so to speak. I arched, back bowing until it was almost painful and I thought I was going to snap in half when he grazed over that sensitive place just right and I completely shattered underneath him.

I crashed into the mattress and felt my body ripple and convulse around his beautifully invading cock. His eyes slipped shut and his head bowed, an expression of pure beatific ecstasy taking over his face and it was the most perfect thing I had ever seen along with the most perfect thing I had ever felt in my life and I suddenly knew what it felt like to be a couple of stars streaking across an infinite sky.

Ghost stilled inside me and knelt with our bodies still joined, panting as hard as I was as the rest of my senses slowly back filled in. I blinked a long slow blink and lay completely sated. Boneless, liquid and languid and I realized with an almost physical jolt that

Ghost had come *with* me. That he was finished, that he didn't need to move or keep going and the sheer intimacy of that struck me to my core. I had only once, ever come at the exact same time with someone and that had been a sheer happy accident. It hadn't been something shared, I hadn't been so deeply intertwined with them I couldn't tell you where I left off and they began. Not like now, not like what I had just shared with this beautiful, stubborn and inexplicable man.

"You okay? Hey! Hey, what's this? No, no, no, don't cry!" Ghost bent over me and gathered me to him and I wrapped my arms around his broad shoulders.

"Good cry, I promise!" I choked out and he held me warm and safe until the waterworks stopped.

"I'm sorry," I said and he chuckled.

"Scared me is all. Wanna tell me what that was about?" He slipped from me and went up and over my leg to stretch out beside me. He pulled me close against his chest and I let my eyes roam the brightly colored new-school rendition of the Sacred Heart's logo taking up his shoulder. It was still peeling in a couple of places, the ink bright and freshly done.

"I don't know," I said a bit uncomfortably. I wasn't used to the whole talking about my feelings shit. I wasn't sure I ever would be. "I guess it was just a little more intense than I expected it to be. A little more... I don't know, just more." He kissed my forehead and held me to him.

"Different huh?" he asked.

"Yeah."

We were silent for a time.

"Come on baby, I'm gonna take you home," he said and I sat up abruptly.

"Why can't I stay with you here?" I asked and I was ready to be pissed. Really? One of the most profound sexual experiences of my life and no bullshit, I had had *a lot* of sex and he just wanted to dump me off at home? Just like that?

"Calm your tits, Princess," he said laughing. "It's been getting rowdy around here and I want to take you *home*, with *me*. I want you in my bed, in my house... well our house. You get me?" he winked at me and I blinked.

"Wait what?" he wanted me to move in with him? Is that what he was saying? Holy shit, talk about moving at warp speed! I didn't know what to do with that but then he kissed me and my brain shut off, just blank, gone... and shit that wasn't fair!

"Stop over thinking things. Get dressed, I'm going to take you home, I'm going to get you in my bed and I'm going to make love to you all over again," he smiled against my mouth and I caught myself nodding before my brain could catch up and I could be outraged he was ordering me around.

"Bossy aren't you?" I asked when he'd pulled back enough that I could remember what it was to think again. He disrupted every one of my senses when he was close. It was the way it had pretty much always been, from the beginning for me. Maybe it was pheromones or something.

He stripped the condom off himself and threw it in the trash and handed me my bra and panties. I pulled on my underwear and by the time I'd done that my clothes were neatly laid across the foot of the bed waiting for me. He pulled on his boxers and jeans.

"I told you Shelly," his voice was gentle and his tone mirrored the serene smile that caressed his lips, "No going back baby. I keep what's mine, what's more, I take care of what's mine."

I wanted to be indignant about him talking about me like I was some piece of property, be all feminist *rawr*! But I couldn't. Not when his words were like a Siren's call... What he held out in front of me was all I had ever wanted. To be cared for and loved and to belong. Who could possibly say no to that?

CHAPTER 16
Ghost

She looked troubled but not and Reaver's words echoed back to me. *"What she needs is someone to stick it out. She gets scared she starts pushing, testing limits until she breaks it so she can say 'see, it wasn't meant to be'... She's too used to being alone. She needs someone strong to show her she doesn't have to be."*

I aimed to be that person but I could see the wheels turning in her head, the gears grinding and I had no idea what she was going to do but I had to be ready for it when she did. She stood up from tying her shoes and looked at me, sapphire eyes troubled.

"What is it Princess?" I asked her gently.

"Are you seriously telling me I'm moving in with you?" she asked. I smiled. I could see it coming, the fight, but it was a fight I was going to win.

"Yep," I held out her sweater for her to shrug into and she did.

"That's some serious bullshit Ghost!" she cried and when she turned around her frown deepened when she saw my grin.

"Probably, but it doesn't change anything. I want you where I can make damn sure you're looked after." She opened her mouth to say something, closed it, opened it again and I watched her expression go from angry to confused to lost and back again before finally settling on just plain lost. I felt a surge of victory. Whatever argument she was going to use I'd pretty much successfully short circuited.

"Let me take you home, Baby," I pulled her against me and her jaw clenched with steely determination.

"I'll go with you but no more talk about me moving in. Not yet," she admonished and I cocked my head to the side. It was already decided, at least for me, I wanted her. I loved her for as infuriating as she could be some times but damn she was never boring. I could see the fear and unease sliding behind her eyes though and so for now, I backed off a metaphorical pace or two. I would get my way in the end. I could be just as stubborn as she could if not more. Right now, I just wanted her alone. No one else, no distractions, just her and me on my little slice of remote country property.

"Okay Princess. I'll shelve the discussion for now," I conceded. She bit her lips together and nodded.

"Okay," she murmured. I jostled her a little in my arms.

"You're okay," I told her, "You're always okay with me. I will never *force* you to do anything. I'll just craft convincing arguments until you give in," I smiled at her and bounced my eyebrows and her expression was like the sun coming out from behind dark clouds. She laughed and it was high and bright and perfect and the mood in the room lightened considerably.

"Caveman," she accused.

"I won't disagree, now come on. I *need* you in my bed."

We went out into the common room where some of the guys were playing poker, some were watching the game and slipped out front after Shelly retrieved her purse from the kitchen. I opened the door to the truck and waited while she stood tapping a text into her phone. She sent it and looked up at me.

"Reaver," she said by way of explanation. I nodded and she got up into the cab. I shut the door and rounded the front end. The drive out to my place was silent. She stared out the window but I don't think she was worried or thinking too hard. It gave me a thrill that she held my hand on the expanse of seat between us.

I pulled down the long lane, my house and garage was set back from the road. I had enough property here that if I'd wanted I could probably keep a horse or two but wasn't really interested. With work and the MC keeping me busy I didn't even have a dog right now which I'd always had a dog growing up around my parent's farm. I kind of missed having one.

"Dog or cat person?" I asked Shelly suddenly as I rolled up to a stop by the house's back porch.

"Dog," she answered but her eyes were all for the light blue clapboard house with white trim set in the deepening twilight. It was a single story rambler and I liked it. Plenty of room to add on with no real need to.

"What do you think?"

"Awfully big for just one person," she murmured.

I smiled, "Guess when I bought it I was still holding out for that happily ever after." Shelly snorted, a jaded and derisive noise.

"Shit like that is only in fairy tales Ghost. Not the really real world," It hurt my heart to hear her say it like that. We had a long road ahead of us but I'd committed, and part of that commitment meant changing her mind about certain things. I added this one to the list.

"Can't have a real appreciation for the good things in life if there weren't a few bad to compare to," I said and got out of the truck, she was still staring at where I'd been when I opened her door. She let me help her down without thinking about it. Whatever barrier had been in her mind about me touching her, it was gone now and I loved it.

"You can explore tomorrow as much as you'd like," I said letting us into the house. "Right now, I'm beat, I want to make love to you one more time and I want to fall asleep with you in my arms," Shelly laughed at me.

"That is such a chick thing to say," she accused.

"Yeah and you tell any of the guys I'll fucking deny it. Besides, I thought chicks dug a dude in touch with his feminine side." I steered her down the hall by her belt loops and into the master bedroom, my bedroom. She was laughing and turned in my arms.

"Condoms?" she asked and I swore.

"Fuck I don't keep them around the house." She pulled the lot from the club out of her back pocket.

"Good thing one of us thinks with their big head."

I pulled her up tight against me with a surprised yip and crushed my mouth over hers. She kissed me back but it was restrained. I told myself to slow down with her. I was just so fucking elated to finally have her here with me. To be able to call her mine and know it was true to the very marrow of my bones. I kissed her until it was her hands that gathered my shirt beneath my jacket and cut. I slid the leather off from my shoulders and tossed it across the foot of my King sized bed.

After sleeping on narrow cots and worse over in bum fuck Egypt, it was the first thing I'd done when I came home from my first tour, gone out and bought the biggest most comfortable damned bed I could find. Of course *that* bed I'd left with my cheating ex. This one I bought after I'd moved out here. I'd taken everything else but left her the bed. I wanted no part of that. Shelly was the first woman I'd brought to it and I swore that I would do everything in my power to make her the last.

I let her pull my shirt over my head and drop it to the floor. Her hands were cool against my warmer skin and it felt amazing. She explored my planes and angles gently, smoothing her silken hands over my heated flesh which did absolutely nothing to quell the fire burning in my blood, if anything her cool hands stoked it higher. I wanted her more than any woman I had ever met before. It was like something in her blood called to mine. I wasn't into a bunch of mystical crap but the attraction I had for Shelly, I was almost willing to bet that soul mate was a real thing and that she was mine.

I broke my mouth from hers and kissed along her jaw, pulling her in tight against me. I buried my face in the crook of her neck and breathed her in deep. She smelled like fucking candy. Sweet and fruity and I was pretty sure it was the shampoo she used but I didn't care. She just smelled good enough to eat and I couldn't get enough of her. I kissed, licked and sucked the side of her neck and found some place special because she went weak in the knees.

"Oh God, Ghost!" she cried and I went from hard to harder. My hands skated under her fitted girl tee and I let my hands smooth over her perfect skin, along her stomach, curving over her ribs above her hip. She had no idea how hard it'd been to hold out on her before. None at all.

"Ghost *please*," she gasped and it was music to my fucking ears. I pushed the cardigan off her shoulders and helped her untangle from it. She worked at my belt and made a slightly frustrated noise when I took her arms and hands away from it by lifting her shirt over her head. I let her get back to it, toeing out of my running shoes which I hadn't laced back up when I'd redressed at the club. She pushed the denim of my jeans down over my hips mirroring my actions, toeing out of her Chucks while I unsnapped and unzipped her tight, figure hugging jeans.

I stepped out of my pants and went to my knees to peel her out of hers, looking up the long lean length of her torso. I pressed a kiss below her navel and her hands burrowed into my hair. She threw back her head and let out a shuddering sigh and it was the most perfect fucking thing I'd ever seen in my life. She was so damned beautiful and so damned *mine*. I skimmed her panties to the floor and pressed her back, turning her so her thighs hit the bed. She sat down obediently and I picked up a foot and pulled her sock off. I pressed a kiss to her knee where I was crouched at her feet and repeated the process on the other side, quickly skimming off my own.

She unhooked her bra and pulled the straps from her narrow shoulders and tossed it to the floor. I wanted her so damn bad but there was still something I hadn't gotten to do. I pushed her knees apart, my eyes locked with hers and lowered my mouth to her pussy. She watched me and didn't make a single sound or protest, desire filling her eyes making them glow like jewels with flames behind them. She tasted fucking phenomenal. Musky and sweet, like Ambrosia, the food of the fucking Gods.

Her arms, which she'd been propping herself up with to watch me, gave out and she flopped back into the midnight blue comforter with the most succulent groan and I knew I had her right where I wanted her. I slid my middle finger up inside her and caressed the roof of her walls with languorous strokes while I lapped at her lips and clit, sucking the little kernel of nerves into my mouth. She cried out and her hips bucked off the bed involuntarily. I felt her convulse around my finger and my cock twitched out of the opening in my boxers.

God I wanted to be inside of her. I snatched one of the condoms off the bed by her hip and withdrew my fingers from her sweet fucking pussy. She made a sound of protest, which I ignored, and I kept working her with my mouth, rolling the damned condom on by feel. I pushed the boxers off most of the way then stopped caring, climbing her body.

"God you're so fucking awesome," I ground out. I wrapped my arms around her thighs and pulled her towards me to get a better angle. She cried out, fear flashing in her eyes which quickly dissipated and I managed to make a mental note to A) slow down and B) never do that again, or at least work up to it.

I knelt up straighter and guided myself to her entrance and she was so wet and ready for me I slipped right in. She was so smooth; satin and perfect around me. Her body tightened and I bowed my head, my eyes closed and I lost myself for a minute in the sensation of her milking my cock. She whimpered and I drew back and thrust forward sharply. She was a fever that had taken ahold of every one of my senses. Driving me wild in just about every way.

I held her hips, caressing the hollows left by her pelvic bones with my thumbs as I set a rhythm of sure even strokes. I wanted to pound that pussy into next week but I knew just by looking at her she was nowhere near ready for the rough stuff. Still, this position was so god damned tempting to do just that...

"Wrap your legs around me Honey," I told her and she complied. She was skin and bones, way too thin that I was able to do this so easily. I bowed over her and slid my arms behind her back, bracing her. She cried out when I stood up with her still wrapped around me, me in her. I sat down on the edge of the bed and her hands braced on my knees to keep herself from going over backwards, but I had her.

"I got 'cha Princess," I held her to me and looked up into those luminous blue eyes of hers and she gasped. Trusting that I held her fast she took her hands from my knees and twined her arms around my shoulders. She kissed me, and held tightly to me and it felt amazing to have her wrapped around me in just about every way possible. She rolled her hips and I made an appreciative and encouraging sound into her mouth.

It wasn't a position that was going to get either of us up and over that edge but I needed to slow my friggin' roll. I didn't want to scare her or do any damage. I wanted to do just the opposite. She writhed in my lap and it felt amazing but even she grew quickly frustrated. She broke our kiss and my name, my real name, spilled from her lips, her voice strained.

"*Derek...*" It was all I needed. I stood us up and walked us up onto the bed better. She clung to me and made a frustrated noise when I slipped from her but it couldn't be helped. I laid her down into the softness of the center of my bed and with as much self-control as I could muster, I eased my way back into her.

Her hands flew to my face and she forced my head up to look at her. I'd been watching where our bodies joined, watching myself slide in and out of her moist, wet heat but she didn't want that. Her eyes were passion filled and at the same time raw, and vulnerable. I searched her face as I made love to her and smiled when I realized that she felt it too. That she was giving me as good as she got.

So. Fucking. Flawless. I don't know how long we were like that. I didn't care. All I cared about was that it was me and my girl in my bed and that there was finally nothing between us but perfect love and perfect trust. Shelly was fucking amazing.

CHAPTER 17

Shelly

It was dark, long past sundown, and creeping towards deepest night. We hadn't either of us moved from his bed. Ghost dozed fitfully beneath me. I lay, my ear pressed to the center of his chest, listening to the ticking echo of his heartbeat. I felt languid and at peace, completely relaxed and drunk off his love and yet I couldn't for the life of me tell you why I couldn't sleep. I traced idle patterns on his skin with my fingertip while I tried to puzzle it out, but as soon as a thought flitted into my head it slid right out again. I couldn't focus like this. I was too warm and comfortable. With a laborious sigh I sat up. Ghost slept on and I smiled wanly. He was so *gorgeous* to me. That all-American Midwest boy with the panty dropping smile.

I slipped out of bed and looked around. I didn't feel like getting dressed in anything we'd been wearing. I slipped back into my panties and pulled them up my legs and with a wolfish grin plucked his jacket and cut off the foot of the bed. The leather was a heavy, solid weight on my shoulders and big enough that it covered me, leaving just a narrow strip of my flesh visible down between my breasts. Really all I cared about was that it was something of his and that it smelled like him, that comforting mix of outdoors, woods and man.

I took him at his word that I would have plenty of time to explore the house after he and I made love and I took that time to be now since I had nothing else to do. The first room, out and to the right of his master bedroom was empty. Just four stark walls and a couple of random boxes. The next, the one on the left was an ever loving treasure trove! It was an office. Likely for his towing business and I was happier than a pig in shit! It was a total freaking disaster area. Filing cabinet drawers open and over flowing with tow slips. The computer monitor on the desk was black and wreathed in yellow sticky notes with hastily scrawled numbers on them. If there was a keyboard, it was buried underneath a drift of gas receipts.

I moved a banker's box of tax papers off the office chair and sat down. I looked back at the open doorway and with a devilish grin decided, fuck it, what was he going to do? Be pissed I fixed it for him? I marveled at the train wreck around me. Ghost was a neat freak judging by his bedroom both here and at the club. His beds were made with military precision to this day. Even his tow truck was organized and clean. So I had to wonder to myself. *How did this happen?*

I found the mouse and moved it back and forth and the fans on the desktop's tower started to whirr. The screen flickered to life and I made a face at the password protected screen. I hit enter but nope, it demanded a password. I tried 'password' but no dice. Then, just to be flippant I tried 'Shelly' and my jaw almost hit the floor when it worked.

"Holy shit," I muttered. The place may be an organizational train wreck but he looked like he at least kept the book keeping software up to date. It looked like he came in, entered shit and then just cast the paper aside. All though some of the receipts on the desk still hadn't been done. Still, I started to see a pattern to the utter chaos after just a few minutes. I rooted around the office and figured out what was supposed to go where after a minute or two and before you could say supercalifragilisticexpialidocious I'd set myself to it.

I fell down the rabbit hole of numbers for Ghost's business pretty hard, adding this; subtracting that, busting out a percentage here or there for this tax or that... It wasn't until I heard the camera function on his cellphone make the shutter noise that I realized he was in the doorway and it had to have been hours after I'd started. I was pretty well into it when he found me. Still the noise scared the shit out of me. I jumped and let out this startled little girl shout and that more than anything made me throw the legal pad I was working on at him. He batted the yellow paper out of the air before it could hit him laughing.

"You scared the shit out of me!" I shouted. That was me, mistress of the obvious, but Ghost was rapt thumbing through menus on his phone's screen. "What are you doing?" I demanded.

"Princess, that is the hottest fucking thing I ever could have imagined. I'm saving it," he said.

I blinked. "What?"

"You, sitting there in nothing but your panties and my coat taking care of my books."

Truthfully he was one to talk, leaning nonchalantly in the doorway, hair sleep mussed, bare feet crossed in just his jeans, the top button not even done and hanging *dangerously* low on his hips. His hip flexors drawing the eye *right fucking there*. Ghost was sex on a stick and it hit me right between the eyes, right then, right there like a bolt from the blue, that he was *mine*. All mine and the reason I couldn't sleep finally came to me. I was scared as shit that I was going to wake up and find that this was all a dream.

"What's that look for Baby?" he asked solemnly. I shook my head so he smiled and changed tact. "What're you doing up?"

"Did I wake you?" I tried.

"Don't answer a question with a question, and no… I woke up and you weren't in my bed where I wanted you to be. Why not?" he cocked his head to the side, rich hazel eyes regarding me.

"I couldn't sleep," which was true.

"How come?" Shit, he would ask that. I sighed. Of course it was the next logical evolution…

"I didn't want to wake up and find it wasn't real. It still doesn't seem real," I looked around and gave him a skeptical look, "What *happened* in here?" I asked. He laughed.

"I hate this book keeping shit," he shrugged a shoulder.

"Good thing you have me to bail your ass out. You're about to be in trouble with the tax man. I think I can fix it but you're going to need to file an extension," I shifted some papers on the desk and Ghost pushed off the doorframe.

"Come here," he ordered but his voice was soft, his tone gentle. I got to my feet slowly and couldn't help but smile a little on the inside at the raw appreciative lust in his expression which was swirled with a healthy dose of protective possessiveness and I suddenly had another epiphany. I went to him and molded my front to his, my arms going around his neck. His arm slid beneath his jacket and wound around my naked body and the feeling made me shiver.

"I got you Babe," he said softly in my ear and I believed him. He really did have me, my best interests, at heart. We held each other in the door way to his office for a long time and finally I blurted it out.

"You're scaring the shit out of me with this whole moving in thing," I swallowed hard.

"Okay, fair enough but let's cut the bullshit, shall we?" he leaned back and gave me a grave look, "I told you, straight up, that if you came to my bed that there was no one and done, that this was it, the end of the line and you came to me, *willingly*, and gave yourself to me. That makes you *mine* Sweetheart, and I'm not saying that you're a fucking object or that you have to do what I say or that it makes you a slave or any of that garbage.

"What that means is that I swear to protect you. I'm going to love you, and no matter how much you frustrate me or irritate me, or piss me the fuck off, or try to push me away or any of that, I'm *here*. I'm not going *anywhere*. It's my duty to be there for you, to hold you to make sure you have everything that you need and hell, some things you don't but you're going to get 'em anyways because it makes you happy. Best way for me to provide any of those things is if you're here, with me."

I shifted slightly and smiled because everything he was saying sounded too good to be true but at the same time...

"What if I want a shiny red bicycle?" I asked and he laughed at my sass and pulled me in tight.

"Done," he said. I laughed with him, feeling lighter than I ever could remember because Ghost... Ghost didn't bullshit. He wasn't like that. In the over two years that I had known him he had never, not once gone back on his word to anybody. That still didn't stop me from being afraid or from worrying that if it was too good to be true...

"I can't promise I'm not going to be a pain in the ass," I murmured.

"Wouldn't expect anything less out of a fireball like you," he said, then asked, "Does that mean it's settled then and we can move your shit?" I made an incredulous noise.

"No! I'm not sure about *moving in* I mean holy geeze! We just started fucking!" Wrong thing to say, so wrong because he had me back against the door frame, one of his powerful thighs between my own so that my sex was pressed to the top of his denim clad leg and my toes barely touched the floor. My heart hammered the inside of my ribs like a damned xylophone and my breath caught in my throat as his gaze bore hot and heavy into mine.

"Don't you ever call it that again Shelly."

Oh shit. He used my name. He never really used my name, just like Reaver. I swallowed hard.

"I-I'm sorry," I said. He kept my gaze pinned with a hard stare of his own and I think I knew what it felt like to be an insect pinned to a board for display.

"While we're cutting the bullshit out of the equation, I'm going to be clear on this. There may be a time when I fuck you, but it hasn't happened yet. You get me?" I nodded not trusting my voice.

"Tell me you understand."

"I understand," I croaked. He softened and let me down, I slid the couple of inches to the floor, the thick leather of his jacket and cut protecting me from any splinters from the door frame.

"You don't have to be afraid of me Baby," he said softly. "I'm sorry I lost my temper there, but I love you and I haven't and won't touch you with anything less. I will never hit you, I will never hurt you but please... don't call it that." I stared fixedly at the colorful Sacred Hearts tattoo on his arm and felt my cheeks flame. He backed out of my personal space and I was a little outraged with myself at the bereft feeling it caused rather than the relieved one I expected.

"Say something please?" he said and his voice was tinged with worry.

"I'm sorry, I didn't mean it like that. I'm um... I'm just really..."

I struggled. I was so not used to talking about my feelings.

"You're just really what?" he asked and the gentleness was back. I closed my eyes and breathed out and felt my shoulders drop defeated. I was suddenly bone weary. I heard him sigh and his hands closed on the shoulders of his jacket. He pulled me into his arms and my hands found the warm skin of his back as I took shelter there.

"Overwhelmed?" he tried. I nodded.

"Okay," he said and flipped out the overhead light in the office.

"Okay?"

"Okay, Princess." He led me back to the bedroom and eased me out of his coat, hanging it somewhere on the back of the bedroom door. He led me gently by the hand and pulled back the blankets on the bed. I crawled in and he got in with me but left his pants on. I kind of appreciated that. He held me close and breathed out a long sigh, his breath ruffling my hair.

"I've been going at my own pace for so long I forget that sometimes the rest of the world needs me to slow the fuck down. I'm trying Princess. You gotta believe me," he kissed the top of my head and I closed my eyes. Of course the room was so dark it didn't make a difference. Open, closed, it might as well be one and the same.

"I know, I'm sorry," I ventured but he shushed me.

"Nothing to be sorry about, we'll figure it out as we go along," and I finally relaxed because it really was as simple as that. We would figure it out as we went along. Ghost was more intense than I had ever given him credit for.

"Instant Karma..." I murmured.

"What?" he asked.

"I've always been the intense one. You're my Karma. Now I know what it's like." He laughed, one of those laughs that starts out slow and then builds up into one of those rich full on belly laughs. I laughed with him and finally he settled down and I settled with him, beyond tired this time. One second I was there and then next I was in what must have been a deep and dreamless sleep.

The next time I opened my eyes it was to a set that perfectly mirrored my own. My cousin Reaver lay stretched out next to me like when we were kids, our noses almost touching.

"Jesus Reave!" I startled. He laughed at me, the laughter cutting off abruptly when I sat up faster than light expecting to be in my room back at his place, my worst fear coming true that it had all been one vivid and intensely real dream, but no... I was in an unfamiliar bedroom in an unfamiliar bed that smelled strongly of the outdoors and woods. I looked down at the deep navy blue goose down comforter pooling in my lap and the oversized General Motors throwback tee shirt I was wearing that I hadn't gone to sleep in.

"What're you *doing* here?" I blurted and looked down at my big cuz, who had his head propped on his hand.

"Ghost called. Brought you some clothes, I had Hayden pack the bag for you so I didn't have to touch your panties," he made a face and I smacked him.

"Hey! Ow! So violent missy!"

"I learned it from you!" I said.

"True dat," then he made a face, "I could swear I taught you to hit harder than – Ow!"

"Hey!" Ghost barked from the doorway, "You abusing my woman?" he held two mugs of steaming coffee.

"No, she's abusing me!" Reave complained.

"Oh, well, carry on then." He strode across the hardwood and area rug already dressed for the day and held out a steaming mug I took it from him and found lightly colored coffee I sipped tentatively. Lots of cream and sugar just the way I liked it.

"What'd you bring me?" I asked Reave.

"I don't know! I told you I had Hayden pack it. Enough for a week, just like Ghost said," I coughed, choking on a sip of coffee. Ghost lifted the cup out of my hands and Reave slapped me on the back.

"A week?" I squeaked.

"A compromise," Ghost murmured, "Stay with me a week, if you're still not sure about moving in then stay with me another."

"How is *that* a compromise?" I demanded.

"You want to move your shit in now?" he demanded back, giving me as good as he got. I glowered at him. Reave bounced between us like some demented tennis match and threw his two cents in.

"Damn I need some popcorn."

"She's mine, she should be here," Ghost said.

"Yeah I get it bro," Reaver said putting up his hands.

"Reaver! I can't believe you're taking his side!" I cried. This was way out of control, I *hated it* when shit got too far out of my control.

"Way I see it, I'm taking yours Baby Cousin. The man says he loves you and wants to take care of you. Who am I to argue?" and that was the point where I think I snapped.

If I had sleeves I'd be rolling them up because I was about to break it off in my cousin's ass. Not that it would do any good. Reaver was as unflappable as they came and truthfully I was only putting up a fight because it felt like they were taking the decision out of my hands. I wanted what Ghost was handing me but quailed on the inside because what if I broke it? So I pushed like I always did to see how far it'd bend before it broke... if it broke.

I started in on my cousin, "Oh! Really? Guys say a lot of fucking things, Reaver!" I threw back the blankets and got up not even caring, not that Reaver did. We were family and might as well be siblings for how close we were growing up. Ghost made a strangled noise and I rounded on him.

"What?" I demanded and he put up his hands, leaving the coffee on the bedside table. His expression was grim and I knew I was about to break it, but I just couldn't help it. Good things like Ghost just didn't happen to girls like me and the dam had burst. I railed. Dropping to my knees and ripping open the zipper on the small suitcase Reaver had brought.

"Remember Tommy Flanagan?" I asked Reaver. "He said we were forever, said nothing would ever tear us apart, until he started fucking Molly Atwood! Oh and what about Marshall Adams? Remember him? 'I'll never hurt you, babe' well it sure fucking hurt when he knocked out those two teeth in the back!" Reaver sighed and looked bored.

"Yeah and I broke his arm in three places and they had to put him in a medically induced coma until the swelling on his brain went down," Reaver said.

"Not the point Reaver!" I shouted and pulled a pair of black running pants on. The fitted stretchy kind. I ripped Ghost's tee over my head.

"Jesus Christ Shelly!" Ghost shouted and I yelled back, "Oh please! It's nothing either of you haven't seen before!" He gave Reaver a weird look and Reaver waved him off like he was being an idiot which he was.

"I *will not* be told what the fuck to do!" I ripped a runner's bra over my head and shoved everything into place. Reaver sighed.

"No one's telling you what to do Runt."

"Well actually, I sort of am," Ghost looked a little guilty.

"Yeah but it's for her own good," Reaver said and I sputtered indignant.

"Stop talking about me like I'm not right fucking here!" I screeched.

"Well fuck! There's no talking to you when you get like this! Go on! Yell, scream, throw your tantrum, run away and wear yourself out like you always do, Shelly! God damn! I've already warned him. You're not going to break this one. That's why I like him!" I fucking hated Reaver in that instant. I hurled the first thing I could grab at him which happened to be one of my Chuck Taylor's and he caught it, snatching it out of the air. A switchblade appeared in his hand and he flicked it open and that calmed my shit right down. I stilled.

"You wanna throw shit Baby Cuz, I'll throw shit too," his eyes had gone that creepy distant that if you were smart, told you that shit had just gotten real and you were about to get hurt and that is when Ghost made good on his word. He pointed a gun at my cousin's head.

"That's my woman you're threatening there Bro," Reaver kept his eyes locked on mine.

"She was my cousin before she was your woman."

"Doesn't matter, she's mine now and I know what you can do with that thing. Make it disappear before my trigger finger gets twitchy." I looked from one to the other of them, back and forth, back and forth and finally my cousin's eyes warmed back up and the blade in his hand was just gone, like smoke like it had never existed. Ghost aimed his handgun skyward and I dropped like a stone onto my ass and burst into fucking tears.

"I can't even fight with you anymore?" I cried and Reaver looked a cross between amused and a little saddened. He dropped into a crouch and stayed a distance away.

"Apparently not Baby Cuz," he said and opened his arms. I crawled over and hugged him and sobbed into his tee shirt and Ghost put up his gun and looked poleaxed.

"What. The. Fuck?" he shouted.

"I told you she'd push limits and be a pain in the ass and try to break it. Reason it doesn't work with me is I fight back. I get a free pass on everything and she does too. We're family," Reaver tried to explain.

"Fucked up and dysfunctional," I moaned.

"Yep. She screams and rages and we have it out about nothing and she feels back in control and we move on," Reaver rocked me back and forth. We'd been doing it since we were kids.

"How about a run, Runt? Will a run make it better?" he asked. I nodded and tried to pull my shit together. If I couldn't fight then a run was the next best thing.

"Okay Baby, you're halfway there. Come on. Up you go," Reaver stood us up and I looked at Ghost who looked confused as Hell and I despaired.

"Finish getting dressed," Ghost said.

"You too Buddy. She ain't going alone," Reaver told him. Reave was pretty much already dressed for it in basketball shorts, running shoes and his ever-present tee shirt and hoodie. Fresh tears welled up and I asked him.

"How did you know?" he pulled me into a tight hug with a sigh. Reaver always seemed to know what I needed before I even did.

"Runt, I was there when you were born and I've been there every day since. I'm always gonna know. I'm magic like that. Now do what you need to do to shove things around and meet me out front so I can try to keep up, just like I've been trying every day since you popped out." He shook me a little and let go and he and Ghost went out. Ghost carrying a bundle of sweats.

I stood still for a minute and got my shit together some before pulling on the rest of my running gear, correctly this time. Lacing my shoes up tight and double knotting them. It was getting to be time for a new pair and thankfully, I was gainfully employed again to be able to afford it.

I looked around the bedroom and sniffed. Angry tears welling up again which just made me friggin' angrier. I hated crying, I hated feeling fucking vulnerable and out of control and I hated that I was doing entirely too much of all of those things lately. I almost, *almost* had myself talked into hating Ghost for causing me to feel these things but there was that damned voice of self-reasoning in the back of my mind! Whispering from the dark corners like it was scared I'd lash out at it next, it said: *Only you can make yourself feel anything. Ghost has nothing to do with that. He's trying to help you.* It was right, and fuck if that didn't piss me off even more.

Bottom line, I was a hot fucking mess and I was more terrified of breaking this, of losing Ghost with one of my epic freak outs than I was of anything else. I needed this run. I needed to put my body in motion and expend all of this nervous energy before I imploded, or worse, exploded. Dr. Hubbard called it a coping mechanism and said that as far as coping mechanisms went it wasn't too bad of one seeing as it kept me physically fit.

My mind was racing, grasping at so many nonsensical and nonessential things it wasn't even funny. I needed to run, to get those endorphins going; to get my body moving like a well-oiled machine so that I could focus again. It was time to see if Ghost really could keep up.

CHAPTER 18

Ghost

"I've never seen her like this, does it happen very often?" I was getting dressed in the middle of my kitchen. Reaver, who was leaning against the counter, gave a Gallic shrug that could mean nothing and could mean everything at the same time.

"You gotta understand how we grew up," he imparted a little sadly. "My mom is a hard core alchie, Shelly's mom though, fucking meth addict. There wasn't any order to anything so it was chaos all day every day. You never knew what Aunt Shari was gonna do from one day to the next. I tried, I really did, to give Shelly some semblance of normal but I was five when she was born and had to deal with raising my own mom who for the most part was pretty functional. Shelly lived two trailers down and her mom would have these spates of normal but for the most part it was sheer crazy. Combine that with what happened… Shit, I'm surprised she's not completely coming apart," he smoothed his hair down in front over his forehead petting it over and over again.

"I think the only normal Shells got was at school and shit. She wants it, she wants the two point five kids, white picket fence, the whole deal and she wants normal so fucking bad but I honestly think it scares the shit out of her at the same time. She doesn't know how to operate in the normal. Never has. She drinks sparingly, doesn't do drugs at all, terrified she'll end up just like her mom but I don't think she sees it, or gets that she just replaced those things with sex as a means to feel good. Then dude comes along and fucks *that* up for her…" he turned his gaze out the window above my kitchen sink and I pulled on one of my running shoes. "Shelly's all mixed up, depressed and doesn't know how to deal with any of it because all she does is internalize all this garbage." He huffed out a sigh.

"Sounds like you been going to therapy," I grunted. He laughed.

"Naw, been getting a lot out of Ashton and Trig. Was hoping therapy would do Shelly some good but she won't talk to him about any of the important stuff. Still hasn't talked to anyone about the attack…"

"Yes, she has," I said quietly he looked at me sharply and I caught a glimmer of hope in his ice blue eyes. He opened his mouth to say something but Shelly stepped into the kitchen.

"You ready?" she asked and sounded like one very unhappy camper.

"You stretched?" Reaver asked.

"Yep."

"Too bad. You gotta wait for us to do it," we trooped out the back door.

"Hurry it up," she stretched some more with us and I took the time to both limber up and inspect her. The turmoil was plain on her face and I was beginning to realize that Shelly had a lot more going on than I had ever realized but she wasn't giving a fucking inch. Reaver leapt up into a runner's starter stance and Shelly dropped into one next to him, I followed suit on her other side.

"On your mark! Get set! GO!" he barked and she was off like a shot. I'd never seen her run before but the girl was part cheetah and part motherfucking gazelle. I pushed myself hard and harder to keep up with her she outpaced me soon enough and by the time we reached the end of the long drive and turned out onto the road she was making long even strides.

"Hope… you… can… go… for a… a while!" Reaver said between breaths. The stride we were in, the pace we were going didn't leave much air for talking. This was going to be a serious cardio session. I simply nodded. I was a Marine damn it. I was no stranger to running and truthfully it was nice knowing I'd be able to do this with Shelly.

We went for miles, way further than I thought she could or would go, all the way into the next town. I had no idea how we would get back. I didn't really worry about it. Probably around three hours after we started we were headed across this municipal park with it's perfectly manicured grass and paved walkways when Shelly slowed then stopped and spinning in place flopped onto her back into a drift of leaves. Reaver, chest heaving laid down with his head meeting hers and I flopped down beside Shelly and picked up her hand pressing a kiss to the back of it. I was too out of breath and covered with sweat to do much else. I think we'd just burned off Thanksgiving and then some. We lay panting in the leaves and staring at the leaden overcast sky as the sweat cooled our skins.

"I'm a mess Ghost," Shelly said between breaths, her breathing slowing.

"Yeah well you're my mess now and I'm not going anywhere," I promised her.

"Stubborn Jackass," she gasped.

"Right back at you Baby Girl," Reaver said.

"Shut up Big Cuz."

"Go fuck yourself Little Cuz."

Shelly laughed at that and said, "Apparently I don't have to anymore," and she squeezed my hand.

"This mean you'll move in with me?" I asked.

"This means I'll stay for," she sucked in a breath and let it out, "A week. Then we'll talk."

She turned her head to the side to look at me and I turned mine to look at her. Her eyes held a pleading she would never speak out loud so I capitulated some.

"One week, we talk," I agreed.

"Thank you Jesus!" Reaver cried, "She does know the meaning of the word compromise. Ow!" Shelly had blindly flailed an arm in Reaver's direction and had smacked him in the face with the back of her hand.

"Ow is right!" she shook out her hand and I laughed.

"Instant Karma," I gasped out and we all lay in the leaves, gasping, panting and wheezing out laughter in between.

Reaver sat up with a groan. "Where the fuck are we?" he asked, looking around.

"Grant's Park, Anderson's Hollow," I answered. I'd done tow work for the town hauling illegally parked cars out of here that illegally parked here overnight.

"Ah," he pulled his cell out of his pocket and dialed. "Yeah Trig, three for pick up, Grant's Park, Anderson's Hollow," he said into the phone only moderately out of breath. I heard the indistinct buzz of a voice on the other end asking if he were taking us back to my place.

"Copy that! Thank You Sir!" I called out.

Shelly heaved herself up and started stretching. I followed suit, before any cramping started.

"There's a water fountain over that way near the parking lot," I indicated. We hauled ourselves wearily to our feet and trudged that direction. I held the button while Shelly sipped. She straightened, waited a bit and sipped some more. Drinking too fast would make her sick and she knew that.

"How long you been a runner?" I asked her.

"Since Jr. High," she said and drank some more.

"All star track and field, blue ribbon in three counties, cross country," Reaver said and the look he gave me was weird like he was hoping what he was saying would make sense on more than just one front. Shelly rolled her eyes.

"Math, running, what do they both have in common Ghost?" she asked and I was both tired and felt monumentally stupid.

"I don't know Princess, I'm not picking up what you guys are putting down, so why don't you just come out with it and tell me?" I stared her down and let the challenge hang between us and she took it, just like I knew she would.

"Control," she said, "I have total control over the situation and the expected result. I like having control and knowing what the fucking outcome is going to be and I don't have that with you! Okay? Jesus Christ."

She took some steps away from me and put her hands on her hips. Reaver was drinking from the fountain where I had the button depressed and I let it go. He made a rude noise and gave me the finger before pressing the button himself.

I went to her and pulled her into my arms. We were both sweaty and in need of a shower in the worst fucking way but I didn't care. I didn't give two shits. I held her, damp and clammy as she was and looked up the couple of inches into her so blue eyes and asked her plainly, "Do you trust me, Shelly?"

She rocked back on her heels and settled flat on her feet and contemplated the question. I mean really thought about it which I appreciated about her.

"Yes but no," she said finally.

"Explain," I said before I let my feelings get hurt.

"I trust you, but I've trusted a lot of people that I shouldn't have and they let me down or hurt me so I trust you, I really do but those past experiences are getting in my way. They're making the road ahead with you foggy and I want to trust you but I haven't been because of those people and those things and I know it's not fair but that's part of what is going on," she looked so unhappy, so miserable and so disappointed in that moment.

"I'm sorry," she whispered.

"I'm not," I said and smiled, "You've identified the problem, now what do you do?" I asked. She startled a bit.

"Solve it," she answered immediately. I nodded.

"We'll work it out Princess," I promised her.

"Baby Cuz, you and me got a mountain and a half worth of issues between us. You don't move mountains in a day, you move them a rock at a time." Shelly nodded at what her cousin was saying but her eyes were fixed on me.

"Why?" she asked, "Why would you want someone so fucked up as me?" I smiled and put my lips over hers in a gentle kiss.

"Maybe I like solving problems too, just not the mathematical kind. Maybe I like a challenge. Maybe the best things in life are the ones you really gotta work for and I see that in you because you are, you know? You are so worth it," I told her and it was true. She really was. I shook her a little.

"I get you!" she said and I teased a small smile from her.

"About time," Reaver said and we turned, he stood there grinning like an idiot and I reluctantly let Shelly go so I could start to hydrate.

"Told you I liked him," he said and Shelly smiled a little brighter.

Trigger picked us up a little while later. Ashton was conspicuously absent and Shelly was the first to comment on it.

"Where's Sunshine?"

"Back at the house," he said and was smiling, "I asked her to do something for me, she's thinking about it." Shelly instantly narrowed her eyes in suspicion. I took her hand in mine where it rested between us on the back seat. Reaver looked over at Trig from the front passenger seat of Ashton's red Jeep.

"Did you get it?" he asked him and I felt myself frowning.

"Yep!" Trig reached into the inside pocket of his jacket and pulled out a little black velvet box. Shelly gasped.

"Oh my God! You asked her?" she let go of my hand and reached between the seats and snatched the box from Trigger's hand.

"No, not yet but I'm gonna. Got to do it right you know?" he said and I grinned at the big man.

Shelly cracked the little box open and gasped again. "Oh Trig, you did good buddy!" she declared and turned it so I could see the ring inside. It was small and dainty like my friend's woman. It had three small diamonds one in the center and two to either side of it with delicate filigree scrollwork around them. He really had done well. It looked like something that should appear in one of her period musicals she loved so much.

"When are you going to ask her? How are you going to ask her?" Shelly demanded. Trigger laughed and took the box back from her and let Reaver have a look. Reave gave a low whistle.

"I'll let her tell you all about it after it's done at the next get together you girls do. Not that I need to say, but you keep your mouth shut!" Trigger said. Shelly ducked sideways so he could see her clearly in the rearview and drew her fingers across her lips, zipping them closed, locking them up and throwing away the key. Her blue eyes sparkled with elation for the small woman and I was glad for it.

Trig dropped us off at my house, and Reaver hugged Shelly goodbye before climbing into his beat to shit white work truck and leaving himself. Shelly turned and faced me and suddenly it was just her and I in the lonely drive.

"It's crazy how remote this place feels," she said and it held an edge of complaint. She hugged herself.

"Used to town?" I asked her.

"Yeah. Out here you can't do anything but think," she scraped her bottom lip between her teeth.

"Would it help if you had your own car back?" I asked. She looked surprised, then thought about it.

"Yes."

I nodded. "Monday," I affirmed, "Dray said it was done but the garage is closed for the holiday," she moved towards me and the front door.

"He and Everett need it, a holiday," she proclaimed with a gusty sigh.

"What about you?" I asked.

"What about me?"

"You need a holiday? Get out of town for a weekend? Go for a ride?" I let us into the kitchen and Shelly gave me a funny look.

"You don't lock your door?" I shrugged and brought the gun Trigger returned to me out of the back of my waistband.

"You were just complaining I lived out in the boonies, didn't stop to think it had its benefits too, did you?" I raised an eyebrow and she laughed.

"Okay, you got me there," she admitted. I set the Glock on the kitchen counter.

"Can I ask you something?" I got her a bottle of water from the fridge and handed it to her, she took it, regarding me carefully.

"Sure."

I cracked the seal on my own bottle. "Why don't you want to live with me?"

She took a considering swallow of water and sighed, "Truth?"

"Always."

"It's not you, it's me," she quirked her little smart assed half smile and I grinned back hoisting myself into a sitting position on the edge of the counter by the stove. Shelly made a face but I didn't move.

"Explain before I get my feelings hurt," I said sarcastically.

"I'm afraid if I live with you that you won't want me anymore because I'm me. That you won't like how I do things or that I insist on things like closing the lid on the toilet before you flush or that the milk has to be on the bottom shelf not the top…" she raised her eyebrows.

"I think I can get on board with these demands. Any other ones?" I killed half my bottle of water in three swallows.

"The office is mine. I do your numbers and book keeping as my way of paying rent," I didn't want it too look like I was to eager but I could see I was winning this particular battle. I tried to keep everything in neutral, thoughtful lines but I must have done a shitty job because Shelly laughed at me.

"Okay, fine. Anything else?" She tried to suppress her smile but failed.

"Yeah. Get your ass off the kitchen counter!"

"On one condition," I said and she raised one pale eyebrow, "Take a shower with me."

"I think I can do that," she agreed and I dropped my feet to the kitchen floor, standing.

"Still think this is a bad idea, Princess?" I asked her with a wink.

"Still on the fence," and her words dripped with lie. I took her hand gently and urged her towards me. She stepped lightly and with only a little bit of reluctance which, I could almost believe, was feigned by the light in her eyes.

"Well we have all the rest of today for me to craft a convincing argument," I closed the gap between us and kissed her gently and thankfully, she kissed me back.

"I'm scared because everything is in flux, I don't have any control over anything and truthfully… it's everything I've ever wanted and it just feels too good to be true," she blurted. I cupped her face in my hands and rested her forehead against mine.

"Just trust me, Baby. I promise, we'll be okay. You'll be okay and when things come up, we'll work through them." She let out a shuddering sigh.

"Don't make promises you can't keep, Ghost… please?" she begged and I stroked her cheeks with my thumbs and kissed her.

"I'll try, Princess, now come on, let's get cleaned up."

CHAPTER 19

Shelly

Ghost led me carefully in the direction of the master bathroom just off the inside of the bedroom. I was surprised at how modern and just plain big it was. It didn't have a bathtub but the shower more than made up for it. I wasn't much for baths anyways. He started the water in the large, stone lined shower and began stripping me, tossing the laundry into a hamper in the corner. I watched him work on us, a slight smile of contentment on his lips and I had some hope that my crazy wasn't going to break us after all. I was really beginning to hate my moods, they never asked my permission before they changed on me lately. I felt a rush of dismay and fear that Ghost was going to get sick of the rapid changes when he caught sight of me.

"Why you looking at me like that Princess?" he asked and I kept my mouth shut. He stilled and stared me down until with an exasperated sigh I gave in.

"I was thinking that there might be some hope after all, that my crazy..." he touched gentle fingers to my lips and got right up in my personal space, speaking close to my mouth, his breath grazing my skin, *my* breath catching in my throat.

"You're not crazy. Your wires may be crossed, you may have more bad days than good right now, but I told you... I'm not going anywhere, and if I have to spend the rest of time proving that to you then that's what I'll do," he didn't let me protest, didn't let me make a sound because his mouth closed over mine and we were kissing and with his hands on my hips he was leading me back towards the gently steamed glass enclosure of the shower.

The water felt delicious on my skin, warm and cleansing, and I felt myself relax even more. The only thing that felt better than the water sluicing down my body was the close proximity of Ghost. He was so close I could feel his energy. He had a stillness about him, he was solid like nothing could or would hurt him without his permission. He was sure of himself in a way I used to be before my very foundation was shaken.

He took his time, first soaping his hands and then soaping *me*. Whatever he used smelled woodsy but not in an artificial man-made way, but in a natural, genuine article kind of way and I liked that, I liked it a lot. He turned me into the hot shower spray to rinse me and then did something unprecedented. He kissed every inch of my freshly washed skin with these soft presses of his lips, softer than the touch of a butterfly's wings. Ghost smoothed his hands down my shoulders and slid his palms along the backs of my hands, lacing his fingers between mine and it was like the spaces between my fingers were made for his to be there. He pressed the palms of my hands flat against the shower's stone wall and treated my back to the same pleasurable kisses.

"Shelly," he said from his knees, just before he nipped my ass.

"Mmm?" I admit, my eyes were closed and I relished his touches more than I could say. No one had ever touched me with as much care and consideration before.

"Time to get out, Baby. I want you to dry off and go lay down on the bed. Face down. You get me?"

"But what about you?" I opened my eyes and turned around. Ghost smiled up at me hands on my hips and pressed a kiss to my stomach just below my navel.

"Don't worry about me. I'm having a good time. Now will you do as I ask please?" I searched his face and finally I nodded, a touch uncertain. He stood in one fluid movement and opened the shower door. I stepped out onto the cushy bathmat and took one of the towels from the bars. I dried myself, Ghost watching me from the shower as he soaped and rinsed himself.

"You look dry enough to me, Princess," his voice startled me, the constant sound of running water lulling me to a point. It was as if his careful ministrations in the shower had gotten my mind to click off. I was in a pleasant state of suspended animation when it came to thought. Things were drifting through my mind but nothing was really sticking or making my brain catch in a loop.

"Shelly, I'll be out in a sec. You trust me right?" he asked. I nodded. "Okay then go lay down."

I wrapped the towel around me and went and did as he asked, laying on my stomach on his big comfortable bed. I was fairly drained, physically, mentally and emotionally from the run that morning and everything that had come with it. I don't think it helped that I hadn't eaten yet and had just had a few swallows of coffee, but I wasn't that hungry and between the soft bed under me and the white noise of the shower I may have dozed just a bit. I remember hearing the shower shut off so I don't know why I jolted just a bit when the bed moved under Ghost's weight.

"Easy, just me," he commented and I felt a tug on the towel wrapped around me. I lifted myself just a bit so he could have it and heard it carelessly dropped to the carpet. I shivered a bit, the air of the room cool against my shower-warmed skin when the warmth of Ghost's hands interrupted the chill. He smoothed them up and down my back, a firm caress. I felt him straddle my legs and thought it was a bit out of place, I mean shouldn't I be the one…

"Ooooooh God that feels good!" all thoughts I'd been having flew straight out the window as he began to knead the muscles in my back into submission. I felt the faint vibration of his chuckle in the backs of my thighs but then his thumbs dug in just a little, just right *there* between my shoulder blades and I was ever so grateful I was face down because I was pretty sure I was drooling on myself.

His hands were pure fucking magic. He knew just how hard to press and where and I was in a blissed out coma before I knew it. I don't know how long he worked on me but when the kisses started to fall across my shoulders and back, he didn't really need them. Just his touch alone had aroused me and I was in this strange semi-state between that and relaxed. I felt absolutely boneless under him and willingly my legs parted when his knee nudged between them.

"Can I take you like this?" he asked and I appreciated so much that he did. I pushed to my hands and knees and arched my back.

"God yes, I want you inside of me," I moaned and he chuckled a little.

"Don't have to tell me twice, Beautiful."

His hands gripped my hips, thumbs smoothing over my back, just above my ass and I moaned, pressing back to find him. His hands disappeared and I heard the wrapper crinkle for the condom and my pussy gave a needy little pleasure filled throb. Ghost lined himself up and pressed into me slowly and I groaned. He filled me out so perfectly from this angle, I loved it. He was just so right, and he moved slowly at first and when I felt him flush against my body I mourned just a little, it felt like he was *almost there* to touching the secret place deep inside me but that he was just shy of it. I moaned and thrust back onto him in hopes that it would make up the difference.

I knew that if he went to town, took me roughly this way; that it would be absolutely fucking amazing but Ghost was trying to kill me, or at least torture me and he was doing a damned fine job of riling me up because, Oh. My. God. Just when I thought the torture he was dishing out couldn't possibly be any sweeter he spoke.

"God Shelly, you feel so good!" his voice was pitched low and deep and I swear to god his words turned me on and turned me up two or three degrees hotter and I wasn't above fucking begging at this point.

"Derek..!" I gasped.

"What is it Honey?" he asked and the fucking bastard! I could *hear* the smirk in his voice. He knew exactly what he was doing to me!

"Harder!" I cried.

"Harder? Now why would I want to do that? Hmmm? Maybe I like taking your pussy soft and slow like this. I mean Christ, you have no idea how amazing you feel wrapped around my cock," he pulled back on my hips and thrust just a little bit harder to punctuate his sentence and oh holy hell he had me, he had me right fucking there. I mean a few more thrusts like that and I would be coming apart at the seams and I wanted that, I wanted it so bad I couldn't even *say*...

"Oh God yeah!" I cried and tried to meet him for his next thrust but he held himself back just enough from making the same impact.

"Ask me nicely," he said and I could almost hear the devilish grin. I gasped slightly indignant.

"You are *so not* going to make me beg!" I cried. He thrust harder and I gasped. I was so wet, it felt so good! I arched my back, low to the mattress and prayed he would do it again.

"Come on baby, ask me nicely and I'll give you what you want, I'll make it good for you I promise, all you have to do is ask," he smoothed his hands up my back, so warm against my cool flesh and I shuddered. I wanted to come so bad but I'd never had someone demand that I ask for it.

"Please, Ghost, harder!" I tried and he was an insufferable shit.

"Nope, you gotta tell me exactly what you want. I wanna hear it Shelly," I could tell he wanted to thrust harder as much as I wanted him to.

"Please Derek, fuck me harder?" I tried and then I had to yelp when his hand came down in a stinging slap against my ass. Ow! Fuck me that hurt!

"Not fucking you Shelly, that shit's impersonal and I'm very much feeling it. What do you need Baby? Tell me," he stroked into me sure and perfect and maddeningly kept me just on that edge. I needed just a little bit more, a little bit deeper, God why wouldn't he just... and then it dawned on me.

The dirty manipulative, insufferable...! I stiffened and was about to get pissed off but then he gave it to me just a little bit harder and I cried out, he eased back off after just a couple of strokes and my triumphant cry turned into a frustrated wail.

"God! I need you to thrust harder! I need to come, please Derek! Please make me come!" he stroked into me harder and it was almost perfect, it was so much closer and felt so good but he was still purposefully missing that mark, I felt that heavy sensation in my pussy, the one that foretold an orgasm was building, a big one, one of those earth shattering soul melting orgasms and I wanted it, I wanted to feel good so badly and to forget how crazy and awful my day had started out. I felt my body tighten around him as he pressed into me and I was close, so close and I told him as much.

"Oh God I'm close, I'm so close!" his hands smoothed up my back and he faltered just a bit but then those beautiful hands of his closed around my arms just above the elbow and he pulled back and *oh my fucking God* it was the most intense and exquisite thing I had ever felt in my life! It was as if he were going so deep inside me there was no way to tell where I left off and where he began. Usually being taken from behind felt great, Hell it felt awesome and just plain really, really good but it had never felt really *intimate*.

This though, *this* felt incredibly intimate, incredibly close and oh-my-god amazing. It was rough, it was so much pleasure it twisted and almost, *almost* became pain but I didn't have time to choose which side of the dividing line I fell on because I was falling apart beneath him, crying out, screaming through one of the most intense orgasms I had ever experienced. I felt him shove tightly into me and spill, twitching into the condom that separated us and for the first time ever I was disappointed that there was a barrier between me and a partner. I wanted so badly for us to be skin on skin in that particular moment.

I collapsed on my stomach, chest heaving with panting breath and felt his forehead come to rest between my shoulders. He'd slipped from my body and I mourned the loss of the intimate contact keenly. He sat up with a groan and breath sawing in and out of his chest in a cadence to match mine, I heard rather than saw him strip the condom from himself and a second later heard it hit the trashcan liner.

"Turn over for me Princess?" he asked and his voice, uneven along with his breathing, was so sweet to my ear I didn't think I just complied. He knelt between my thighs, his eyes lovely dark and deep with desire and he shook his head. "I'm sorry, I need more. I need more of you, can you take some more?" he asked.

I felt my head nodding even while my brain was still trying to catch up. Wait? *He was already ready for a round two?* Was that what he was saying? It hadn't even been five minutes! Sure enough that was exactly what he was saying because he was already rolling on a fresh condom and the sight of it made my body throb and fizzle with aftershocks and excitement. I didn't get to think about it though, because he was bending over me, sliding inside me and his lips were pressing hungrily to my own before I could form any more coherent thought.

My legs wound unbidden around his lean hips, my arms around the tight swell of his shoulders and I clung to him as he moved in and out of me with sure even strokes. He was going for another long and slow build and I was okay with that because I never wanted it to end at this point. I drank of Derek's soul through our kiss and let him have his fill of mine and loved that he could do this to me. That he could make me *feel* with his touch and his kiss; that it wasn't about the physical with him. He looked at me and I saw a deep understanding in the depths of his eyes. He saw me, every last sharp and gnarly bit and there wasn't one iota of indifference in his stare. Just complete acceptance. He accepted every part of me and that rocked me to my core.

I kissed him with a renewed vigor, finally understanding. He'd waited for me, for this to happen. He'd waited so patiently and so *not* so patiently for me and he'd waited for a very long time. Since he'd first laid eyes on me, God! Well over two years ago now. As he pressed deep into my body, touching off pleasure in nerves I wasn't even aware I possessed, I wondered how I ever missed it. How I could have been so blind to it, but my thoughts, they still weren't sticking, and as Derek rocked into my body and kissed me with a feverish passion I had only ever dreamed someone would hold for me, I was okay with that. I was content to simply let this man love me and to let myself be his and belong and *God it was all I ever wanted!* I belonged to someone. Finally, I really belonged and was completely, one hundred percent accepted by this man for who I was and all he wanted was for me to be *me* and to be his.

It was as if Ghost read my mind because he looked deep into my eyes and asked me, voice barely above a murmur, tone beseeching, "Tell me you're mine?"

I smiled serenely and told him the truth, "I'm yours Ghost. I'm really yours," he bowed his head as if it were the sweetest music he'd ever heard and he kissed me and everything crystalized and snapped into place and I have never felt like I was in such perfect harmony as I did right then, with him, and I swear by everything, I never wanted anyone else ever again because there wasn't another man on the planet that could compare. Not with this, not with him, not with my Old Man, Ghost.

CHAPTER 20

Ghost

She looked so peaceful when she slept this time. Her head resting against my chest, I watched her and marveled. Something was different about her after this last round of love making. I wasn't sure what, but I was totally cool with it. We'd both fallen into a blissed out coma after finishing and now that the day was deepening on into dusk I realized that neither of us had eaten. I was starving and in the middle of a pretty hardcore debate with myself on if I should wake her when those gorgeous sapphire eyes of hers opened up and pinned me with their jewel bright gaze.

"Hey," her voice was soft and husky with sleep and I felt my cock stir beneath the sheet. I resolutely told it to get down, I didn't think my thighs could take any more of a work out, but her voice interrupted my thoughts.

"What's wrong?" her brow wrinkled with concern and I laughed.

"You're so damned beautiful, like a fucking angel when you sleep," I said and she blushed faintly her eyes slipping shut in pure bliss. I didn't want to get sidetracked from the immediate need so I cleared my throat and asked her, "You hungry?"

"Starving now that you mention it."

"I don't have anything except beer in the fridge. Not much sense in me cooking for one, so uh, yeah… Up to you, what do you want to do?" I watched her carefully and she smiled a little sadly.

"Damn. I don't really want to leave the house, but I bet you there is plenty left at the club house, I mean Ashton had us cook enough to feed an army. Not sure what would be open the day after Thanksgiving, at least not restaurant wise," I smiled at her.

"Club it is," I said. She leaned up carefully and brought her lips to mine, tentatively like she wasn't sure it was okay. I returned her kiss and tried very hard not to get so turned on I had to take her again.

"You good?" I asked her and she smiled at me.

"I'm good. Not sure I'll ever walk correctly again but I'm good," I laughed.

"Up you go Princess, I'm starving too."

We dressed comfortably and she took a couple of minutes to smooth down her platinum blonde hair in the bathroom mirror. She looked stunning in just jeans and a tee but it wasn't warm enough for that and the thin sweater she had on the day before, while comfortable looking... no. Just no. I pulled down my Marine Corps black hoodie out of the closet and held it out to her. She smiled and lit up and pulled it on. It was way oversized on her thin frame but she looked good.

"Thanks," she murmured and I nodded.

We went out to my pickup truck and I loved that she took my hand in hers on the short walk from the door. I opened up the door for her and she let me help her up into the cab. I smiled.

"Thanks," I said and she blushed.

"I like your hands on me," she admitted and I could see it cost her some effort to admit her feelings out loud. She searched my face, a little anxiety in her eyes. I stepped up onto the runner and ducked into the cab to kiss her. She was trying. She was trusting me, but she was still afraid some dick comment was going to fly out of my mouth and hurt her. I could read her like a book sometimes but only when she let me and she was letting me. Something about our last round of intimacy had opened her up and I needed to show her it was okay to be that way. That it was safe for her to be her around me.

"I like my hands on you Shelly," I murmured against her mouth and she smiled.

"I need to feed your other appetites. I can't have my ol' man getting as skinny as me," and I swear to God her words made my heart swell to three times its size with elation in my chest, pressing hard to the inside of my ribcage almost to the point of pain. She'd called me her Old Man. I backed out of her personal space reluctantly, grinning like a god damned fool and went around to the driver's side. I drove us to the club on cloud nine and we talked on the way. Mostly about inane things that didn't really matter, but now wasn't the time for any heavy shit.

It was a Friday night but surprisingly fairly sedate in the front room when we arrived. There were three brothers at a table cleaning their guns, talking quietly. Chandra came out of the kitchen with a heaping plate and a smile like the cat that ate the canary.

"Was wondering when you two were going to show," she smiled at Shelly, "Plenty left in the kitchen, Baby... you'd better eat something." Shelly laughed.

"Sort of why we're here. He doesn't keep food in the house. Plenty of beer though," Chandra rolled her eyes.

"Pffft! Just like a man," she said and walked back towards, presumably Doc's room. Shelly giggled and I pulled her closer into my side.

"I'll fix us some plates," she kissed me quick and spun out of my grasp and sashayed that sweet ass of hers into the kitchen. I went over and pulled out a chair at the table of brothers and spun it around so I could straddle it. I hung off the back of the chair nonchalantly and watched for a second as they cleaned their guns. There was no smell of fresh gunpowder hanging in the air, so they weren't recently fired. I raised an eyebrow at Blue and Duracell and looked over to Zeb.

"Getting ready for a party?" I asked.

"Got some info on The Suicide Cunts," Zeb said in his rich New Zealand accent.

"There gonna be trouble?" I brought out my Glock which Shelly and I had fired, Jesus! Just yesterday, and began to disassemble it. Blue, a fair skinned dude with gray eyes the color of dirty window glass, shoved some of the cleaning supplies in my direction wordlessly. He blew a lock of his medium brown hair out of his eyes and went back to plunging the depths of his barrel, the white wad of cleaning cloth blackening quickly.

"Trouble for them," Duracell smiled and it wasn't friendly. His light eyes glimmered wickedly.

"Oh yeah, what's going on?" I'd been out of the loop and buried in Shelly and had apparently missed a lot. Wouldn't trade the time I'd spent with her for anything though.

"Yo, Ghost!" Trig called from the open chapel door way. I looked up from my task and caught movement out of the corner of my eye. Shelly stood with two plates of food, she'd been making her way over. Trig smiled at her.

"When you finish eating and doing what 'cher doin' get in here," Trigger said and disappeared back into the glass fishbowl, which is exactly what it was. Wire reinforced glass, it had been an overlook spot for the juvie's cafeteria when it had been in operation.

"Sure thing," I told his retreating back and he waved over his shoulder, shutting the door tight behind him.

I caught a glimpse of Dray and Reaver bent over the table, a roll of paper... a map or blueprint or something big like that, sprawled over its top. Something was up but when I looked at Shelly, her expression was a mix of troubled and fearful. I went back to work on my handgun, finishing what I'd started while she pulled a smaller two seater table near and set up places for us to eat. She didn't comment about what I was doing, didn't nag me to come eat before my food got cold or any of that. She simply sat nearby and ate her food silently, waiting for me to come join her. It was so unlike Shelly it worried me to a small degree.

"What's the matter Princess?" I asked her.

"Nothing," she said, but the pointed look she gave me said otherwise but it also screamed 'don't be dense' and so I let it go for now.

I finished cleaning my gun and reassembled it. Zeb passed me a box of ammo and I reloaded the magazine Shelly had emptied the day before and let the loaded spare ride in the gun. Once the spare magazine was at capacity I shoved it into my hip pocket and tucked the gun in the back of my waistband and joined my woman for a meal. I was a little surprised, she'd loaded my plate with pretty much all my favorites and left off the green beans of which I wasn't a fan.

"Good?" she asked as I took my second big mouthful. I nodded and tried to slow down. I was eating like I was back in the Corps and pounding sand. When you took meals over there you never knew how long you would go between 'em or if it would be your last so you tended to scarf them. The tension in the club was like that now. Like we were heading into hostile territory and were preparing for a firefight. I felt myself scowl for a second and caught Shelly smiling at me a little sadly.

"Feel it too?" she asked softly. I nodded and kept eating.

"Hey Runt, give us the floor?" Reaver asked from the chapel doorway. Shelly looked up and whatever she saw on her cousin's face, which admittedly was undecipherable and a total mystery to me, made her arch an eyebrow and then go very somber. She picked up her plate and wordlessly ghosted back to the kitchen. I frowned hard.

"What the fuck am I missing here Reaver? She's not acting like herself at all and it's starting to freak me out a little," Reaver dropped into the chair Shelly had vacated and sighed.

"Shelly knows what's what. Atmosphere around here is what it was like before the club went legit."

"I feel you. Just what the fuck is going on?" I asked. I didn't stop eating, I was fucking hungry.

"Suicide Kings did us wrong. We took retribution, they got butt hurt and have been doing these penny-ante strikes and feints. Well they've been messing with the big dogs and we haven't bitten back yet," he leaned back in his seat and raised his eyebrows.

"Time to bite back," I mused.

"Yep."

"What 'cha got?" I asked.

"Found their meth-cook operation. Seems they really do have a death wish spreading that poison around," Reaver had a gleam in his eyes I'd seen only once before, and truthfully, I *never* wanted to see again. I mean shit, I was no fucking saint. I'd killed people over there, and Sparks had what was coming to him in a bad way for what he did to my girl. Sparks was a son of a bitch and had deserved to die, bottom line, it was as simple as that. So why did I have to keep reminding myself of that fact? Because the *way* that man had died was pretty much too horrible for words. Reaver *enjoyed* what he did to Sparks way more than anyone should enjoy killing. It made me sick to think about it so I simply shoved it aside. Put it into that little box of horrors right alongside the shit that probably kept Trigger up at night too and I locked those things down tight.

Reaver was a split personality if I ever saw one. In the light of day, with his son, with his wife and with his brothers, he was a good and just man. Right there beside you and willing to do anything, including die, for his people. That darker half of him though. It was the worst, most nightmarish thing I had ever seen and I'd seen some seriously fucked up shit before. Reaver was looking me over and it must have showed on my face because he suddenly looked frustrated and uncomfortable.

"Sorry man," I shook it off and he nodded solemnly.

"Anyways, the guys sent me out here to make sure you were up to speed before we filled you in about all that. You know we weren't always legit and Trig told you about the runs we used to do, trying to fix the other chapters and get The Sacred Hearts across the board on the right side of the law?" he asked. I nodded and slid my gaze sideways to the three at the table.

"Don't look at us man. We wanted out of the drugs and the guns. Blue did six years hard time because of that shit," Duracell said, Blue nodded. "I had no interest in doing hard time and that shit got my brother dead. My *real* brother, flesh and blood. I went Nomad to fucking bail on that scene, see if they could clean up their fucking act but most of them went down in a massacre seven months later when their drug shipments stopped making it to their destinations," he ran the magazine home on his handgun and pulled back the slide, tucking what appeared to be a very nice Hi Point C9 into a holster under his jacket and cut. He leaned back into his chair, tipping the front legs up off the floor.

"Not something I wanted to be a part of. Blue here got out of the state Pen and we were still members in good standing, just with no chapter to call home, the rest of ours was fucking dead or still in prison. I saw what that shit did to my brothers. The greed, some of them getting hooked, going to prison, getting themselves dead. Not fucking worth it man and I don't want my new home to turn into a fucking cesspool of that shit either. I'm a Sacred Heart's man. A real one. I'm in it to win it here with my brothers."

Interesting. He disagreed with his brothers but had stayed true to his colors, to his oath. He'd gone nomad and ridden, he hadn't turned rat but hadn't participated in the drugs either. Blue had gone to prison for this club, yet he remained true as well. I could see why Dragon had gone out of his way to recruit these two back into the mother chapter.

"I come from the North East chapter. Most of them went down in a RICO case. I was in New Zealand, my granddad had died. I get back and the whole chapter is shut down. I knew what was what but tried to stay out of it for the most part. Kept my head down. Did what my Pres. asked me to do when he asked me to do it, but I was barely a patched member when I went back home. Got in touch with Dragon and he said to come here, that's my story," he shrugged and tucked his completed weapon into the front of his waistband and pulled his tee shirt over it.

"Apparently shit's been falling apart all over the place," I commented dryly. Reaver gave me a hard look and I took it for what it was, that some of these outlying chapters may have had a little help going down the drain when they were resistant to getting on board with the mother chapter's morals relocation program. Dragon was one smart and seriously crafty motherfucker. I wouldn't put a god damned thing past him.

"Anyways, if we're done trading campfire stories and braiding each other's hair?" Reaver said and was met with a round of chuckles.

"Sorry, finish telling me what you were going to tell me," I said and couldn't suppress my smile. Reave could be funny as Hell.

"Right, so working on us has obviously taken a back seat when we got problems much closer to home. We know the Suicide Kings are cooking, we know where that cook operation is and we want to send a message, if its war they want its war they got and we don't take it laying down. You finished eating?"

I pushed my plate to the center of the table.

"Yep."

"Cool, let's go play," Reaver got up and I followed suit. I glanced toward the kitchen and Reaver smiled. I followed him into the chapel and the other three followed us in, it was fucking crowded with the five of us, Trig, Dragon and Dray all piled in the curtained off fishbowl.

Reaver pushed through us and said, "I know I'm pretty boys, but hands off the goods." He took up post by Trig and I got a look at the contents of the table. It was a topographical map of part of the region.

"How we get this intel?" I asked.

"Combination of Data monitoring their communications and we got a man on the inside," Dragon grunted. I felt my eyebrows go up. A man on the inside. No idea how we pulled that off but again, Dragon was a crafty bastard.

"So what do you need me to do?" I asked.

"You got your tow truck out there?" Dray asked.

"No, my pickup," I frowned. I didn't much like the idea of bringing my business into things. Dragon read my look plainly.

"Not asking you to use it for this, we got one, old as dirt but reliable, no markings just need someone practiced in operating it. You drive stick?" he asked.

"I drive anything on two, four or more wheels. Piece of cake," I commented.

"Good, you ride with me to the rendezvous point," Trig said, "It's up to you and me to keep these happy bastards occupied," there was a light tapping at the fishbowl's door. Dray stalked over and whipped a curtain aside revealing a man in his forties, graying hair cut short, wearing a dirty SHMC cut over a worn and scaly looking leather jacket.

"Lucky!" Reaver crowed. I'd heard of Lucky but hadn't seen him. Dray opened the door and Lucky came in, hands shoved deep into his fraying jeans pockets. He was around my height, a smaller dude and pretty unassuming. Up close I put him closer to fifty rather than in his early forties. He gave Dragon and Dray a grin and laugh lines bracketed his mouth and crow's feet fanned out from his light blue eyes.

"Somebody call for a demolitions expert?" he asked and Dragon and Dray grinned a matched set of wolfish smiles.

"Glad you could make it brother," Dragon put out a hand and they clasped forearms and pulled each other in to a bone crunching back slapping hug.

"So what needs blowed up?" he asked and cast his eyes to the map sprawled across the table.

"So this is what we're thinkin'..." Dragon started in and we all listened, rapt.

The plan was an eye for an eye on a bit grander of a scale. It was my job to tow Grizzly's big boat of a car from out front of his house with Trig, Reaver and Lucky. If all went according to plan, our other boys would raid the farmhouse, pull anyone inside out of there and have 'em phone home. When the cavalry started to amass, they'd run into our little road block and pop goes the weasel. We were supposed to drop the car out in front of the Suicide Kings' club house driveway which had only one way in or out with the chain link fence they had surrounding it. Once we dropped it we were to GTFO so Lucky could blow it.

Meanwhile, back at the ranch, or in this case, the Suicide King's cook house which was out at an abandoned farmhouse, the real eye for an eye shit would be going down. It would be getting blown up in retribution for Open Road Ink.

The whole thing was supposed to prove that one, we had bigger balls than they did and two, that if they wanted to fuck with us they were fucking with the wrong dudes because we didn't back down and we protected what was ours. The fact that we were blowing up Griz's car for the road block was purely because we were dicks and it entertained us... well, it entertained Reaver, he thought it was hysterical and that part had been his idea.

It was going to be Dragon, Dray, and Duracell taking out the farmhouse with Zeb and Blue on back up. Apparently Duracell knew how to blow shit up too, he was a demolition's expert when it came to construction or some shit. Lucky's explosives expertise is how he came by his road name. He apparently just liked to blow shit up, doing it as often as possible. He was just plain lucky he hadn't blown himself sky high in the process.

Trig and Reave were my cover while I did my tow magic and while Lucky set the car up for explosion. The whole thing felt pretty fucking cracker jacked together and sort of on the fly. I looked to my old CO and his best friend.

"Were you guys drunk when you thought this up?" they traded looks and the big man shrugged.

"Maybe," Reaver said with his cheerful psycho grin. I rolled my eyes.

"Girls learn nothing of this," Trigger said and Dray snorted,

"Everett would have my nuts in a vice," Dragon slapped his son on the back after he said this and laughed.

"Anybody gonna pussy out on akind of yer women, best do it now," he commented dryly.

"Fuck no. I'm gonna do this *for* my woman," I said grinning.

"Bullshit!" Zeb coughed behind his hand, "You're going to do this one for you mate. You did what you could for your lady already I reckon," I nodded.

"Yeah, okay you got me there," I said with a feral grin. "You know this is stupid right?" I asked.

"Boy, how do you think we got the badass reputation we did? Half the time we planned shit it went sideways in the middle. We plan, we go do and the rest is just balls to the wall." Dragon shook his head.

"Pretty much. Reckless and stupid and we get lucky," Lucky agreed, "God damn it's good to be home!" he cried.

"We going to spend all night standing around talking about it or are we going to do this shit?" Dray asked.

"You in a big fucking hurry there Veep?" Duracell asked.

"Unlike you, I'd like to get back here and fuck my girl at some point tonight," Dray intoned but his expression was serious as his dark eyes roved the map like he was committing it to memory.

"Let's stop standing around with our cocks in our fists circle jerking it out and get to it," Blue said wearily and we all turned. Blue was like a silent fucking Bob, he just about never spoke. Duracell slapped him on the back of his cut.

"Best go make peace with your little women and make sure it's okay that we go out and play. Ain't no one holding my fucking leash," the ginger said with a wink.

"No one holding ours either," Trig said with a peaceful little smile and we traded looks. I knew how he felt on this one. We piled out of the chapel. Shelly, who was tiptoeing from the kitchen through the archway leading to the back and presumably where the other girls were at, froze.

"Runt," Reaver grunted and Shelly's shoulders dropped like she'd been caught. Reaver crooked a finger at her and she gave him a look that was like 'really?' and shuffled over to her cousin.

"I don't know, I don't want to know and just please be careful," she said and hugged him but her eyes were on me and pleading.

"C'mere Princess," I said and she came to me and folded into my arms like she was meant to be there. "Be back before you know it, Baby," I said softly and she sighed.

"Lucky, you blow up my Ol' Man, I'm kicking you in the balls," she said over my shoulder and Lucky laughed.

"Good to see you too Shells," he said and sounded amused.

"Go on, go do whatever you're going to do and just be careful," she kissed me and wandered into the back. I watched her go.

"Well fuck, who knew Shelly had it in her to be an Old Lady? Didn't think anyone was gonna tame that one," Lucky said.

"Watch it," Reaver and I chorused in unison and we looked at each other, everyone busted up laughing.

"Let's roll," Dragon said when we got our shit together, and we moved for the club's front door.

CHAPTER 21

Shelly

Fuck Reaver and Dragon and Trigger and Dray and everyone else! I got around the corner where they couldn't see me and scrubbed my face with my hands. I was a club whore before I was an Ol' Lady and I'd heard some really fucking wild stories in my time. They were going out to go do something stupid. I could see it, I could feel it and hell I could even *smell* it but that was before any of them got attached and that was before *Ghost*.

Karma sucked balls. I used to sit around the club in whoever's lap and think to myself how I was glad I wasn't an Ol' Lady and that I only had Reaver to worry about and I didn't really have to worry about *him*. My cousin was slicker 'n owl shit. He knew how to take care of business and himself... Now they were going out enmasse to do God knows what and for the first time freaking ever my food was sitting like a rock in the pit of my stomach and I was friggin' *worried*.

More worried than you could imagine knowing *Lucky* was headed out there with them. He wasn't crazy like my big cousin, if anything his variety of crazy was even scarier because if something went wrong and Lucky ran out of luck there wouldn't be enough pieces left to put in a Ziploc baggie.

"Hey Shelly, didn't know you were here! Wait, what's wrong?" I groaned inwardly and brought my hands down from my face. Everett stood a few paces away but blessedly she was by herself. I found myself thanking my lucky stars it was Everett and not Ashton or Hayden. Everett was made of sterner stuff, like me and Chandra, so I could say something and not have her dissolve into a puddle of girl-goo.

"Boys went out," I muttered. She raised an eyebrow like she wasn't impressed.

"Doing something stupid?" she hazarded. She didn't know

Lucky like I did and I wasn't going to be the one to fill her in.

"Oh yeah," I said and pushed off from the wall. She rolled her eyes. Better to let her think they were up to their usual shenanigans and that the shit wasn't about to get real wherever they were off to.

"Probably be a few hours then?" she asked, searching my face.

"Yeah probably," I agreed.

"Come on. We're binge watching Once Upon A Time," I pushed off the wall and went with her, back further into the depths of the club house towards the media room.

It was dark inside, mostly because the walls were painted black and all the furniture was too. The big black leather couch was something like a ten seater and curved around. There were several sections of it that footrests popped out recliner style and there were also a couple of those too, recliners I mean. There were pillows in the club's colors of red, white and blue here and there, mostly on the floor in front of the biggest big screen TV Ashton's money could buy. The system also boasted surround sound and the room had been unofficially declared an Ol' Lady safe haven when the boys were doing club business the women were to have no part of. Mostly because the women were tired of being sent to their men's rooms like errant children. It was Ashton's gift to the Ol' Ladies as much as it was to the men of The Sacred Hearts. A gift to the club as a whole.

Personally I thought the media room makeover was fantabulous. The side walls boasted big black bookshelves that were heavy enough the men had bolted them down so they couldn't fall. These shelves were slowly filling up with books on one side and DVD's and Blu-ray discs on the other. Hell, even some PlayStation and X-Box discs were working their way into the mix. Sure enough someone had brought and hooked up their gaming consoles to the big screen. I rolled my eyes. Boys.

I went around and dropped into an empty seat on the couch. A few of the men were sitting around with the girls, mostly looking bored and messing around on their smart phones. Well the two that weren't Disney and his boyfriend Aaron. I dropped into the vacant seat by the gay brother whose boyfriend was practically in his lap, his head on the taller man's shoulder. Disney had his brightly colored arm curved protectively around Aaron's shoulders, holding him to his chest. His other arm snaked around me and pulled me in.

I loved Disney like a brother from another mother and cuddled in gratefully, wishing wistfully that it were Ghost that held me fast. But no. My man had gone off less than a day after becoming my man to go do something stupid, something stupid that likely involved explosives and the Suicide Kings. Dis kissed the top of my head.

"Don't worry about it. They'll be fine," he murmured and I frowned. It was the wrong thing to say because Ashton and Hayden's heads popped up like Meer Kats sensing danger.

"Who will be fine? Where did they go?" Hayden demanded, her green eyes piercing even in the dark.

"Boys went to take care of some business that's none of yours," Grinder said unhappily from the other end of the couch, adding a belated, "Don't worry about it."

Ashton's eyes widened. "Did Ethan go?" she asked.

"Trig, Ghost, Reave, Dragon, Dray, Duracell, Lucky, Blue and Zeb all went," I said. Ashton looked like she was ready to cry. Probably because Trig had slipped out without saying 'goodbye', or 'I love you' or some shit. Which I couldn't be one to talk, it had stung that Ghost had simply told me he'd be back before I knew it. It felt like a promise he potentially couldn't keep.

It was about this point I realized that not only did I love him, that I could finally admit to myself how deep those feelings ran and all I wanted was for him to come home safely so that we *could* figure things out. I wanted a life with Ghost. To start to build something lasting, and now he was out there…

I slammed the lid on those thoughts and took some deep even breaths. Disney's arm tightened around me and his hand smoothed up and down the shoulder of Ghost's hooded sweatshirt. I tucked my nose into the front and breathed my man's smell in. It calmed me, comforted me and I liked that it could. We all watched the show but to glance at any of us women should have been enough to tell you that our thoughts and even some of our prayers were back with our men who were out there doing who knew what...

I just wanted him to come back in one piece. In fact, I wanted him to come back in one piece so bad that if he did, I swore to myself and to God that I would move my shit into his place, no questions asked. Just as long as he came back to me without a scratch on him. Yeah. That is exactly what I would do. Now here was to hoping I didn't just jinx him in the worst kind of way.

CHAPTER 22

Ghost

The drive out to the rendezvous point took a while but there was a reason for that. We didn't want our crazy and sometimes very illegal dealings anywhere near the house. I rode in the back seat of Trigger and Ashton's rig, while Reaver sang poorly and intentionally off key to some country music up front. It was one of my favorite songs and the son of a bitch was mangling the lyrics to boot. Trigger was laughing his ass off as they made fun, I was pretty sure at my expense, but I didn't care. When you were heading into heavy shit, you tended to laugh at anything. It was a coping mechanism for a lot of guys.

"Jesus H. Christ you sing pretty! You sing so god damned pretty it's making me hard," I said and Trigger lost his shit. Reaver did too.

"Sorry bro, I don't swing that way!" he said, but mission accomplished, he'd stopped warbling like a half mangled cat.

Trigger made the turn off onto the gravel and dirt lane leading back onto the random property out in the boonies. I don't think any of us had been out here since the deal with Ashton's douchebag ex. I caught Trig's ghostly silver eyes looking at me in the rearview. I locked eyes with him and nodded once. Steady. Rock solid. We had each other's backs and God fucking help anybody who got in our way. By the time we pulled up outside the big old corrugated steel building, Dray was rolling back the big bay door. Trig threw it in park and we all bailed out.

"What the fuck, over? You didn't say it was a fucking ramp truck!" I cried. I looked at the big, red Chevy, that *shit*, must have come out of the 80's. The bed of the truck a giant silver flatbed ramp. This complicated things.

"Why? Is that bad for what we want to do?" Reaver asked and was bouncing on the balls of his feet.

"More chains, more hook ups… to get the damned car up the ramp requires I drag it and that shit takes *time*. The longer we're at this the longer we make a target of ourselves," I scratched my head and thought about it.

"Ah shit, what the hell! This whole thing is pretty fucking half assed and stupid. I don't suppose it makes too damned much difference. So this is how this is going to go…" I was the one with tow experience, I made the rules on this. We could do it but we had to do it fast and sacrifice some safety in order to do it. I was okay with that and so were the guys. I laid out what I needed from them in excruciating detail.

While I spoke, Trig handed out body armor. I took off my hooded sweatshirt and strapped into the vest, knocking into the plate over my heart. My knuckles clacked hollowly against it and I nodded. It was the hardcore ballistics shit. Meant to stop a bullet cold. Still would hurt like a fucking bitch if I got hit, but I wasn't planning on getting hit. I had a beautiful woman I wanted to go home to.

Once we were all agreed on what was what, and were finished laughing our asses off, I got up into the driver's seat and began the process of starting the old diesel engine up. I turned the key Dray gave me and waited for the glow plug to tell me the ol' girl was ready before I threw the key the rest of the way over and started her up. She may have been an old truck, and not much to look at from the outside, but she was kept in fine working order. She fired right up. It was a tight squeeze, with me Reave and Trig in the cab and fuck no there wasn't any room for Lucky, but that crazy bastard straight up said not to worry about it. That he was happy to ride on back. I pulled down the lane and Trig's radio squawked to life.

"Let us know when you have the package Big Man. We'll be waiting for your call," Dray said.

"Copy that, VP," Trig grinned in the dark and Reaver bounced between us in his seat like some kind of little kid.

"This is gonna be fun!" he crowed, his assessment was punctuated by Lucky out the back.

"Woo Hoo!" came the rowdy cry and the elevated mood was

infectious. I just had to laugh.

We got real quiet when we rumbled up the street where Griz lived. "You guys sure about this? I mean this is breaking all kinds of codes we live by and we don't live by many."

"I know how you feel man, it's weird as fuck going to one of their homes but he started this shit the minute he had our women watched. They played dirty first and all we're doing is boosting his fucking car. We're not touching the house or any of his family that might be inside." Reaver clapped me on the shoulder, his icy blue eyes cold and colder still where they shone in the dark.

"There it is," Trigger pointed. It was a big fucking beast of a land yacht and parked perfectly for us, *in the street* outside the driveway which contained the man's first love. His motorcycle.

"He made it easy for me," I said and piloted the big truck into place in front of the car, gauging how much room I'd need for the ramp. I threw it in park and Reaver scooted over into the driver's seat as I dropped to the ground outside the cab. I pulled on my gloves. Lucky leapt off the back of the ramp and went for the car, Trig covered my ass, sighting down his arm over the hood of the truck at the house. Watching for any movement. I heard the spray from a can of paint as I put the ramp into motion. Lucky was free handing something on the side of Grizzly's car. I rolled my eyes. At least he was out of the way.

The truck operated smoothly. I just hoped that wherever Grizz was in the house, he was far enough away not to hear what we were up to. I did my job, moving quickly and efficiently.

"*Lucky!*" I whisper-shouted, "*Stop fuckin' around with arts n' crafts and get the winch!*" he scrambled up the ramp and I started rolling out the winch to get the car up the ramp. He kept it from making any noise and soon enough I had him at the controls while I was on the ground up under the old Caddie.

I got it hooked up and rolled out of the way and spun my arm. Lucky flipped the lever I'd showed him and the massive old car began to lumber up the ramp, the tires making a god awful squealing where they dragged over the aluminum ramp bed.

"Fuuuuuuuuuuuuuck," I heard Trigger hiss when the sound

started and I couldn't agree with him more. I took over the controls while Lucky got to work getting whatever explosive rig he had ready to hook up to the car. The fucking ramp truck's controls were on the driver's side, just behind the cab and the driver's side happened to be the side the house was on so if douche pickle came out guns blazing my ass was straight in the line of fire.

We were about half way up the ramp when the god damned barking started. I heard Reaver giggle like a fucking ninny from the open driver's window and I damn near shat myself when I heard the loud boom of a voice from the house.

"Shut up! Fucking dog!" punctuated by an animal's frightened cry, or cry of pain. I scowled and Lucky's expression echoed my own. It was a tense couple of moments waiting to see if the man would look out the window or come out front for anything but we were fortunate so far and that luck held. He either went back to whatever he was doing inside the house or remained in the back. Just about a foot more...

Success! Phase one basically completed, I started the ramp back down into the flat position, the old truck groaning with some protest at the sheer size of the load it was undertaking. Lucky hoisted himself onto the ramp as soon as it was in a position where he wouldn't slide right off and Trig handed him an old canvas carpet bag. I didn't know and I didn't want to know what he was up to I just wanted to get this up and get going. Adrenaline was fizzing through my veins, making me feel light and shaky and as soon as I realized it I put a lid on that shit.

I swallowed hard and the ramp clicked home. I hoisted myself up and over the side and lay flat, rapping twice on the back of the cab. Reaver threw the truck into gear and had it in motion before Trig could even shut the passenger side door. Reave drove through the neighborhood and out and as soon as we were about a mile away, rolled to a stop. I jumped down and retook my place behind the wheel.

"That was way too fucking easy," I gasped and threw the switch to get the heat going. Trigger grinned savagely in the dark.

"Why do you think I wanted Lucky?"

"Never figured you for superstition," I sniffed, proud of myself for leaving off the 'sir' this time.

"I wasn't 'til I met that fucking fool," he said and Reaver chortled.

"Dude you remember that time, after we got clean that we ran some of the shit for Dragon and Lucky laid his bike on fucking *purpose?*"

"How could I fucking forget it? We're being chased by this fucking rival gang and Lucky, he fucking whips it around and goes at them like he's playing fucking chicken, right?"

"This mother fucker lays his bike and is skidding along after it along the big slab," Reaver says.

"Shit you not, he turned his fucking bike into a bomb. Timed it just perfect. He's sliding and his bike goes up under this fucking fancy ass Hummer they're chasing us in," Trig paused and Reaver picks right up where he left off.

"Yeah and Lucky, he *stands up* like it ain't nothin'! His bike goes skidding along and goes up under this damn thing and fucking *explodes* and he goes loping off into the woods on the side of the highway. It was like something out of a James Bond movie!"

I stared out the windshield and tried processing what the fuck these guys were saying, finally I spoke, "You guys are pulling my leg!" I said incredulously. There wasn't any fucking way that this had happened but I believed Trig, and was suddenly real grateful for my choice of words when Reaver sniffed and said:

"You're right, we are."

"Man fuck you guys," I said plaintively and they both started to howl. Trigger got on the radio.

"VP this is Big Man, you copy?"

"Yeah Big Man, go ahead."

"Got the package, no complications, ETA 30 minutes, phase two."

"Copy that, Big Man we're in position."

We rolled along in the deepening dark and the mood changed in the truck. We went from lighthearted stupidity to all business the closer we got to the Suicide King's territory which *had* been part of ours. We'd pretty much conceded them being there out of the goodness of our hearts at one point. Somehow I got the impression that was about to change.

The Suicide Kings holed up in an industrial park just over the county line in this sort of no man's land where the sheriff of our county didn't have jurisdiction but the sheriff of the next county didn't *want* it and the city cops sure as fuck weren't going to have nothin' to do with it. It was actually a well thought out place to be for them but it wasn't exactly a fully defensible position. Ours was a better set up for that.

The Suicide Kings tried to make up for the lack of cover and the like by ringing their lot with a twelve foot, razor wire topped fence with only one usable driveway. It was good at keeping people out. They were about to find out that it was good at keeping people *in* too. The Suicide Kings had brought this fight to our door by blowing up Open Road Ink, we were about to sock it right back to them.

I pulled up in front of the drive and slid out, Reave took up position in my place and while I started raising the ramp Lucky started releasing the chains holding the Caddie onto the bed. We had to move fucking fast.

"Hey! What the fuck are you doing man? Hey! *Is that Griz's car?*"

Oh shit, I think our luck had just about run the fuck out.

"Go! Go! Go! He went inside, hurry it the fuck up man!" Trigger said Lucky hit the last chain and smashed the window on the driver's side. He leaned in while the ramp tilted ever so fucking slowly and I started to sweat a little. *This crazy son of a bitch.* He hotwired the fucking car in less than thirty seconds flat and put the fucker in neutral. The car started to roll and he yelled out,

"Reaver, punch it!" I leapt up onto the runner board and hooked an arm through the open driver's window. Reaver slammed the truck in gear and gave it some gas and it lurched forward. The ramp was up just enough, the Caddie rolled and careened off the back. Lucky ran back up to it and dove through the window to jerk the shifter into park and the passenger side door on the tow truck

185

slammed. I looked in and Trigger was reaching across Reaver, he grabbed me and hauled me bodily into the truck. I kicked out against the door to slide in and connected with I think Lucky because I heard a sharp curse.

A shot rang out and I fucking ducked and scrambled the rest of the way in but there wasn't really any place for me to go!

"Stop fucking squirming Ghost!" Reaver grated and I stilled half in his lap and half in Trig's. My former CO was popping off shots out the passenger side window and I heard Lucky shout,

"Reave I'm good!"

Reaver put us in gear and we started moving, a heartbeat, then two and the whole fucking world lit up like a god damned Christmas tree when Lucky blew the fucking Caddie! We pulled through the maze of industrial parks and buildings until, satisfied we weren't followed; we stopped so I could put the truck to rights before we drew any suspicion from anybody lurking. I backed out the driver's side door and turned to look at Lucky who was laughing hysterically.

"Did you see their fucking faces?" he demanded. I hadn't but I could see his and I grimaced. He was bleeding pretty freely from a cut over his eye.

"Shit man you all right?" I asked working the levers, putting the bed back down.

"Yeah you fucking kicked me. 'sallright though," he shrugged grinning like a fool.

Trig came around the front of the truck and pulled Lucky into the beams from the headlights. He was grinning like a fool too.

"Didn't *exactly* go according to plan, nice light show though," he commented dryly looking at the gash. Then, "Meh you're fine. Don't even need Doc to look at it. Might get you some pussy though." Trigger grinned.

"Been a minute since I tapped anything, takin' care of the 'rents, Moira still coming around?" he asked.

"Last I saw she was at the club," Reaver said grinning.

"Sweet, she's got some good pussy," I got the bed into place and stepped back.

"We're good," I declared, "Where to?"

"Rendezvous point," Trig grunted. I nodded.

"Hey Lucky, what'd you write on the side of the Caddie?" I asked before I climbed up into the cab. He grinned.

"Eviction notice," he said and I felt a savage grin of my own take over.

"Nice," I chuckled.

We made it back to the rendezvous point and locked the ramp truck inside, what Trig assured me was a barn. Never saw a barn that looked like that but whatever blew his skirt up. We drove back to the club and went straight for the bar where Reaver poured us each a shot of cinnamon whiskey. Lucky raised his injured eyebrow.

"You grow a cunt Reave?" he asked and Trig and I laughed.

"No, it's pretty good shit. I like it. Shut up and drink it, asshole. Last time I pour you a drink," we took the shots and Lucky looked around. There were a few guys sitting around drinking and talking and more than a couple of whores straddling laps and making out like teenagers.

"Ouch! Lucky. Need me to have a look at that?" Cherry asked.

"Naw bitch. You seen Moira?" he asked. Cherry's face collapsed into a scowl.

"Bathroom I think," she tossed her long brown hair over her shoulder and walked away. The four of us exchanged looks and shrugged. Cherry *was* a bitch and no one particularly liked her because of it. She liked to instigate shit and didn't always keep her attitude in check, like now.

"Hey Cherry, last question, you know where about my Ol' Lady's at?" I asked.

"I don't fuckin' know! Go look for her!" she snapped and that's when Reaver leapt the bar, his eyes gone wintery and distant. He went up to Cherry who was at the pool table and seized her by the upper arm and hauled her to the front door.

"Hey! Quit it!" she said.

"You're forgettin' your place Darlin' and I for one have kind of had it with you so I'm giving you a new one," he said.

"What? What the fuck are you talking about?" she demanded.

"You don't disrespect a brother, you're starting to get the impression your shit don't stink, well it does and so now, off you go," he shoved her out the club house front door and shut it in her face on whatever protest she was trying to make. Some of the guys around the tables watched the goings on with mild interest before turning back to whatever conversation was at hand.

"I'm going to go find Shelly," I said and Trig nodded.

"I'll come with you, she's probably in the media room with the rest of the girls," we trooped towards the back, the four of us. Lucky encountered Moira in the hall and the much younger girl smiled and cooed over his eyebrow and dragged him into the nearest bathroom with a medicine cabinet.

We left them, Lucky sitting on the closed lid of the john, Moira straddling his lap and fussing over his minor injury. Trigger and Reaver chuckled and I felt the exact same sentiment clearly. There was something like an eighteen to twenty year age gap between those two but again, whatever blew their skirts up.

The media room was dark and some fantasy show was playing on the big screen. Hayden and Ashton were huddled at one end of the couch under some blankets in a girl cuddle pile. Ashton was facing the television so we couldn't see her face but when Hayden turned around and saw us, her eyes first lit on Reaver and relief flashed across her face but Trigger... Well he got twin green laser beams of heated fury leveled on him.

I grinned. Somebody was in seven different kinds of trouble. I lost the smile pretty quickly when Hayden nudged Ashton and the slightly smaller woman sat up and turned. She'd been crying and looked absolutely devastated and when she saw Trig her eyes welled up fresh.

"Baby what's wrong?" he cried and went for her. Ashton crumbled and fresh tears slicked down her pale cheeks.

"You didn't say goodbye! You just left and didn't say I love you or goodbye or *anything!*" her slight shoulders shook and Trig went forward and lifted the small woman off of the couch like the small child she resembled. She automatically wound her arms around his shoulders and her legs around his waist and clung to him, burying her face in the crook of his neck while her tiny frame hitched with her sobbing.

"Ohhh Baby I'm sorry. I didn't think!" he held her close and murmured to her. Disney and Aaron looked on concerned but said nothing and Hayden looked like she was ready to put a boot in Trig's ass until Reaver's hand fell onto her shoulder. She glared up at her husband who grinned like a son of a bitch, ready to take one for his friend. I shook my head and asked Dis...

"Seen my woman?"

It was Aaron who replied, "Went to bed. She looked worried, everything all right?"

"Yeah man, everything's cool," I said which wasn't exactly a lie, as far as things went, they were cool, for now. We hadn't heard from Dragon's team yet but no sooner had I thought it, Trigger's cellphone went off in his cut. Ashton had calmed down considerably and the big man went over to one of the recliners and sat with his woman curled in his lap. He answered his phone on the third ring.

"Yeah?" he listened carefully, "Yeah... Uh-huh... Good deal man. Yeah. See you when you get here," he gave me and Reave a pointed look and nodded and I felt myself smile. Mission accomplished.

I nodded back to both of them and went for my room, opening the door and sliding in. I shut it tightly behind me and was met with one of the most exquisitely beautiful sights I had ever seen. Shelly lay on her stomach at the edge of the bed closest to the door, her face turned towards it, slack and angelic, lashes making perfect crescents against her high, pale cheekbones.

The blankets had slipped and so the long, perfectly smooth line of her back lay exposed. It was a fairly full moon out and the light from it shone down through the high window above the bed, bathing her in a silvery light and I felt my heart give a hard twist in my chest as I looked her over.

My woman, nude and sleeping peaceful, waiting for me in my bed. It made me hard to the point of pain but I didn't want to disturb her. I set about undressing quietly, hanging things and setting them around the room where they belonged. Shelly's clothes were folded neatly atop the dresser and I appreciated that she had kept the room tidy.

I went around to the other side of the bed and just looked at her for a long time. She was so fucking beautiful.

CHAPTER 23
Shelly

The bed dipped and I think that's what startled me out of my slumber. I woke with a start and was immediately pulled backwards into a warm and equally nude, hard body. I gasped and Ghost murmured in my ear,

"You are so fucking beautiful," he punctuated the remark by kissing the edge of my ear, his lips silken and hot, sending a course of tingles in a wash down the side of my neck that swept over my shoulder and across my back.

"Oh!" I gasped in surprise and I couldn't see it but I was pretty sure he smiled. My suspicion on that was confirmed when I could *hear* the smile in his voice when he asked me,

"Did you like that?" he kissed my ear again and then pressed a light kiss behind it, trailing fine kisses down the side of my neck, over that sweet fucking spot, along the back of my shoulder... He cupped a breast with his hand, teasing the nipple with thumb and forefinger and I gasped at the answering throb of arousal in my pussy.

"God I love your reactions," he said with this desperate heat in his voice that seriously lit my fire.

I squirmed and his arm tightened around me, the scorching length of his erection pressed against my ass and I gasped and went still for a moment before redirecting my wriggling. I ground myself back against him and he groaned, pressing forward, lining up neatly with the crack of my ass. I felt myself moisten in anticipation. God I wanted him.

His arm tightened possessively around my body, fetching my back hard against his chest. He kissed a line along my shoulder and slid his other arm beneath my neck, curving it over my chest above my breasts. His arm over the top of me drifted down to my leg, lifting it. It took him a few tries but finally with a moan of satisfaction he slid into me. I cried out softly and squeezed my muscles around him, taking him in deeper. He rolled his hips forward and the head of his cock went over that spot inside me on my roof and it felt so *good*.

I was dimly aware of my nails biting into his arm, where it crossed my chest and he slowed the rocking of his hips.

"You okay baby?" he asked by my ear.

"Your arm, across my chest like this, it's freaking me out," I told him. Clinging to Ashton's advice to talk about those things, he immediately took it away and slid from my body and I mourned the loss but he wasn't gone from me for long. Just when I had a spark of panic, thinking I should have simply kept my mouth shut and let him hold me like he was, he was laying me flat and vaulting over my leg.

"I'm going to pull you," he warned me, his arms going around my thighs and I smiled as he dragged me down the bed, into a better angle for him to do what he wished. He reached between us and positioned himself before passionately thrusting back into me. I arched. I knew there was nothing between us and I just couldn't bring myself to care.

"Derek, kiss me!" I pleaded.

"I love it when you say my name," he growled and bent over our entwined bodies to crush his mouth over mine. I wound my legs around his hips, opening myself to him further and cried out into his mouth as he drove forward in these short little controlled thrusts that were pure, sweet, blissful torture. The head of his penis riding over my g-spot sending a warm suffusion of pleasure throughout my body, causing my blood to effervesce in my veins.

I moaned, these helpless little mewling sounds which he quickly ate up, his lips curving into a smile against my own and I found myself smiling too. His hands roamed my body while he loved me, smoothing over every last reachable inch of my skin. When his mouth broke from mine it was so that he could take one of my nipples into his mouth. I arched and then cried out when his thumb found my clit. It was too much sensation all at once and I was wound tighter than a Timex beneath him to the point that when things built, winding down tighter and tighter still, I came, springing apart. All of my cogs and gears, coils and springs bouncing off the walls of the room until I lay panting and empty and winding down and out until nothing but the faint, hollow ticking of my heart remained.

Derek laughed a little above me and kissed my chest between my breasts, just over my heart. He twitched inside me and I jerked, small little aftershocks causing my legs to quiver and twitch to either side of him. He smoothed his hands up and down my legs and sat up, his warmth retreating. I made a small sound of protest which morphed into an overwhelmed cry of protest. He was moving inside me again and it was too soon! But he didn't stop. He wasn't done, though he did me the favor of twining his fingers with mine, holding my hands while he watched our bodies come together.

He was getting close. It was spelled out in the lines of tension all over his face and body. He grunted and threw back his head and made to pull out but I didn't care. I knew it wasn't the responsible thing to do with how much of a mess I was, with everything still being so new but I wanted it. I wanted the closeness and so I wrapped my legs around him and held him. His eyes snapped to mine and whatever he read there, it decided him because he thrust hard into me and with a cry, bowed over my body and came inside me. No barriers, no protection, but it was beautiful and I loved it, I loved *him* and I was so fucking grateful he'd returned to me in one piece, without a scratch that I could see, that I was willing to take this risk.

If I were pregnant, so be it. It was time for me to grow the hell up anyways. I would know, one way or another, in a couple of weeks.

Ghost collapsed over me and stayed rooted deep inside my body, gathering me in his arms and I made good on my silent vow of earlier that night. He was here, he was safe and so I opened my mouth and I told him, "I'll move in with you."

He took a deep breath, then two and asked, "Did you miss me then, Princess?" I smacked his shoulder and he laughed, "Ow! Hey! Quit it."

"I was scared okay?" I demanded. He pushed himself up so he could look at me and I felt my eyes well with a cross between angry and grateful tears. Angry that so soon after us getting on the same page that he would go out and do something stupid, and relieved that he'd come back to me safe.

"Oh hey…" he kissed me, and then kissed me again. I sniffed and forced the tears back down before they could spill over.

"I'll always come back to you Shelly. Always," he intoned.

"Don't," I said harshly.

"Don't what Honey?"

"Don't make promises you can't keep, Ghost. Its bullshit and I had too many of 'em growing up." He searched my face for one very long minute.

"Okay Baby, okay," he cupped my face with gentle fingers and kissed me long and slow. He'd grown soft inside me and it was a unique and decidedly delicious sensation when he grew hard again, filling me from the inside out while we kissed. I'd never experienced anything like it before and I marveled at how many firsts he took me through in the bedroom.

I gasped when he began to rock with a slow and loving cadence in and out of me. I loved what he did to me, that he wanted me; that he wanted to help me fix me. I wrapped my arms around his hard shoulders and raised my hips to meet his thrusts, loving him back while he loved me slowly and deeply. It was so different than anything I had ever experienced before and I cherished it for the precious gift that it was.

Here was to hoping that we would survive living with one another. I closed my eyes and came with a gentler explosion this time, the pleasure washing out to my edges and then gently lapping back in towards my center. My Ol' Man certainly knew how to make a splash with me.

CHAPTER 24

Ghost

I didn't waste any fucking time. Shelly had agreed to move in with me, I asked a couple of prospects if they'd help us out since most of the guys had something going on Sunday. The prospects agreed and with them on board, I had her moved in that weekend. After, of course, stopping at the drugstore and loading up on condoms which I discovered needed to be stashed in just about every corner of the house, truck, garage, bike, club room, you name it. I couldn't get enough of her. I just couldn't. It was impossible, but all good things must come to an end and unfortunately the weekend was over and I needed to take my ass back to work.

I propped my foot onto the old country wooden chair in the corner of the bedroom by the bathroom door and pulled the laces tight on my work boot, tying them off. Shelly was quickly becoming the mistress of her domain which once had been my office but I was happy to have her there. I found her on the floor in a pair of skin tight gray leggings and an oversized tee. She was pulling on one of those thin sweater things that draped artfully in the front and I asked her, "Want me to build a fire in the stove before I go?" she smiled up at me, her face the most tranquil that I'd seen it and shook her head.

"I'm handy-capable," she smarted.

"I always wondered which one was the retarded cousin," I gave her a one sided grin. She stuck her tongue out at me.

"Speaking of... Reaver is supposed to come by and go for a run with me tomorrow. Is that okay?" she chewed her bottom lip.

"Shelly, this is your house too. You can have whoever you want over here whenever you want. You're my girl, not my prisoner or captive sex slave... all though I kind of like the sound of that last one," she balled up the piece of paper she had in her hands and threw it at me. I put up my hands and batted it away.

"Hey!"

She was smiling brightly and my heart felt lighter, "Better get to your Rescue Ranger gig."

I frowned at her, "Where'd you see them?" I asked. I mean I knew about 'em being in my thirties but Shelly was barely into her 20's.

"I grew up poor, remember? When my mom was sober enough to remember she was supposed to give a fuck about me she picked up a VCR from good will. VHS tapes were like twenty-five cents apiece or less. I had a pretty impressive Disney collection at the trailer. If Reaver heard my mom and her boyfriend du jour going at it from his place he'd climb in my window and would put whatever on and we'd huddle there and watch it while they screamed and crashed. When Reaver was there things were a lot less fucked up and scary," I leaned against the doorway and listened to her. It was the first time she'd spoken frankly about anything from her past, or her feelings on it...

She blushed faintly and bit her lips together and I had this funny feeling in my chest and felt my muscles relax. She was trying with me, trying so hard and it was written in the faint lines of worry in her forehead, between her eyes, that she was trusting me but was so very afraid.

"If it turns out you're pregnant," I said softly, "I promise you, we'll do much better with our kids," her expression softened and she dropped her eyes to the papers in her lap. She nodded but the set to her shoulders betrayed her level of fear.

"Shelly," she looked up at me and swallowed hard, "Whatever happens, we're going to be okay." I said but didn't add the 'I promise' at the end that I wanted to.

"You better git," she said and smiled faintly. I went into the office and dropped into a crouch beside her.

"You better kiss me goodbye then," I told her and she nodded and kissed me, slow and patient, savoring the contact. She broke away from me and swallowed hard, she looked like she wanted to say something but then she rubbed her lips together and smiled.

"Be back before you know it," I said and stood.

"Take a shower before you come to bed. You went out with the boys you smelled like gasoline and fire when you came back," she looked over a line of figures and I smiled.

"Too smart for your own good. You gonna be a handful?" I asked.

"Would you really have it any other way?" she asked pointedly.

"Nope," I ducked out of the office with a raging hard on in my jeans and made it to the kitchen. I paused with my hand on the door handle and forced myself to turn it when all I wanted to do was go back to her and make love to her and make her feel safe. I pulled on the door handle and went out to the tow truck.

Huge progress was being made. I wasn't sure it could be made any faster than what it was. Still, it was frustratingly slow. I passed the old Volvo she drove and made a face. She needed something better, newer, more reliable but it was going to have to wait for now. I got up into my truck and turned her over. She started right up and I called in that I was in service and pulled out of my driveway leaving my girl to swim in a sea of her numbers.

CHAPTER 25

Shelly

"It's too fucking quiet!" I moaned into the phone. Hayden laughed.

"How long has he been gone?"

"A little over two hours. I swear to God it's actually too quiet out here for me to concentrate. I like, need noise or something." I could swear I heard my cousin-in-law roll her eyes at me through the phone line.

"Better get used to it. Turn the TV on or something and leave it on in the other room. Works for me..." Truthfully I was feeling creeped out now that I was in the house by myself for the first time. It felt like I was being watched or something which I knew was both crazy and stupid. No one would be out in the boonies like this. I shook it off and tried one more time...

"Going to leave me out here to suffer huh?" I asked.

"You suffer so beautifully Baby Cuz!" I heard Reaver growl into the phone and that pretty much sent my last hope of getting Hayden to come over down in flames. *The fire, it burned.* I sighed, but put my hand over the phone so they wouldn't hear it.

"Okay, I need to have a girl kind of something out here soon though. It's a sea of ugly country prints and mismatched furniture and I'm not about to take it." Hayden laughed.

"I solemnly swear I will help you guys find a happy medium when it comes to the interior decorating for the low, low fee of you double checking my taxes," she said and I raised an eyebrow.

"Deal," I said.

"Okay," Hayden squealed and laughing said, "I gotta go bye!" before the line went dead. I pulled my headphones from my ears and tossed them down onto a stack of manila file folders next to my phone.

"So much for that," I muttered but decided that the whole TV thing had pretty much been a solid tip. I got up and went out into the living room and rooted around for the remote. I found it wedged between the arm and seat cushion of a shabby but comfortable looking recliner. I was looking over the buttons to familiarize myself with the operation of it when I heard the noise. It was a thump followed by a scrape and it was just outside the kitchen door.

I froze, my heart squeezing painfully in my chest as panic hooked its claws in my throat. I couldn't swallow, although I wanted to. I took a slow deep breath and tried to quell the urge to freak out. It was dark outside, just past ten now, Ghost was working the overnight shift. I took a halting step and stopped. He'd shown me the gun safe in the office closet but the kitchen was between me and the office and even supposing I could make it...

Bam! Bam! Bam!

I jumped and cried out, slapping a hand over my mouth to quell the short terrified sound.

"Shelly it's Blue!" a strange voice I'd never heard called out from the kitchen door. I dropped the remote into the recliner and breathed out. Blue never really talked so it could be him... I went to the kitchen and pulled a big blade from the butcher's block on the counter, holding it the way Reaver taught me. I jerked back the blue and white gingham curtain over the kitchen door's window and let out a breath, shoulders dropping.

Blue regarded me plaintively through the glass. I unlocked the deadbolt and opened the door, he stepped into the kitchen and eyed the butcher's knife along my forearm. He raised his eyebrow and smirked at me which earned him a scowl.

"What?" I demanded. He raised a shoulder indelicately and dropped it.

"Ghost isn't here," I said and put the knife away. Blue ran a hand through his light brown hair and blinked like he was willing me to just get it. I rolled my eyes in exasperation.

"What? You here to babysit me?" he nodded and shifted slightly on his feet.

"You can talk, you just did... so talk," I folded my arms across my body and he gave my tits an appreciative once over where they rested above my arms.

"I'm not club property anymore," I said softly, and shifted on my own feet, uncomfortably.

His dove gray eyes widened and his expression seemed a tad upset, he put up his hands and waved them like he was warding something off. "Didn't mean it like that," he said and I scraped my bottom lip between my teeth. He had a nice voice.

"Sure you did. You all do."

He looked a bit dejected, "Yeah, you have a nice body and I'm male. Still, I should have had some fucking tact, you're Ghost's Old Lady," It was the closest thing I was going to get to an apology and a pretty good one, so I nodded.

"Thanks. So you're here to babysit me huh?" He shrugged and a stubborn scowl crossed his features.

"Can I use the bathroom?" he asked ignoring my question.

"As long as you tell me what you're doing here," I crossed my arms and he stared at me with a similar look that Reaver got when he went all cold and scary, except Reaver was much, *much* better at it so I told him so.

"Reaver is way better at the scary face and he's my cousin, so how about we cut the bullshit, you tell me why you're on babysitting duty and then you can go piss or whatever while I contemplate how hard I need to kick my Ol' Man's ass." I raised my eyebrows.

"Girls aren't supposed to know we're watching them," he grunted.

"Secret is safe with me, oh white knight. Why are we being watched?" he frowned, I sighed, "Fair enough, go do whatever it is you need to do and I'll put on some coffee. Should have come in a lot sooner, its cold outside." he nodded and went past me stopping at the mouth of the hallway.

"First door on the left," I said and with another nod he went in and flipped on the light. I started the coffee pot and after the first grunt and the hiss decided to see what was up for myself. He'd left the door open and was standing in the harsh bathroom light trying to peel a square of taped down gauze off his side. I sighed again and he jumped.

"Let me have a look," I said gently. He swallowed hard and nodded. The bandage wasn't in the most convenient location for any do-it-yourself and it was soaked through pretty good. I got it off and saw a pretty decent stitch job, considering.

"Doc do this for you?" I asked. He shook his head. I frowned. "Why didn't you have Doc do it?" he gave a one shouldered shrug.

"This looks pretty bad, were you with Ghost when it happened?" he shook his head.

"Don't talk much do you?" again he shook his head, "Lift your arm up?" I showed him what I wanted and he complied. I cleaned and dressed what looked like a pretty serious knife gash and he lowered his arm.

"Wasn't so bad was it?" he shook his head and picked up his shirt from the top of the closed lid of the toilet. It was a pretty decent stain in the side. I took it from him and put it in the sink.

"I got it," I pulled down the hydrogen peroxide and poured some on the fresh blood. It foamed like mad. Blue's eyes got wide.

"Take your cut, I'll get this stain out and bring you one of Ghost's shirts," I told him. I wasn't happy with having a babysitter but I was secretly grateful not to be alone in the house at the same time. I would grow accustomed to it with time but this was my first night alone and yeah, okay, I was a chicken shit, who was I kidding?

I finished getting the majority of the blood out of Blue's tee in the bathroom sink and threw the offending and peroxide soaked material into the washer. I went into the bedroom and found a black Jack Daniels tee shirt in one of Ghost's drawers.

"Here, use this one," I said and held it out to him rubbing my eye. I was suddenly very tired. Blue stood up and shrugged out of his cut which he'd put on over his bare chest. He wasn't bad to look at but he certainly wasn't my Ghost. He pulled the tee on which was just a touch too snug through the shoulders and chest and a bit on the short side. Ghost was a large, looked like Blue took an XL. I smiled and laughed a little.

"It'll do for now. Coffee?" I asked. He nodded carefully.

"You aren't pissed," he stated.

I shrugged. "What's the point of being pissed at you? It'd be like shooting the messenger. I've been around the club for a long time. You wouldn't be here if it weren't serious, at the same time I'm not an Old Lady like Ashton or Hayden who are new to the MC lifestyle," he searched my face and nodded.

"All the Old Ladies have a protective detail?" I asked. There was a slight flinching around his eyes, but other than that, no other tell or change in his expression to tell me anything. Time to work my hoodoo. I had a fifty-fifty shot at getting this right.

"I see. Don't let Chandra or Everett catch you. They'd be fucking pissed," he pursed his lips and looked to the side like he was pissed, a classic 'Fuck! She got me!' expression. I laughed.

"I told you, I've been around for a long time. Cream and sugar?" I asked.

"Cream, no sugar," he eyed me speculatively. I poured us coffee and motioned for the couch. He sat on it and I curled up in the recliner.

"Let's see what's on," I fished under me for the remote and turned on the television. It took a minute or two to find a happy medium but we finally settled on The Expendables movies.

I must have fallen asleep because when I woke, it was to Ghost smoothing back my hair and the On Demand screen telling me all about the latest next big thing. I looked over at the couch and shifted. I was under the blanket from the back of the couch and Blue was gone, his coffee mug and mine had disappeared too.

"Come on, Honey. Let's go to bed," Ghost kissed me and whatever I had been about to ask him flew out the window. I let my man take me to bed.

CHAPTER 26

Ghost

She was so beautiful, asleep in my tired old recliner when I got home. I stood there for I didn't know how long and just looked at her. She was just so damned angelic when she slept it was hard to believe that when she was herself, when you took away all the sadness and doubt that she had just a little bit of devil hidden in those sapphire blue eyes. I let her sleep and went in and took a hot shower, remembering her admonition about coming to bed smelling like work. Fresh and clean I pulled on a pair of comfortable pajama bottoms and padded back down the hall.

I didn't want to scare her, I wasn't really sure how to go about waking her, so I went with a gentle approach and figured if she swung on me I'd deal. I knelt down and smoothed her hair back off her forehead where it'd slipped down over one eye. She jerked, startling and brought her hands free from the throw but I was already talking. Low, like you would sooth a frightened animal or child,

"Come on, Honey. Let's go to bed," I murmured and she looked up, her posture easing when she realized it was me. I leaned forward and kissed her, and her arms twined around my shoulders. She sighed out against my mouth and I helped her to her feet. She plucked the remote from the recliner's armrest and turned off the television and gave a long stretch full of feline grace. I had a sudden and extreme urge to run my hands over all that smooth skin exposed along her stomach and ribs where her tee rode up. One I would likely be acting on as soon as I had her in my bed.

I drifted up the hall behind her, my hands resting lightly on her narrow hips, thumbs tracing lazy circles on her lower back, above the waistband of her leggings. We slipped through the portal of my bedroom door and I gently swung it shut behind us. It was dark, and

I reluctantly let her go just long enough to switch on the bedside lamp. The room was instantaneously suffused with a warm golden glow, muted enough to remain relaxing but bright enough to easily see by.

I turned and went back to her, she was smiling this tiny devilish smile and wasn't shy or timid at all when I stepped into her personal space. My hands found her hips and I drew her tight against my body, her hands found my arms and smoothed up the outside, along the swell of my shoulders, sending an electric jolt coursing through my blood as her smooth fingertips traced either side of my neck before she captured the back of my head in her hands.

She molded the front of her body tight to mine and kissed me back just as deeply as I kissed her and I felt such a fierce sense of pride in her that she would be willing to take back what was stolen from her because this time, right here, felt different than the other times we'd come together. It was like Shelly was more engaged, surer of herself, back to being bold and unafraid. She was the girl that had caught my attention and lit my very soul on fire from the moment I'd laid eyes on her that very first time all that time ago and so I let myself go, let myself be consumed and just barely had the forethought to tell her, "You need me to stop you tell me to stop," before I let my body do all the rest of the talking for me, beginning with my hands.

I smoothed my hands under her shirt, along her skin, pushing the cups of her bra out of my way so I could palm her breasts. She groaned into my mouth and I felt myself tent the front of my pajama bottoms that much more, which was suddenly an issue for me. The fact that there were this many clothes between my skin and hers was just totally unacceptable. I pulled up on her shirt to the point she had to raise her arms or she'd be trapped in it. She let me take it from her and drop it to the floor but that put a mild distance between us and I wanted her close.

I pulled her body right up against mine and our mouths found each other again. God my girl could *kiss*, she was brilliant at it, her tongue stroking along mine, taking her time; the thing I was loving about her now was that she was just *losing* herself in it. Giving herself over to my hands on her skin, my kiss on her mouth, my body against hers.

I went for her bra and undid the little hooks in the back, pulling it off her and letting it join her shirt on the floor. She immediately pressed tight against me and I loved the feel of all that warm satin flesh against mine. She didn't so much as flinch when I went for the waist band of her leggings and I wasn't exactly taking things slow, or gentle. I peeled both sides down, the material rolling down effortlessly and for once I used my shorter height to my advantage, breaking our mouths apart I trailed kisses and slight love bites down all that smooth and creamy skin.

"This okay?" I growled and sank teeth into one of her perfect breasts, just enough to leave a slight imprint behind. Shelly gasped, her fingers which were threaded through the back of my hair, tightened against my scalp and pressed me in tighter against her.

I chuckled darkly, "I'll take that as a 'yes'," I murmured against her skin.

"Just shut up and make me feel good," she said, a wicked curve to her lips. I slapped her ass lightly through her lace panties and she gave a mock-indignant cry.

"Any other time, any other place you can be mouthy, Sweetheart. It's one of the things I love about you, but not right now and never this place. Okay?" my phrasing was a little off, as I took time out from my demand to kiss down the rest of her body, until I ended up on one knee in front of her. She looked down at me only slightly apprehensive and I met her jewel bright eyes with a steady gaze. She clasped her bottom lip between her teeth and nodded slowly.

"You need me to stop, you say so." I reminded her softly and she met my gaze with a much steadier resolve, nodding a bit more rapidly. I peeled the fabric of her leggings down her long and lovely legs and she stepped out of them obediently. I looked my fill, *she was just so fucking stellar*, before settling my gaze on those bright inquisitive eyes of hers again. I hooked my fingers in the waistband of her panties and drew them down her legs. Her fingertips lightly resting on my shoulders for balance as she stepped out of those too.

"So fucking beautiful," I breathed and pressed a kiss to her stomach, running fingertips from the inside of her ankle all the way up her leg. She shivered but it had absolutely nothing to do with the temperature and I smiled, letting my fingertips graze her most sensitive flesh.

"God Ghost, yes," she breathed, her eyes slipping closed. I nudged her thighs apart with my hands and she widened her stance. I slid my fingers back and forth along her opening before plunging two up inside her and her reactions were just so damned *fine*. Her head tipped back, her fingers digging into the tops of my shoulders she moaned as I worked those two fingers in and out of her, my thumb pressing and teasing her clit.

Man it took everything I had to stay down. To make her come just once before I took her. I wanted to take her so bad. To have those long limbs wrapped around me to hold her close and breathe her in but I needed something baser and more primal than we'd done to date. It was taking a while to work her up but finally with a flick of my fingers and a swish of my thumb through her wet, she came apart, arching and crying out, legs trembling with the effort to hold herself up. I gave her a little helping hand, a little shove and with a short indignant cry she fell back onto the bed.

She panted, and looked up at me with a fire in her eyes, and I gave her a feral grin in return. Fear flashed and was quickly overwhelmed by a determination and a trust and even though I didn't have to I reminded her, I said low and harsh, "You need to stop, you just say so Baby Girl," before I dropped my pajama bottoms. She pulled herself back onto the bed and crooked a finger at me, a darkness of her own filling her expression.

"I don't want to stop, come here," she ordered, her voice husky and demanding. That was my girl.

I joined her up on the bed and settled between her thighs, kissing her fiercely, teasing her and myself with some dry humping action. She made me feel like a fucking teenager again and it was just one more thing I loved about her. Well that and the way she writhed underneath me. Shelly, for having a toned runner's physique, still managed to be *all woman*. She wasn't flat as a board, no, she was sweet supple skin and mouthwatering lush curves. The girl managed to have a perfectly rounded ass and a pair of tits that were just a perfect overflowing handful for me.

It had become entirely too easy to lose myself in her, to just give up all thought and just *feel* when we were like this. Just me and her, her and me and a seemingly inexhaustible amount of time with which to explore every inch, every bit... right down to the things that couldn't be seen or touched or tasted in a physical sense.

I locked hands with her, threading the fingers of my left hand through the spaces between her own, palms pressed seamlessly together and I slipped effortlessly into her, my cock sliding inside her sleek wet heat as if it were meant to be there all along. Shelly's entire being arched off the bed and pressed into mine, meeting in the middle as I pressed deep, my body meeting flush to hers in every way that counted between two lovers.

I kissed her lovingly and held her close before I started to move. She gripped my hand and turned those jewel bright eyes on me full force and I was so fucking lost in them, lost to her. This beautiful creature who had been in my thoughts, in my heart and on my mind non-stop since the first time I'd ever laid eyes on her back in that club room just after I'd set myself up here.

Shelly had tripped my trigger with her sheer force of will, her sass and her personality from the moment she first parted those gorgeous lips in my direction. I was slain, smitten, whatever you call it and despite my damned pride and both of our stubborn fucking attitude problems here we were and I was never letting her go again.

"Harder, oh please Derek! Harder!" she gasped. I smiled and untangled my hand from hers, and reared up. I palmed her slender and delicate waist and gripped firmly, but not hard.

"You tell me if it's too much." I reiterated and for the first time I deviated from just simply making love to her and I gave us what we both needed, a deep rough *fuck* and it was amazing. Shelly balled her fists in the comforter to either side of her lean hips and gasped deep and satisfied into the night, her eyes never leaving mine. I drove into her hard and fast and deep, the cadence of our uneven desperate breathing and the sharp report of my flesh meeting hers filling the bedroom, the entire experience was deep and erotic and just so damned *fulfilling* I couldn't hold on. As soon as Shelly started to come around my cock I went with her, giving her two or three more sharp but uneven thrusts before collapsing on top of her.

I pressed my ear to her chest between her breasts and listened to her frantic heartbeat and the cadence of her ragged breathing. Her fingers swept through my hair, combing it back from my forehead and the sensation made me shudder. She laughed and scratched her nails along my scalp and holy Jesus that felt good. I settled against her, crouched over her and just relaxed, enjoying being with her.

"That was amazing," she commented dryly when her breathing had calmed enough to allow for speech.

"Yeah," I agreed.

"No don't move!" she cried when I moved to get off of her. I was worried I'd been crushing her, but no dice. She gave a little wiggle beneath me to settle into the cloud of a mattress. We lay together for a long time just catching our breaths as I grew soft inside her.

"Can't stay crouched like this much longer, Babe," I murmured against her skin. She sighed and uncoiled her arms from around me. I sat up and gently vaulted her leg, letting my body collapse boneless onto the bed beside her.

With a wicked little smile she sat up and straddled my hips, lowering herself down over my body to softly place her lips over my own. We kissed, a slow and languorous thing full of weight and heat and promise.

"Hmm, you doin' okay?" I asked her.

"Mmm, yeah. Always knew you'd be amazing," she smiled against my lips and I laughed and gave the outside of her thigh a swat which made her yip and then *really* laugh.

"Always loved talking with you, loved the banter and the barbs, every time you parted those lips of yours with a zing or a parting shot it made me so fucking hard..." I sighed out. Shelly folded her hands one atop the other on my chest and rested her chin there, sliding a bit down my body which made me shiver, and my cock stir. She raised an eyebrow.

"I just wish we'd really *talked* to each other, much sooner..." she confessed and that made two of us.

"You and me both, Sweetheart, you and me both…" I kneaded the back of her neck with thumb and fingers and her eyes drifted shut in pleasure. I swear to God, if she were a cat she'd be purring.

"I'm yours Ghost, you know that right?" she asked softly.

"I know Baby," her words caused a contented sigh to escape me, I leaned my head up to kiss her and she returned it, so perfect, so sweet my arms curved around her and held her to me. By now I was hard again and after a few missed attempts I let her go so she could straighten. She slipped me back inside her and sank down over the top of me so slowly, the sight was just so fucking… Mmm!

"Ride me, Baby," I ordered and she smiled this brave and at the same time wicked little smile and complied but she did it *her* way which seemed to be doing a whole hell of a lot for her, getting her worked up and the like but for me, all it did was drive me crazy. It just wasn't fast enough, wasn't hard enough, she was such a fucking tease! I laughed and let her have her way. I knew I'd get mine in the end but the thing was, for right now, I was enjoying the hell out of watching my woman take her pleasure off of me. My woman… The sound of that was just as perfect as she looked in the muted lamp light.

I watched her move above me for I don't know how long. Her hands on my chest, her long legs raising her up off of me only for her to glide back down. She was so *wet*, so beautiful and her shell pink nipples hard and all but begging for attention. I grasped them with thumb and forefinger and teased them for her, tugging gently until she cried out, and came, pulsing and fluttering around me, milking my cock but it still wasn't enough. I gripped her hips firmly and held her as she bowed over my body and *finally* I was back in the driver's seat and driving up into her and *shit* that felt good. I felt my balls tighten with my impending release and I drove up into her the same time she came down on me and I came, deep and hard inside of her.

No other feeling like it in the damned world… Shelly came again, the same time I did and it was probably the most perfect thing I'd ever felt. Like our bodies were meant to fit together. We kissed, and lay in the circle of each other's arms and it wasn't long before both of us ended up fast asleep. I felt determined that this would so not be the last night for us to ever be so perfect. She fit against my chest just so damned well...

CHAPTER 27

Shelly

The week passed quickly. I didn't see Blue again, nor did I see anyone else for that matter. Still, I felt a lot better just knowing a Sacred Heart was out there. I got busy and stayed really busy with my numbers and never did get around to asking Ghost why there were protective details on the Old Ladies. I figured it had something to do with The Suicide Kings and when it came to that, I firmly admit to wanting to be an ostrich. I kept my head planted right in the sand where I didn't have to see it, or deal with it.

Things with Ghost were really good. Almost idyllic. He would cook with me either before he went out or after he came home from work, we made love quite a bit and he just seemed to *know* what did it for me. I was satisfied, content, in just about every aspect of this new life and even though the week was winding down, I was comfortable enough that I didn't have a single thought towards going back to my cousin's or of moving out. I was startled to find that I was really comfortable here, that it felt just as amazing as I had always imagined it would to have someone to fall asleep beside every night and even better that he was there to wake up to in the morning.

It was Friday when he called from out in the house somewhere, "Hey Babe! Where's my blue Ford motors tee?"

"Check the dryer!" I called back. I was parsing through his receipts from the month before when he stepped into the doorway, I looked up and frowned, the expression on his face was as hard and closed off as I had ever seen it.

"Ghost what's wrong?" I asked, worried.

"This isn't my shirt," he held up the gray tee Blue had been wearing.

"Oh, no it's Blue's," I said matter-of-factly and recognized my mistake too late. Ghost's face looked like he had just been shot in the chest and his expression immediately turned cold and nasty.

"You fuck him?" he asked and I froze. I blinked slowly and took a deep breath. In an instant the entire week of peace that had been cultivated between us, shattered... What I said next I shouldn't have but what he had just asked me... *it hurt*. It also proved to me he didn't trust me, not one bit.

"Yeah, of course, we had a great time!" I said voice heavy with sarcasm. I crossed my arms hugging myself. He slapped a hand on the wall by the door frame.

"Don't fuck with me on this Shelly! Did. You. Fuck. Him?" he yelled.

"No, I didn't fuck him you asshole!" I shouted, jumping to my feet, "What the fuck is wrong with you? He showed up the beginning of this week and had a pretty heavy gash in his side, it was bleeding through his shirt! I patched him up and gave him one of yours, got the stain out of his but it was wet and needed washed so I dumped it and left it in the washer! I can't believe you don't trust me! That you would even think that!"

"Do you blame me?" he cried, outraged and it crushed a decent sized chunk of my soul...

I looked at the floor so he wouldn't see the tears starting to well up in my eyes and said, "Well I guess that's what you get for taking a club whore as your Old Lady." I shrugged my shoulders indelicately.

"That's not what I meant..." he said trying to back pedal.

"Yeah. Yeah it is Ghost! Don't even try to lie about it!"

"Why didn't you tell me about it then huh? Why do I have to find this," he shook the tee shirt in both his fists, a look borne of pure rage on his face, "In my fucking laundry for it to come up?" he demanded and he was right, sort of... I just hadn't thought anything of it at the time.

"I don't know!" I screamed back, "I just didn't think about it! I have a lot on my fucking mind lately Ghost! What do you want from me?"

"I want what I've always wanted Shelly! I want you to be mine!

Just *mine!* No other man's!" he threw the tee shirt onto the floor.

"Well we got a fucking problem there Ghost because you obviously haven't been paying attention! Because I'm mine now! I gave myself to you, you insufferable ass, but apparently that isn't enough!" I glared at him chest heaving.

"Yeah, me and apparently Blue too! You just couldn't keep your legs shut could you?" I gasped incredulous.

"You know what? Just fuck you! Go to the club without me. I might not be here when you get back!" I glared at him, I knew I would be here. I knew deep down that as much as he was hurting me right now that I loved him and that I wanted this to work and that in order for it to work it would *take* work but I was hurt and mad and just wanted some time to breathe.

"Fine, fuck, do whatever Shelly! You always fucking have!" He punched the door frame and left, went out the kitchen door slamming it so hard I expected the window to break rather than just rattle in its glass. I dropped into the desk chair like a sack of stones and stared at the gray tee on the light cream carpet. Laying there like the dirty accusation it was. I hated to fucking cry but this was definitely the time and place for it. I scrubbed my face with my hands and took several deep breaths and tried to squash it down but couldn't.

Fuck Ghost! Fuck him six, seven, no, *a million* ways to Sunday! The son of a bitch! I put my hands over my lower stomach and really fucking prayed hard I wasn't pregnant for the first time since we'd made love – no, *fucked* without protection. I felt so fucking stupid for trusting him. It was about this point I couldn't keep the flood waters back anymore and burst into noisy wracking sobs.

Why did this shit always happen to me?

CHAPTER 28

Ghost

I'd fucking trusted her. Believed what she'd said, that she was mine and only mine. I pounded my fist into the steering wheel and cursed savagely. I went to the club. We were supposed to go together but she'd fucked that up. Couldn't keep her fucking legs together. I felt sick, a small voice in the back of my head telling me, *way to go asshole, what if she's telling the truth? What if you just crucified Shelly for the sins of your exes all over again?*

I jerked the wheel of my pickup savagely and turned up into the MC's lot in a wash of pinging gravel. I shut it off and got down, slamming the door behind me. I stood, chest heaving in anger and couldn't tell you exactly who I was angry at, Shelly, Blue... or me.

I strode across the lot past the line of bikes and an arm shot out from the dark and caught me by my jacket sleeve. I turned a black square of cloth thrust at me with white writing on it. I took it without thinking and looked stupidly down at my favorite Jack Daniels tee shirt and up into the crooked smile of Blue. He shrugged and I glared hard at him chest heaving.

"Did you fuck her?" I demanded. His eyes got real wide and he put up his hands waving them.

"Answer me you son of a bitch!" I screamed, "Did you fuck my woman?"

"No man! I was bleeding like a son of a bitch and I was on watch!" he lifted his tee and there was a snowy white rectangle of gauze taped to his pale skin.

"What's going on?" Reaver asked from the club's front door, Duracell right beside him. My stomach churned with acid and rage.

"Found a shirt that wasn't mine in the laundry," I grunted. Reaver's eyebrows went up.

"And?"

"It was mine," Blue said and looked at Duracell, as if for help.

"Yeah, you said you knocked on the door, Shelly patched you up and gave you coffee," Blue nodded.

"They watched The Expendables, she fell asleep in the recliner; he covered her up and rinsed the cups and put 'em in the dishwasher. That's *all* that happened man. He figured he'd give you your shirt the next time he saw you. Said to me you got a Hell of a woman. She's smart and nice and funny," I glared hard at the silent man who was wide eyed and nodding at everything Duracell was saying.

"Where's my cousin, Ghost?" Reaver asked and everyone turned towards him. His voice held that hollow creepy as fuck tone that was scary with how calm it was, I swallowed, suddenly queasy.

"Back at the house," I answered.

"Alone?" he demanded but it was too late, I was already climbing back into my truck.

Shit, Blue had nothing but honesty shining out of his eyes when Duracell spoke, there'd been no lie there. She'd been telling the truth and I'd let my hang ups and past experiences rule the day. I picked up my cell phone and dialed Shelly's number. It rang... and rang and rang and rang.

"Hi this is Shelly, you know what to do, and if you don't, well I can't help you," her voice sang out the next bit, *"You're retarded!"* the message cut and the phone gave the tone signaling I should speak.

"Shelly, Baby, I'm gonna call you again. Answer the phone, Princess. I'm a fucking fuck, just answer the phone, Babe, I owe you an apology." I hung up and dialed again.

"Hi this is Shelly, you know what to do..." I hung up and dialed yet again...

"Hi this is Shelly..."

"Fuuuuuuuuuck!" I shouted and threw the damned phone into the passenger side floorboard. I cursed me and my god damned temper and drove, breaking every speed limit. I didn't even care. I just needed to make it right.

CHAPTER 29

Shelly

I tried to be adult about this. Ghost was going to go to the club. He was going to get lit, stay out overnight and then come home tomorrow and we'd talk. Or not... I didn't know. I got over my crying jag pretty quickly and went into the bathroom and splashed cool water on my face. I was red and blotchy and gross which made me sigh. We were both pigheaded on a good day, he'd told me more about his two ex's, about how much it'd hurt, how much it'd ripped his guts out, their betrayal. I should have remembered about the damned shirt, now he was super upset and I felt super guilty for letting my smart mouth run unchecked yet again but at the same time, I was angry too!

I went back into the office and sat down again. It felt as if I had been cracked wide open and everything that was *me* was spilling out onto the carpet in a horrible painful rush. I was so hurt and mad, and guilty and it was all very confusing and over the top of it all I kept trying to logically tell myself, *it's okay, this isn't the end, he'll come home and we'll talk and we'll figure this out...* Because as douchey as his accusation had been, I understood. Didn't I? I sat in silence as all of these thoughts and feelings agitated inside my skull, until my thoughts were interrupted by a tapping at the kitchen door.

Ghost was my first thought but I hadn't heard his truck and so with a sigh I resigned myself to the fact that this was likely a Sacred Heart on watch duty who had seen Ghost storm out or was sent over here when he'd gotten to the club all hot headed and was coming to check on me or get the full meal deal on what was up. I opened the door without checking. So stupid, so fucking stupid...

"It's fine, I'm fine I..." my words died when I looked up at a tall, beefy motherfucker in a Suicide Kings cut.

"Heard you like to fuck!" he said and I swung the door shut but it was too late. The door bounced off one of his boots and he reached for me. I barely dodged and didn't quite make it because when he didn't get me by the arm he lunged and *did* manage to get me by the back of my sweater. I shrieked as I was hauled back against a wall of muscle. I made another lunge to get away.

"Woah, woah, woah! Where you going sweetheart? I want to play!" he pulled me back again and I struggled to get free of the sweater and just managed to do it, whipping around as I yanked my last hand free of the sleeve to put the kitchen counter between us. I ripped one of the knives from the butcher block and held it between us, but in my panic, I was holding it all wrong. I slashed at him and he bounded backwards. Laughing he taunted me.

"Woo! Kitten has claws!" he laughed harder and I lunged again to go around him but he was ready. He caught me by the wrist and *squeezed* until my bones ground together and my hand popped open and the knife clattered to the floor. He backhanded me next and I saw stars and tasted blood and the world phased in and out for a second flashing photo negative, then positive; then negative again and suddenly I was face down over the kitchen counter.

He held me, one meaty hand in the middle of my back, the stench of stale cigarettes, motor oil and sweat invading my nose and mouth, cloying and sickening as he struggled to keep me still and get my leggings down with one hand. I didn't make it easy for him. I fought, *hard* but I had fought hard in the woods at Lake Eversong too and it had gotten me nowhere.

Not again, not again, not again... was the mantra in my mind as he gripped the back of my head and reared me back. He slammed me face forward into the counter and blood spurted from my nose. I choked on the copper tang and gagged, trying to breathe around it. It didn't stop me from fighting as much as he'd have liked because he pulled me up and bodily slammed my back against the counter.

The guy was *huge*, like Trigger big! I didn't stand a chance without some kind of weapon! He gripped me by the throat and I brought a knee to my chest and kicked out hard when he began to squeeze. My vision started going black and my kicking remained ineffective, my hand scrambled blindly over the edge of the counter at drawers as I choked and coughed and tried to get enough air. The drawer slid out I scrabbled around inside of it and my hand closed around the familiar grip of a gun.

I found the trigger guard and got my finger in it and scrambled with my thumb for the safety and got that too. I brought it around shoved it in the dude's face and the world *exploded* in sulphur and a riot of sound that left my ears ringing. He flew backwards off of me and partially took me with him. I slid off the counter, my back to the cupboards and fired over and over into his prone figure which was sprawled with half his face gone against the wall.

I dropped the gun with a clatter to the linoleum next to me and chest hitching in these hiccupping sobs, I took a deep breath and *screamed*, long and loud, over and over even though I couldn't hear it for the ringing in my ears. It just felt good to let it out. I howled my injustice and my triumph into the empty house and thanked god that the man who'd both picked me and broken my heart was a gun fanatic and that he kept one in almost every room of the house.

I'd fought back this time. I'd won this time and I'd survived something awful *again*. Me. No one else. Just me… so why did I wish against wish that he'd just fucking killed me?

I didn't have long to ponder it because suddenly a pair of denim clad knees were skidding to a stop beside me, gentle hands were touching me, but I didn't want to be touched! Not now! Not ever again! I batted at them, shrieking, shoving at them and wondered in my confused haze if I were being attacked again but then those hands gripped me firmly on either side of the head and his voice registered and I was staring into gravely concerned eyes the color of winter come to an end, the brown wreathed in the color of new spring leaves.

"Shelly stop! Princess it's me! It's me Ghost! You're safe! You're safe, Baby!" I looked at him and crumbled on the inside.

"I'm not safe… You broke my heart. You broke me Ghost," I told him and then he was suddenly gone, yanked off me and flying backwards and I was being lifted into a strong set of arms and the familiar and really safe smell of my cousin and the wind from a wild ride wrapped around me and I don't remember shit after that.

CHAPTER 30

Ghost

Reaver took her from me, and I wanted to be pissed about it but I couldn't be. Not after those wounded sapphire eyes over all that blood looked into mine and the bitter broken truth poured from her swelling lips.

"I'm not safe... You broke my heart. You broke me Ghost."

Reaver had gotten into Trigger and Ashton's Jeep with Shelly and left his bike in my driveway. He had arrived right on my ass and Trig had pulled up with a bunch of other brothers on bikes as he'd strode from my house with her.

I looked at the dead man on my kitchen floor and felt a surge of pride. She'd got him. Her leggings may have been down but her panties had still been in place and she'd shot the son of a bitch. Dray looked down at the body dispassionately from beside me and rattled off a string of insults in Spanish.

"We got this," Duracell said from the doorway. I looked up and met Blue's eyes which looked incredibly sad and at once apologetic and I barked a bitter broken laugh. What the fuck did he have to be sorry about?

"Jeeeeesus Christ!" Grinder said from behind the two men.

"Come on man, I'll give you a lift back to the club," Dray held out his hand and I grasped it. He hauled me to my feet.

I was numb and not quite there the whole ride to the club house. I stared out the passenger window of my truck sightlessly and wordlessly and thought about how many times I'd watched Shelly do the same. Like me, Dray didn't press. I was first through the door at the club and walked straight into Reaver's fist and I was okay with that, but I was also a Marine and didn't take a beating like a fucking pussy even if I did deserve it so I swung back.

He launched himself at me and caught me around the chest, I

landed against something hard and sharp and was vaguely aware of Hayden screaming at Reaver to stop, but I'd earned this. I brought my elbow down hard between his shoulder blades and his hold on me loosened. We grappled in the wreckage of chairs and the table we smashed through. There was shouting and screaming and hands closed around my arms and my cut and hauled me back. My chest was on fire, heaving with breaths as I fought to get my wind back.

"She fucking trusted you!" Reaver screamed. Trigger and Revelator had a hold on him. Dragon had me and a couple of the new guys.

"I know!" I bellowed back.

"You stay away from her!" Reaver pointed in my direction. Blood seeped from his nose and I felt a trickle of my own down my chin from what was sure to be a busted lip.

"I can't do that man! She's mine!" I shouted back and Trig and Rev had to renew their efforts to hold him off of me. I was pretty sure that the only thing keeping his knives in his cut was the fact that I was his brother in leather.

"She fucking loves you and that shit you poured on her! Pure fucking poison you cock sucker! If she didn't love you so help me I'd fucking kill you! I'd kill you!" Trigger and Revelator hauled Reaver out the door and Dragon shoved me forward.

"Fucking Shelly, she really knows how to cause a mess," he commented dryly and with his typical humor but I was having none of it, I rounded and fucking cold cocked him right in the fucking mouth. A round of shouts went up and I was hauled back again. Dragon spit blood on the floor and grinned savagely at me.

"Now I'm going to let that go, boy. Seeing as I have no fucking idea what's going on! But somebody better fill me in right fucking now or there's gonna be hell to pay!" Dray stepped up to his dad and spoke low. Dragon's expression went from as hard as obsidian to resigned in varying stages, the more Dray talked, the more his expression fell until finally, he sighed.

"That changes everything," he said. "As soon as Reaver calms his tits, get his ass in the chapel. Time for church."

"Ghost!" I looked up. Chandra was standing, arms crossed in the archway leading back to the rooms. "She's asking for you, baby. Try not to bone it any harder than you already have, okay?" she gave me a disapproving look and I heard Doc,

"Chandra, I will slap the shit out of you I hear any disrespect come out of your mouth!" Of course he didn't mean it. Things didn't work that way around here. No women, no children... unlike the fags in The Suicide Kings.

I went for my girl and prayed I could do something to fix all of this but was at a complete loss as to how.

CHAPTER 31

Shelly

I never actually went unconscious, I just can't remember the car ride to the club or getting cleaned up or changed out of my bloody and torn clothes into one of Trig's giant ass Sacred Hearts tees. I just remember the vague pinch of a needle and Doc asking a bunch of questions. I stared at him blankly for a long minute and then the horrible and stark reality crashed into my consciousness.

"I killed him, I shot him in the face," I said and it sounded hollow and wounded and just plain awful because I didn't feel bad for what I'd done and I should feel bad, I mean am I right? I shot a man in *the face.* Ended his life, snuffed out his existence and I really should feel bad about that *except I didn't.* I covered my face with my hands and cried out, it hurt! My face did.

I looked up at Chandra, "Where's Ghost?" I asked. I was afraid he would be mad at me, he was always so neat and orderly and I made an absolute mess of his kitchen. A hysterical bubble of laughter crawled up my throat and I bit down on it with a moan.

I killed someone. I should feel bad about that right? Except I didn't feel anything. Did I? I mean I felt bad about a mess in a kitchen when that mess was a man's *face* that *I* shot *off*! What was wrong with me?

"What's wrong with me?" I asked and Doc sighed.

"You're in shock honey, just give the medicine a little time to work," he held both my hands between his and I looked down at them. He was rubbing them as if to get them warm but I wasn't cold was I? I mean I was shaking, but I didn't feel hot or cold or anything, I just *didn't feel anything.*

I heard a crash out in the common room and shouting. I squeezed my eyes shut and shook my head which made it swim. I needed to think, I should be thinking about what to do. I killed

222

someone. The cops, I would be arrested! Yes! That's what happened wasn't it? You killed someone and they arrested you. I looked at Doc and pleaded.

"Please don't let them take me away..."

"Who Baby?" he asked softly.

"The police," I answered. I mean, he should know, *I killed someone.*

"Just rest Baby Girl, no one is coming to take you away. We got things all taken care of," he made soothing sounds and I nodded. Doc was trustworthy. Doc I could count on and always believe in. Doc and Reave and Trig and Ghost. I could believe in Ghost, couldn't I?

"Where's Reaver?" I asked. I wanted, no needed my big cousin. Reaver had always chased the nightmares away, and this was what this was. A big bad dream... or at least it really felt that way.

"Hey," soft, so softly I looked up into eyes the color of winter being chased back by spring and I crumbled just a little.

"I'm sorry I made a mess of your kitchen," I said because that was important right? Ghost liked things in order. Ghost likes things orderly, except for his office. That was the only room in his house that was messy and I was fixing that for him. That room was mine now, or wasn't it? Did Ghost still hate me for something I didn't even do?

"Hey no, don't cry Princess," he reached for me and I flinched. I wasn't sure I wanted to be touched and I blurted out,

"No don't touch me! I'm not clean!" Ghost's face collapsed into lines of anger and I recoiled, his expression immediately smoothed out. Doc said something or other to him, I wasn't paying attention. Ghost sat down slowly on the edge of the bed.

"I don't care, Baby. You're my girl and you look like you need a hug so can I hold you?" he asked. I nodded and sniffed back tears which hurt and reached out my arms. He murmured at me to scoot over and I did and he sat down next to me putting his feet up on the bed. He put his arms around me and I laid my head on his chest the way I had grown to like to do over the time we'd been together which was far too short and I just wanted to lay here like this for a while.

I was certain, like all good things, that this was going to come to an end and quickly and so I just wanted to lay here for a little bit. Close my eyes and pretend that it was yesterday and that we were happy and bright and still looking forward to a future together. A future that, it was killing me, would never happen now because Ghost thought I was unfaithful, that I wasn't his and I'd killed someone, and when you do that you have to be punished. There were only three things I cared about in life anymore. My Cousin, this club and Ghost, any of those three would be incredibly painful if not devastating to lose and I'd killed someone. I'd shot a man in the face. That meant I would need to be punished and I would lose one of them right?

"Shhhhh, I know. Shhhhhh... It's gonna be all right Baby," Ghost rubbed my back and kissed the top of my head and held me against him. Whatever drugs Doc had given me were working. My senses dulling around the edges, the world becoming hazy along with my vision. I closed my eyes. Warm and safe and solid in Ghost's arms. A hand closed around mine and I opened my eyes to the familiar face of my big cousin, his big blue eyes just like mine filled with love and concern.

"I'm right here Shells. It's okay," he said and his voice sounded loud, but I was starting to drift, warm and protected and safe. I twined my fingers in his and he lay down on the floor by the bed between me and the door and Jimmy if he were going to come and try and mess with me again.

"Jimmy ain't here Baby Cuz. I got you," I heard and I closed my eyes and let the comforting dark of oblivion swallow me whole.

CHAPTER 32

Ghost

Shelly was so much dead weight against my chest and I was almost too warm but I didn't care. I kissed the top of her hair and held her a little tighter, afraid to let her go.

"She'll be all right after she gets some rest," Doc said. Reaver lay stretched out on the floor by the bed, his hand upraised and tangled with Shelly's where it hung limp over my body and off the edge.

"Who the fuck is Jimmy?" I asked with a scowl. Shelly had been spouting a lot of random things, like every thought she'd been having had come pouring out of her mouth in a confused and jumbled mix of past and present.

"Her mother's boyfriend when we were growing up. He started coming into her room and touching her, trying to mess with her. I was fourteen, she was nine. I started crawling in her window at night and doing this," he shook his hand that held Shelly's. "I'd sleep on the floor, her hand in mine and when he opened the door and saw me, he would just close it again quietly. He knew he couldn't say or do nothin' or Shari, Shelly's mom, might ask questions," he sniffed.

"She comes out of this, she takes you back, you ever hurt her again, I'll fucking disappear you. You get me?" he asked coldly.

"Man I want to disappear *myself* right now," I growled and it was true. I felt like the biggest asshole in the history of, well, ever.

We stayed silent. I stared at the water stained ceiling tiles and wondered vaguely whose room we were in but it didn't matter really. Shelly was down for the count and I had every intention of being here when she woke up. Reaver though, he didn't get that luxury.

"Yo Reave, man, Dragon wants you in the Chapel," Dray said from the doorway. Reaver nodded and carefully untangled his hand from his cousin's. Shelly moaned and shifted a bit in her drug induced sleep but went still. Reaver gave me a look that was glacial and I nodded. I don't think we could be what you would consider friends anymore, which sucked, hard. Reaver left with one last worried look at his cousin. I stared at the ceiling for a long time before my eyes finally drifted shut.

I jolted awake, disoriented for a second, and realized it was the pressure from Shelly pushing off my chest and scooting a distance away that had roused me.

"Whoa, hey, easy Honey," I soothed but her face held none of the confusion or distress it had when I'd come in. Instead it held everything I should have expected, fear, mistrust, hurt and yes, even hostility.

"What are you doing here?" she asked. I sighed and thought about it for half a second.

"Trying to take care of you. Feeling like I'm always trailing seven steps behind when I should be right beside you. I love you Shelly and I am so fucking..." she stopped me, putting up a hand.

"Save it," she said disgusted.

"Princess..." she threw a pillow in my face.

"First off, *stop fucking calling me that!* I did just fine *by myself* where *you* left me. Second of all, I don't want to hear it!" her expression cracked and she looked like she was going to cry but then she wrestled whatever it was back into submission and gave me a hard look, her eyes as hard as the sapphire stones they resembled.

"You didn't know what I was going to say," I said and she scoffed.

"You were going to apologize, probably because you feel bad about the poor little abused club whore," she waved her hand up and down in front of her and turned her face to the side.

"Just get out!" she snapped at me and I'd reached about my limit.

"No," I said and I captured one of her hands between mine. "I'm not going to leave you. Not now, not like this, not ever. I told you this was for good Shelly and I meant it," she glared at me.

"You sure, or is it only until you get jealous and decide not to believe me?" she gave me a disgusted look and I bowed my head and bit my lips together. I nodded.

"I earned that and probably quite a bit more, got anything else you want to say?" I asked. She blinked, a bit stupefied and opened her mouth then closed it. I got the impression she wasn't told she was right very often.

"You hurt me," she said finally and I could tell it cost her to admit it.

"I know. All I can say is I'm sorry," I sat there and looked at her.

"What if 'sorry' isn't good enough?" she asked.

I slipped off the bed and stood up, "That's up to you, Princess, but 'I'm sorry' is all I've got. I don't want to lose you, Baby, I really don't, but if I do… That's on me and no one else. No one's gonna blame you if you walk now. Least of all me," she stared at me openmouthed and God she looked like hell, so swollen and bruised and it killed me. It fucking killed me that I wasn't there to protect her.

"I'll go find Reaver for you," I said and she looked up.

"I don't know what to do with all of this," she said and the look on her face was so raw and stark and honest I paused.

"Can I ask you something?" I asked softly, she gave me a curt nod.

"If we were laying up on that mountainside and a star streaked across the sky, what would you wish for? Right now?" she sniffed and the first tears spilled over.

"I would wish for…" she hung her head, "I would wish for a lot of things, I would need more than one star," she said and I nodded.

"Tell me Princess," I urged softly.

"I would wish that this had never happened, that we were home, and still getting ready to go out. I would wish that I felt bad for killing that man, and not… I feel bad that I *don't* feel bad and that scares me Ghost! What does that *mean?* What's wrong with me?" her hands shook and I went to her, I sat on the bed beside her and took her hands in mine.

"Baby he was hurting you, you did what you had to do to protect yourself. You fought so hard and I'm so proud of you for that," she gave a broken little sob and I hooked a hand behind her head and pulled her against me. She came into my arms willingly. Her slender ones curving around me and clinging to me.

"I'm so sorry I didn't protect you. That I let my past and my own hang ups…" I didn't fucking care that I was a man and that I wasn't supposed to fucking cry. This was my fucking fault. All of it. I held her tight and swallowed hard, choking up.

"Never again. Never going to leave you like that again. Even if I have to spend the rest of my fucking life earning back your trust," I vowed. I expected her to be jaded and cynical like always, I expected her to tell me to not make promises that I couldn't keep but all she did was give me a watery and broken 'Okay.'

I held her and rocked her and there wasn't a God damned thing short of the Reaper himself that was going to get me to let her go. I had been such a God damned fool and it had nearly cost me everything.

Someone cleared their throat from the doorway and I looked up. It was Dragon, looking apologetic. I gave him a chin lift and he gave me a watery smile.

"Sorry about the punch," I said and he smiled a little wider.

"Yeah, we voted on that, yer fined a hundred bucks, pay Reaver by next week," he said and I nodded. I continued to rock Shelly who had gone very quiet.

"How you doin' Chica?" Dragon asked and she turned, ashamed by her looks which were pretty fucking rough.

"I don't really know how to answer that question," she said solemnly. Dragon looked judicious and nodded.

"Stay as long as you need to here at the club Sugar," he said.

"Actually, I really want to go home," she said and her true blue eyes met mine. I had to ask her even though it pained me to do it.

"Which home, Princess?" she looked so fragile before she said,

"Ours," and I nodded. Forgiven I was not, but it was a start.

"We're gonna stay here tonight," I looked to Dragon, "I need to go back to my place and get it cleaned up," Dragon shook his head.

"Your brothers got that shit handled but we *do* need to talk," he said. I nodded. "Club meetin' in three hours. That'll give everyone enough time to get their ass back here," he turned to go and then turned back to Shelly.

"You did good Chica. We're all proud as hell at how you

handled yourself. You need anything, you let us know," Shelly nodded and looked a touch overwhelmed.

"I killed a man Dragon, I don't know if he had family or if he had kids... I just don't know any of that," she covered her mouth with her hand and Dragon's look softened.

"You did what you had to do Baby Girl. Ain't no one, not even God his self can fault you for that," and with that parting shot he went back out into the hall and disappeared in the direction of the common room.

"That's cold comfort," she whispered and I looked her over.

"Not meant to be a comfort, Princess. It's just the truth," she tucked her head under my chin, folding her tall lithe frame against me to do it and put her ear over my heart. I held her and rocked her, glad she was back and just wishing I could put all the broken pieces back together somehow.

The girls came and took over when it got to be time for me to go out front for the club meeting. They'd put Shelly in Reave's room when they'd arrived not knowing the full 411 on what was up and I was glad for that. I tucked her in and kissed her carefully. There was no TV in here so Evy, Chandra, Ashton, Hayden and Red made do crowding around a laptop while they watched some show or other that they were all in to.

I went out front and gave Reaver eighty bucks out of my wallet. "Get you the other twenty when I can hit an ATM," I told him and he nodded. A hard set to his jaw. I sighed.

"She wants to go home," I tried and he looked at me, and I was grateful his expression was heated instead of empty.

"Fuck you man," was all he said and I nodded.

"Fair enough," that was all I could say because Dragon was calling the meeting to order.

"Right, so this is what's what!" he said and laid everything out on the line. The eye for an eye we'd taken the night after Thanksgiving, and the attack carried out on Shelly tonight.

"We did use this to our advantage some," Trigger said quietly.

"What'd you do?" someone called. Duracell answered for our Sergeant At Arms.

"Strung up their trash on their fucking front gate with a message," Blue looked positively feral. Dray nodded and Dragon spoke up.

"This is what I want. Data, get me everything you can on the dude broke into Ghost's place and got himself perished. No one rides alone, or if you do you do it slick backed until further notice. So far these cunts are on the losing end of things. I want to keep it that way," he looked judicious.

"I also want to see what else we can come up with on getting them to relocate. Put a strangle hold on their money makers and operations. Go on the offensive a bit. Remember! No women, no children! Protect what's ours and fuck these motherfuckers!" Nods and murmurs of agreement swept through the assembled brothers. I just wanted to get back to my woman.

Dragon went through some other things and the meeting was adjourned. Guys got up and some went for the bar, others back towards the media rooms and one went for the front door to let in some of the women who hung around and were freezing their asses off in short skirts in the parking lot. I turned to go and Reaver caught me by the arm.

"You fucking hurt her again..." he intoned and I jerked my arm out of his grasp.

"Yeah, I get it! For fuck's sake man! I fucked up, and you can stay fucking pissed at me for as long as you like but right this second my girl is in there hurting and needs me, so fuck you and your high horse, I got shit to take care of!" I stalked off back to his room without a backwards glance stopping in the doorway. Shelly looked a little strained around the edges and was talking softly with the girls. The laptop was closed and resting in Everett's lap, her friend Mandy sitting cross legged on the floor.

"Hey," I said and watched the reactions, Ashton and Mandy both startled as did Shelly but with Shelly's recent trauma and Ashton's history of abuse that was to be expected. I focused on Mandy for a second but Everett, ever her best friend's human shield, got up and stole the attention away from the redhead.

"You want we should stay?" she asked Shelly in that thick Irish brogue of hers. Shelly shook her head.

"I'll be fine," she murmured. The girls were all giving me a mix of disapproving looks ranging from eye rolls to glaring daggers.

"Get the fuck out if all you're gonna do is judge," I told them. They rose to their feet, and painted on scowls and I didn't give a fuck. They left casting Shelly worried glances and shut the door behind them. She sagged a bit and I went to her, tucking her in a bit at a loss for anything else to do.

"Hungry?" I asked her.

"And thirsty. The girls wanted to get me something but the meeting was between them and the kitchen."

"What do you feel like?" I asked her and she laughed a little.

"Why do I feel like a kid who just had something happen so the parents let them eat whatever junk food they want?" I smiled.

"I guess it's kind of like that."

"Ice cream doesn't fix nearly getting raped again and shooting a man in the face," she said bitterly.

"No it doesn't," I intoned gravely. A long silence ensued.

"Could I just have some water?" she asked finally. I nodded.

"Whatever you want," I kissed the top of her head and someone cleared their throat in the doorway. I turned. Reaver stood with a bottle of water in his hand.

"He still being a dick to you?" Shelly asked me.

"Yeah," Reaver answered petulantly and I couldn't help it, I laughed which earned me a scowl from the scary ass motherfucker.

"Well knock it off," Shelly said irritated, and she leaned back tiredly. "You don't know everything Reave and it ain't your business but I'd like to hope that we're going to be grownups and work through this," she said it with her eyes closed and opened them, pinning me with a pleading gaze.

"I'd like that," I murmured.

"I mean it," she said, "I can't handle any more shit falling apart around me. I want a normal, a constant, so fucking bad. One that doesn't fall on just Reaver's shoulders anymore," she looked at her cousin, "You've been babysitting my ass since the moment I was born; you can't do it forever. You have Hayden and Connor and I need to put my big girl panties on some time."

"Oh, Honey. No one is expecting you to bounce back so quickly from all of this," we all turned to see Hayden in the doorway. She went to her husband and twined her arms around his waist.

"She's right Baby Cuz. I just want you to be safe, to be okay. I don't like seeing you like this. Especially when it could have been prevented," he looked at me pointedly.

"Blow it out your ass, Reaver!" Shelly scoffed. "That son of a bitch could have gotten me at any point. Leaving that fancy therapist's office, or what if Ghost had to go out on a tow and the protection detail you secret squirrel decided we all needed without giving *us* the heads up we needed, didn't show up? Whose fault would it have been then? How about you stop *blaming* everyone except the person whose fault this *really* is?" She stared her cousin down.

"It's not Ghost's fault. It's not *my* fault either!" she put up a hand to stop him when he opened his mouth. "It's Sparks' fault. It's the man who attacked me's fault. It's The Suicide King's fault! Now I don't care what you have to do, but do it. Just don't get arrested," she looked from me to her cousin, "That goes for all of you," she said and Reaver looked taken aback.

"When the fuck did you grow up?" he demanded.

"Obviously when you weren't looking," she said wearily. Hayden glowed with pride. I had no fucking idea what the girls had talked about but it had done Shelly some good.

"Anything else there Princess?" Reaver asked adopting my nickname for his cousin.

"Yeah, fucking feed me. I want a god damned burger and I want my Old Man to cuddle me."

And Shelly was back to her old fireball self, sort of. She sent Reaver and Hayden out and demanded they close the door behind them. Suddenly it was just her and I and no distractions.

"Never again," she intoned and her sapphire eyes welled, she sniffed and pinned me with a fierce look that I *more* than deserved.

"I'm a flirt, I'm not a cheat and if you *ever* accuse me of being unfaithful, say such ugly things to me ever again, I walk. I won't do it, Ghost. I don't deserve it and I won't be crucified for the sins of some crazy bitches I've never met."

I nodded slowly, "I hear you loud and clear Princess. I… I am so sorry. I found that shirt and just all common sense flew out the fucking window. I saw red. I didn't even give you the chance to explain I just let fly with my temper and I… I don't deserve a second chance, but I'm gonna take it. I'm going to do better, do right by you. I p–" she put up her hand stopping me cold and swallowed hard.

"Don't make promises you can't keep, Ghost. I've had too many of them," she murmured and tears slipped down her battered and bruised face. I felt my heart dissolve into a pool of acid and I shook my head.

"I promise. I can keep it, I *will* keep it or I'll fucking die trying. Just say you're mine, and it's done, Baby," I held my breath while she looked me over.

"I mean it Derek. Never. Again."

"I am so tired of fucking up with you," I hung my head and shook it. I was so fucking pissed at myself, I wanted to hit something, to scream, to rage and let it all out but there wasn't any way to do that here, now, not without fucking everything up even more.

Shelly took one of my hands between the both of hers and sighed, "We keep butting heads over the past, over history neither of us can fix or rewrite or erase… I get how deeply they hurt you Derek, but I'm not them… I'm a slut, sure, but in my world that isn't mutually exclusive with a lack of monogamy. I want you, for whatever reason, my heart chooses *you*," she gave me a pleading look and I nodded gravely. I massaged her hands with mine and kissed her forehead gently.

"Okay," I murmured and nodded, "I hear you, Shelly, loud and clear and I'll do better, I really care about you, what happens to you, and I've been so wrapped around the axle…" I sighed, "So yeah, okay. I'm here and I want to build a life with you. I want to see you smile again and I want to make you feel good about yourself and maybe I just need you to teach me how to do that."

She smiled wanly, "It's really easy Ghost… Just love me, believe in me and try to trust me," she murmured.

"I can do that," I agreed and never had I been more determined to do anything in my life.

"I'm still here," she said softly and brought the back of my hand to her lips, she placed a reverent kiss there and it was the most achingly beautiful thing I had ever felt or seen. Her forgiveness.

"I'm not going anywhere," I promised her, she folded against me and I held her close and we stayed like that for a really long time. I would never be such a god damned fool again.

CHAPTER 33

Shelly

"Let me get your door," Ghost was driving me slightly insane. It was nearly a full week before we had come back to the house. He'd had me stay at the club where he knew I would be safe while he worked. He kept using the excuse that the house needed work or to be cleaned or this and that or the other.

Now finally I was here and about to get out of the truck and I would be lying if I said I wasn't dreading it from the top of my head to the bottom of my toes. Ghost helped me down from his truck and lifted down my small suitcase I'd been living out of at the club from behind the seat. I hugged myself, breath fogging the early December air and followed him to the kitchen door.

"You sure you're ready?" he asked me concerned and I scowled at him.

"Just open the fucking door! It's freezing out here!" I snapped and his expression softened, he knew I wasn't snapping at him, that my anxiety was just running at an all-time high.

"I love your face," he said and I made one at him. I still looked like shit and would for another week or so. He'd started saying it when I'd started complaining about how awful I looked. He laughed a bit and opened the door and I let my feet carry me forward. I stopped on the threshold and his hand went to my lower back. I startled and he gave me a nudge. I went in and he stepped inside behind me shutting the door tightly.

The house was warm and almost cheery, and it was as if nothing awful had ever happened. Not a trace of disorder in the comfortable, homey kitchen. I waited for a flashback, for something to happen, for a meltdown, anything, but there was nothing. I guess talking to Dr. Hubbard really had done wonders. I'd gone back and sat in stony silence three days ago before I finally asked him if it was true that whatever I'd say to him couldn't be repeated at all to anyone. He'd assured me, shown me the laws governing that kind of thing and the consequences that could come of it for him.

He'd said, "Shelly, my clients depend on me. I'm here to help people, not judge them," and he'd waited patiently and boy was I glad I was his last client for the day because I told him a lot of shit and he'd listened and taken notes and then, while I waited with a pent up breath he'd said exactly opposite of what I'd been terrified he was going to say…

"You're not crazy."

That had meant more to me than anything I could ever even say. Now, standing in the kitchen and staring at the place where the man's body had landed, I wasn't entirely sure that was wholly accurate.

"You okay?" Ghost asked me and I startled.

"I killed a man. Right here," I said softly.

"About that," he said setting down my suitcase and stepping around me. He took me by the hands and pulled out one of the stools beneath the kitchen counter. I sat down obediently. He put a hand flat down on a manila file folder and slid it down the counter at me.

"What's this?" I asked softly.

"Dragon had Data find everything he could on the man you killed," I blinked and held the folder in my hands with suddenly very numb fingers.

"What's in it?" I asked hollowly.

"You really want me to tell you?" he asked.

"Would I have asked if I didn't?" I said a bit sharply. His hands came to rest on my shoulders.

"Just tryin' to look out for you, Princess," I bit the inside of my cheek to keep myself from popping off with something shitty and unfair but Ghost still wasn't done flogging himself apparently because he said the first thought that came to my mind.

"I know, I've done a bang up job of it so far but I'm trying here," he said.

"I know, and I love you for it," I murmured and he gasped a bit and I froze, realizing what it was I'd just said. I blinked. It was the first time I had admitted it out loud and it felt pretty good. I looked him in the eyes.

"I love you," I said, much stronger this time and his eyes closed and he turned his head savoring the sound. Ghost looked at me and brought his lips carefully to mine. I kissed him. Minding my healing lip and swallowed hard looking at the file folder I held in my hands between us.

"You going to tell me?" I asked.

"His name was Robert Heindland. The Suicide Kings called him Heiny, partially because his last name but mostly because he had a habit of showing his ass. He's been in prison twice, once for armed robbery and once for rape. She was seventeen and he uh," Ghost cleared his throat, "he cut her up pretty bad."

"Jail multiple times for drunk and disorderly, he's dodged several assault charges. Into drugs, manufacturing, selling, you name it. All around bad dude. No woman, no kids, although that's not a for sure, it's probably safe to say that if he has 'em they're better off without him."

I opened the folder and flipped through police records and investigation reports and all manner of things likely taken illegally from one database or another. The man who had tried to hurt me was pretty much scum but I still had a hard time with this. I looked at Ghost.

"Is this supposed to make me feel better?" I asked quietly.

"No, Princess. You wondered about it and Dragon got you the answers you were seeking but it's not supposed to make you feel better. Killing someone has serious weight to it," he said and I stopped being a bitch for a second and hugged him to me. He was taller than me standing while I was seated like this and I fit perfectly under his chin. I startled when I heard the gravel of the drive crunch under tires.

"Shhhh, it's just Trig. He wanted to talk to you," I pulled back and frowned at him.

"What does he want to talk to *me* for?" I asked.

The Big Man rapped lightly at the kitchen door and Ghost

opened it. Trigger's massive frame filled the doorway and he edged into the house.

"Hey man," Ghost said and they clasped hands and pulled each other in for a hug. Trigger looked me over and sighed. He opened his arms and cocked his head questioningly and I smiled. I appreciated that he asked and didn't just go in for the hug. I looked at Ghost who seemed fine with it and I opened my arms and Trigger hugged me gently.

"Get gone D," he said to my man and Ghost slipped out the kitchen door and shut it behind him. I blinked, stupefied by the exchange. Trigger pulled out a stool and sat facing me.

"What?" I asked.

"Derek knows what happened because he was there that day, but this is something I haven't even told Reaver, or Ashton," he said and he pulled his e-cigarette out of his cut and put it in his mouth. He sighed out and took a long thoughtful drag.

"We were in this fucking podunk village in one of Afghanistan's eastern provinces doing surveillance, trying to catch this piece of shit lead of this terror cell. We'd been set up on this ridge for fucking hours. Sun beating down on us, hotter than Hades balls and we're just about ready to call it a fucking day when this God damned Mercedes pulls up outside this mud hut," he took a couple more drags off his e-cig and looked at me with haunted silver-blue eyes.

"There he is. Just comes popping up out of the car and we call for confirmation, right? Well it takes a minute and while we're waiting for the green light to take this mother fucker out, here comes his *kid* running out of the hut, and this dude he doesn't know I'm looking down the scope at him. He picks his boy up and he's holding him up in the air and it's this joyous fucking reunion going on down there," he bowed his head and was silent for a long minute.

"And we get it. Confirmed. Green light. Take the motherfucker out, but he's got his *kid* in his hands and he's bouncing this boy who is six maybe seven and I got it buzzing in my ear to take the fucking shot and I'm telling them, negative that I ain't got a clear shot and the order keeps coming in, take the shot, to take the fucking shot and D. he's like 'I know man but you gotta take the shot, it's orders' and so I sight and I pull the fucking trigger and..." he looks at me agonized and I stare back horrified and his next words drop into the silence of the house like a thousand pound boulder... "I missed," my shoulder's dropped in relief and Trigger, he shakes his head and looks like he's about to puke and he tells me... "I hit the kid."

I stared at him, several moments of silence stretching between us and all I can do is blink, stonily, sitting there and Trigger, he takes my hands in his and he tells me, "You did what you had to do to *survive* Shelly. He was hurting you. He was gonna rape you and nobody, I mean *nobody* should have to live through that once let alone twice. You did what you had to do to save your life. Big difference from the stain I got on my soul, Sugar. So stop torturing yourself." He got up and I stared at him openmouthed and horrified.

"What about the man?" I asked hollowly, "The one whose son you shot?" Trigger looked at me incredibly sadly.

"It was the only time I've ever missed Shelly and I haven't ever since for a reason," he intoned and then to make things crystal clear he said, "I got the son of a bitch with the second shot but I can still never take back the first." I nodded and pressed the heels of my hands hard into the seat of the stool I sat on, straightening my arms between my legs to hide their shaking.

"Why did you tell me this?" I asked him and I wanted so badly to cry for him. The pain I was living with for ending the bastard who attacked me must be nothing in the face of what Trigger was living with, I mean it explained *so much*. Trigger looked me over a little sadly.

"Because I thought it might give you some perspective, Baby. That it might get you to stop torturing yourself over a piece of shit male I would have gladly killed with my bare hands for putting his hands on you like he did. That wasn't a man Shelly. Real men don't hurt women, or children," and with that parting shot he disappeared out the kitchen door, shutting it firmly in its frame.

I turned my head and stared at the place where the man had lain after I had shot him. I pictured all that red blood, some of it my own from my busted face and decided that Trigger was right. I needed to work it out and be done with it and move past this little slice of Hell quicker than any of the rest. That the dude I'd shot didn't deserve any more of me.

I pushed to my feet and went down the hall into mine and Ghost's room. I moved through the dark and flipped on the bathroom light. I wanted a shower in the worst kind of way all of a sudden. A symbolic washing myself of this whole last ordeal. Ghost joined me as I was rinsing the last of the soap I used down the drain. He pressed a kiss to the back of my shoulder, his fingers curving around my upper arms to draw me back into his chest.

"You okay?" his voice was husky and soft with concern. I nodded, not trusting my voice to speak and he sighed and cuddled me back in to him.

"Do you want to talk about it?" he asked. I shook my head no… I didn't want to talk. I wanted to do the furthest thing from talking, but we hadn't been intimate since this new attack.

"Why… why haven't you touched me?" I asked softly, half afraid of the answer.

"Is that what you need?" he asked gently, lightly setting his teeth into my shoulder in a slight nip, "Me to touch you?" he asked.

"I need to know why you haven't."

Ghost sighed out and rested his forehead at the base of my neck, between my shoulder blades. His arms tightened around my waist and he pulled me back against him, more skin on skin. For a long time the only sound filling the bathroom space was the sound of the pulsating showerhead.

"I want to. I've wanted to, I just didn't want to push, Princess. I'm not sure what's okay and what isn't, I don't want to make you hurt, or make you cry, Baby. I'm just not sure how to go about things with someone who's been through what you've been through," he murmured the words, so stark and honest against my skin and the sensation was incredibly unique.

While the physicality of it, the sensation of his lips moving against my back, sent delicious waves of sensation sweeping down the rest of my back. The words he spoke were a sharp but sweet pain that pierced my heart. They made me incredibly sad and at once incredibly, incredibly angry. Not with Ghost, but with the men that had done what they'd done. I didn't want to be this ticking time bomb with my lover. I didn't want Ghost to feel like he was sweating it out, like he stood poised with clippers and every touch was a choice between the red or blue wire. That if he touched me here or kissed me there, that if he held me the wrong way or got rough with me that it could be like clipping the wrong damned one and *boom!* Instant emotional disaster.

"Look, I don't want you to treat me with kid gloves. I don't know if or when or what sets me off and I'm probably not going to know, but you treating me like something that needs to be bubble wrapped on a shelf... So not helping. I feel like I have orange traffic cones around me and that just drives me nuts! Makes me think about it *more* not less and truthfully," I struggled to turn around and he let me, I looked him in the eyes and sighed, "The last thing I want to think about when you touch me is *them*," I willed him to understand where I was coming from and I watched his grave expression lighten as he processed through what I was saying.

"I get you, Baby," he murmured and I felt myself relax in the circle of his arms. I was so grateful that this wasn't something that we needed to butt heads over that I kissed him and he really did get it, because he kissed me back and there was nothing careful about it. Our mouths tangled in a wild, passionate abandon and I felt the constriction around my heart ease.

Ghost backed me right against the cold stone of the wall and I squealed into his mouth which was met with the vibrations of his dark chuckle. He wasn't giving an inch, he wasn't giving any quarter and I felt like I was *on fire* from the inside out with every kiss, every nip, and every touch as he slid his hands over my body, slicking them through the moisture on my skin.

He kissed his way from my mouth, along my jaw, to the side of my throat, spending a couple of moments working the sweet spot on the side of my neck that turned my legs to Jell-O, before dropping into a half crouch and paying some extra special attention to each nipple. Pretty soon I was leaning back hard into the wall just to keep myself upright. I tangled my fingers into his wet hair, the strands that were normally sable soft to the touch, clinging wetly to my fingers as he dropped to his knees and with his stature that put his mouth *right there* and oh God yes, I wanted him to.

"Trust me, Baby. I got you," he murmured and braced one of my knees over his shoulder, draping my leg down his back and with one final look up the length of my body to make sure I was doing okay, that I didn't feel like I was going to fall, he licked one provocative wet line from my opening to my clit and *oh man* did Ghost know how to please with his mouth! I tipped my head back against the stone and cried out, pressing his mouth tightly to my pussy, fingers gripped through his hair. I closed my eyes to better concentrate on the sensation of his mouth on my most sensitive parts all the while encouraging him with my voice.

Not that any of the sounds pouring from my mouth, bubbling up from my throat were articulate in any way. Far from it. Ghost was one of the most orally talented men I had ever been with and as he flicked his tongue through my folds he'd successfully short-circuited my brain rendering me completely incapable of coherent thought, or the ability to speak intelligibly.

It felt so good, *he* felt so good and he kept me there, right on that precipice for what felt like forever. The cries coming from me were taking on a tone of begging and I was completely devoid of any pride by that point. I would have begged him, pleaded; gotten on my knees if only he would give me what I needed to come. I felt him chuckle darkly against my body, the vibration of it creating a new dimension of pleasure. Something fuller and more robust that had me gasping. He skated fingertips from my knee, up the inside of my thigh in a feather light touch and I wanted it, oh God yes I needed something inside me, to fill me out, to get me there. My core throbbing and empty, aching for the presence of his cock or his fingers, for the sweet bliss of having something, *anything* for my cunt to clench down around, to have that sweet spot inside of me touched and teased to pitch me into the whirling velvet dark of orgasm.

Ghost slid his middle finger into me, to the hilt and I clenched my pelvic floor muscles, drawing him in, welcoming him into my body. He pressed his tongue to my clit, lapping at my body while he searched for that one damned spot and when he found it I yowled in bliss and wouldn't you know? Something actually articulate came out of my mouth.

"Oh God yes! There! Right there!" I cried and I felt him smile and grin against my body but Ghost didn't give one fucking inch and with a come hither motion of his fingers and a final press of his tongue I came, pretty sure I did it screaming and had it not been for his palm flat against my chest between my breasts, pressing me tight to the shower's smooth stone wall I would have fallen but Ghost wouldn't let me fall. He held me up with his body. Bore my weight and held me on that high, milking every last bit of pleasure from my body with fingers and mouth until the pleasure became too much, too overwhelming and I whimpered, trying to scoot away.

I'd let go of his hair at some point and now my hands were pressed, palms flat to the shower wall behind me as I panted. Ghost placed a final reverent kiss on my shaved smooth mound and looked up at me, his eyes filled with a deep and dark passion, with a touch of smug pride for good measure. He stood slowly and pressed me back into the shower wall with the warm hard length of his body against mine.

"Kiss me," he demanded shortly and I was oh so willing to comply. He held me against the wall and kissed me until he was sure I could stand on my own before gently pulling back. He gave himself a final rinse under the shower spray, probably more to warm up than anything before shutting off the tap.

"Come here, Baby," he helped me out of the shower and we dried each other off. There was still a lot of languorous kissing and lazy touching, which was enough to both relax and arouse me at the same time. Pretty soon we had each other worked up to the point where we were both damned near tripping over the other in our haste to get to the bed. Ghost grasped me by the hips and pulled me back against him when I turned to climb up onto the mattress. He smoothed one hand up my back to my neck and kneaded the muscles to either side before applying gentle pressure.

I bent obediently at the waist and grasped the comforter in my hands. He kicked my feet into a wider stance and I gasped just before he found my entrance with the head of his cock. I was wet and ready for him and I wanted so bad for him to just fill me that I pressed back to meet his thrust. Oh my God, coming together like that was such a powerful feeling. Incredibly passionate, incredibly intimate and such a pure, sharp and sweet pleasure it was damned near bordering on pain.

The sensation of having Ghost go that deep, of bottoming out against my cervix and pushing just that little bit more had us both crying out, his masculine to my feminine. The sharp pleasure filled report echoing back at us through the dark, from the ceiling, from the dark glass of the night filled windows. I gasped and begged him to do it again, for him to touch me deeper, give it to me harder and oh man did my man give it to me.

He gripped me by my hips, fingers digging, damn near bruising and I loved it! I had always been partial to taking it kind of rough when it suited me and Ghost gave it to me with no exception. He gave me everything, his love, his hurt, his anger and frustration as well as his longing and comfort. He wrapped me up tightly, until breath panting, body slicked with sweat, I came apart beneath him screaming in pure unadulterated bliss. The bed holding me up as he rode me through my orgasm.

I lay on my stomach, limp and full of grace as he took his time, finishing himself and when he finally came, his cock jumping and pulsing with his release inside me, it was so perfect, so exquisite I came again too, a much less wild, a much gentler blush of emotion and pleasure sweeping through my body, but another, quieter orgasm none the less.

"Mm," I heard him, and it was the sound one made after savoring something so fine, so beautiful you wanted the flavor of it to last forever on your tongue, the sensation of it to go on forever and it was knowing that *I* was that fine thing to him, that it was *me* that he was savoring that mended some of the tatters in my soul. He smoothed the palms of his hands over my ass and all the way up my back before gripping my shoulders. He pulled me back onto him even though he was seated as deeply as he could go and I felt an answering pleasurable throb from my body.

"God you..." he blew out a breath, "I don't even think there are any words, Baby, you're just so..." he made that sound again, "Mm," and I couldn't help but smile.

"Thank you," I whispered. Derek withdrew from me slowly and I gave a little ecstatic shiver.

"Can you get up? Need help?" he asked gently. I crawled the rest of the way up onto the bed and he followed, pulling me in against his chest. I rested my head onto his shoulder and sighed out, content. He kissed my forehead and echoed my contented sigh with one of his own.

"Damn I love you," he murmured and I smiled, it wasn't long though before I was sound asleep.

CHAPTER 34

Ghost

I waited impatiently on the stool Shelly had occupied while Trigger had talked her out of her self-flagellation over killing the fucking douchebag that'd attacked her. I was staring at the closed bathroom door off the kitchen, knee bouncing in agitation. She was late. Only by a couple of days at this point but enough that I'd procured a pregnancy test in the midst of my last round of tows so that we could just *know* and stop stressing over the unknown.

The door opened and I looked up at her solemn expression expectantly. I didn't know if I was excited or terrified, if I wanted her to be or if I didn't. She slipped up on the stool across from me and cast her eyes to the floor and shook her head, scrubbing her face with her hands.

"Negative. I'm not pregnant. It's probably just stress that has me late," she chewed her bottom lip and wouldn't look at me. I felt both disappointed and elated at the same time and it was the most bizarre combination of emotions I think I had ever encountered.

"I don't know how to feel," she said finally and frowned, I smiled.

"I was just thinking to myself that I was feeling both disappointed and elated at the same time," she looked up sharply.

"I know right?" she asked and I smiled a little bigger. When we weren't busy clashing and butting heads over stupid shit, Shelly could easily be like a best friend to me. We were so much alike. At any given time, we were discovering, we were thinking or feeling the same way about this or that. It was really nice. Still, there was enough apprehension over how either one of us would take something that it made what I said next difficult to say for me. I pressed on ahead anyways.

"We really should plan things better and stop flying by the seat of

246

our pants," I said and she looked at me thoughtfully, so many emotions and so much confusion on her beautiful pixie like face. I held my breath and waited to see what she would say, how she would take it. I was finding my beautiful girl had a very hard time taking criticism over anything, that she was sensitive and would just tear into herself for doing something wrong even when that wasn't the case. Likely it was a product of her erratic upbringing. I didn't know, all I knew was that we needed to take things one step at a time and part of doing that, was planning things a bit better.

"Yeah," she said in agreement but her mind was here, there and everywhere. Didn't take a degree in rocket science to see it.

"Feel like a run?" I asked her and she looked at me stunned, before smiling appreciatively.

"You're learning," she said with a secret smile.

"Maybe I am," I conceded and stood up. I took her into my arms and held her close for a few minutes.

"I love you," I said.

"I love you too," she said back.

"Come on. Let's go," I took her gently by her fingers and helped her to her feet. We changed into running gear and stretched in the living room on the floor. Her face was healing, the bruises were at least something she could cover with a thicker than normal layer of makeup which was heart breaking in its own right.

Dragon and the President of The Suicide Kings, Griz, had a meet in the coming days. No telling what would come of it, but we'd have to see. Shelly looked at me.

"I'm not sure kids is a good idea until the whole thing with the Suicide Cunts is resolved," she said gently.

"Who knows how long that could be, Princess," I murmured.

"I know, I was going to say, I'm not sure I want to put it off for too long, maybe a year or two at the most, but Ghost... I don't ever want to be a single mom."

I paused in my stretching at the flash of real fear in her eyes at the thought. My woman liked truth. It was one of the things I loved about her. She wasn't into the pretty little lies. I couldn't promise it would never happen because I'd promised her I would try not to make promises I couldn't keep and no one knew what tomorrow would bring. I could die doing a tow for Christ's sakes.

"I can't promise it won't happen," I said finally, "What I can promise is that you and me, we can do whatever it takes to have a plan in place in case of that eventuality. You're my Ol' Lady Shelly. I love you and you were part of The Sacred Hearts long before I showed up and they will *always* be there for you. So let's go for a run, and we'll come home and we'll sit down and talk and try to make some plans for a future together and try to leave some shit in the past. How does that sound?"

She smiled and it lit her up from the inside out. She leapt lightly to her feet and said, "Think you can keep up?" and I grinned.

"I'm always going to try."

She laughed and I followed her out into the freezing December air. She may not believe it, but I was determined. I would always be right behind my girl in this life, or the next. No matter how much of a bitch she was to keep up with.

I shot off a text behind Shelly's back and caught up with her and hoped that the guys would pull through for me on this one. Okay, I knew they would pull through. I was more hoping they could get in, get out and get gone before we got back to the house.

We ran and ran and ran some more until she finally came to a stop, jogging in place, "Turn back?" she asked, breath pluming the frigid air.

"You ready?" I asked, I know I was *more* than ready. The cold made my lungs burn and I just generally wasn't a fan.

"Uh huh!" she nodded and breathlessly we turned and started back and I hoped it would be enough time. I felt my pulse throb in my temples more with a slight spike of adrenaline. They'd pulled it off. It was sitting on the back porch all shiny red and white with a big red bow on the handlebars. Shelly slowed just ahead of me and came to a stop.

She turned slowly, eyes wide and I smiled. She turned back to the porch and breaths pluming the air in measured puffs turned back to me. She pointed, her eyes wide and so blue it hurt.

"Did you..?" she asked. I nodded.

"I told you, Princess and I meant it. I'm here, I love you and I may have my moments where I fight with you, where I'm a total idiot wrapped in moron, dipped in dumb shit like with the whole Blue's shirt thing, but I'm not going anywhere," I said. She turned back to the back porch with its shiny red bicycle perched on it and turned back to me.

"I didn't *really* want a shiny red bicycle Ghost!" she exclaimed and put a hand over her mouth and turned back to the sight.

"Does it make you happy?" I asked.

"Strangely yes!" she cried.

"Then that's all that matters Princess."

Shelly turned and launched herself into my arms and I held her tight. She was a little less tattered and I was a whole lot less torn but we both had an extremely long ways to go. A long road to travel before either of us could declare ourselves good or healed or whatever.

"I'm so sorry for what happened, Baby," I murmured into her shoulder. She drew back to look at me.

"Don't," she said, "It was a big black ugly rock that dropped from the sky," she said, "It's only in our way for as long as it takes us to go around it and keep going. I want it behind us. I want to stop going at it over stupid shit neither of us had control over in the past and I want to move forward," she pinned me with her gaze.

"I can do that," I told her, "Whatever you want. Whatever you need. Just tell me and I'll do it."

She rested her forehead against my own. "Is that a promise?" she asked.

"Do you want it to be?"

"I need it to be," she said.

"Then yes, it's a promise and it's one I can and will keep," I told her. She kissed me and I held her tight against me in the cold December early afternoon. She shivered against me and pulled back.

"Take me home?" she asked and it was the meekest I'd ever heard her. I smiled and stooped lifting her up. She shrieked and laughed and I carried her up the back steps.

She took one lingering last look at the bicycle as we passed by, "Good thing I didn't say 'pony' she murmured, and I laughed. I stooped and she twisted the knob on the kitchen door and I carried her across the threshold, kicking the door shut behind us.

We didn't make it to the bedroom. I made love to her on our hallway floor just outside her office.

It was good to be whole.

EPILOGUE

Revelator

I dropped into the open seat beside my mentor and VP, Dray. He turned and raised an eyebrow at me and took a sip of whatever he was drinkin'. Looked like Scotch. He looked me over with somber dark eyes and I took his measure right back. He wasn't here with Everett, which usually meant she was hanging with Red, which was what I wanted to ask him about.

"Yes?" he drawled out.

"Question for you," I snapped out and he set his glass down on the bar. One of the new guys, Blue, moved off to the other end from where he was wiping down the old worn wood surface to give us the illusion of privacy.

"I'm waiting, dude. Spit it the fuck out." Dray's look turned tempestuous and I couldn't help but grin. Everybody thought Dray was a miserable fucker but I'd figured out a while ago he was just short on patience and wanted the short version of everything.

"Red single?" I asked.

"Oh, you thinkin' you finally got some time for her?" he asked. I rubbed the back of my neck where it heated up with my embarrassment.

"More thinkin' I'd better make some fucking time," I muttered and it must have been the look on my face because whatever wicked smart assed remark Dray was about to let fly, died on his lips.

"Yeah man, she's single," he said and sighed, "Good luck with that though. Don't think you're going to make it past my girl. She watches over Mandy like a mama bear does her cub," he grinned at that and I smiled. I remembered *his* mother. She'd been much the same way and I tilted my head to the side.

"You thinkin' about rug rats of your own?" I asked.

"With Em? Shit yeah, eventually, not now but if I had to pick a mother for the fruit of my loins, she's it!" he tossed back the rest of his drink and I shook my head laughing.

"Wouldn't fucking let her catch you putting it that way," I said with a grin.

Dray smirked, "Yeah no, I plan on having sex again this week, hell, *tonight* if I'm lucky. Em and Mandy went to catch a movie. She's supposed to be dropping my girl off to me later," his smirk turned into a grin, "Got a couple of hours yet."

"Thinkin' what I'm thinkin'?" I asked.

"Been a while since any of us cut lose, we're just waiting on the Big Man and Reave," Dray let out a gusty sigh, "Speak of the devil," he said.

"You called?" Reaver slapped me on the back of my cut as he and Trig came through the front door, a blast of cold damp air wafting in behind them.

"Going to Sugar's you coming?" Trig grunted, putting his e-cig between his lips. I could see his hands just itching to go for a lighter out of habit but he refrained.

"Sunshine still hasn't figured out that you ain't quit the real thing?" I asked.

"I'm pretty sure she knows," he sighed and gave me a dirty look. I put up my hands.

"All you dudes have women, *fine* women, what the Hell you going to the strip club for?" Disney asked from a nearby table where he sat across from *his* little mister Aaron, who was about to leave for some time on the west coast scoring some movie or some shit. Dis had been moping around the house fucking hardcore but Aaron didn't have a clue how bad it was tearing my brother from another mother up inside.

"You like dick, you wouldn't understand," Reaver said but he was grinning like the maniac he was, taking any bite out of the remark. Aaron smirked but remained silent.

"Woah! Don't ask don't tell!" Dray threw his hands up. Disney scowled at our VP and Aaron laughed.

"I think my Ol' Man is desensitized to it, but I'm not. I'll explain it to him later," Aaron winked at Dray who looked slightly uncomfortable until Aaron and Disney both started howling.

"Man fuck you guys," Dray muttered under his breath.

"So we going or what?" Trig asked and I got off my stool.

"Shit, yeah, keep your panties on Partner."

The guys all moved around finishing drinks and grabbing yet more guys asking who else wanted to come. By the time I got on the back of my bike out front I wasn't saying much or laughing at their dumb assed jokes. My mind was firmly on a set of fiery red curls and these hazel eyes that reminded me of the turning of the leaves.

"Rev! You good man?" Trig asked, firing up his bike next to mine.

"Yeah! Yeah! I'm good!" I yelled back.

I'd be even better if I had clue one on how to get Red to give me a shot after things went south the last go around. I sighed. Not like I'd tried to really fix it, I was just tired of waiting and yeah, I knew what kind of a douche that made me.

I fell into line behind the other guys and let some stripper grind her ass over my crotch but my heart wasn't in it. I wanted something much more innocent and much more pure, and no matter how much naked flesh I stared at in the strip joint, I couldn't get my Red out of my friggin' mind.

Damn it, I had it bad for the girl. Worse than bad and I needed to get off my ass and do something about it or I was going to lose my God damned mind...

Read revelator and mandy's story:

FRACTURED & FORMIDABLE

ABOUT THE AUTHOR

A.J. Downey has been a resident of Seattle, WA her entire life, that being said she has lived in many different places and many different worlds through her imagination. She enjoys music, coffee, writing (obviously) and a bunch of other boring things that you probably don't really care about. She is ever so grateful that you either picked up her writing or that you continue to read her stuff!

You can find her on Facebook at:

www.facebook.com/authorajdowney

Second Circle Press

Made in the USA
Lexington, KY
02 August 2017